# Praise for *Wishes and Wellingtons*

"It will ensorcell and entertain any who enjoy a feisty protagonist or the conceit of a wish-granting djinni... Berry mixes classic storytelling with modern feminism as Maeve forges genuine friendships, outsmarts a powerful foe, and matures without losing her edge."

—*Booklist*

"Small details weave together to create an engaging tapestry that becomes more complex and compelling with every page turn. A nostalgic Dickens and Nesbit mashup."

—*Kirkus Reviews*

"This novel spotlights friendship and an athletic, unconventional heroine... Readers looking for a fantastical romp through Victorian England will be entertained."

—*School Library Journal*

"For history buffs and budding fantasy fans with enough twists and turns to keep readers on their toes."

—*The Bulletin of the Center for Children's Books*

"[This] globe-spanning romp balances tongue-in-cheek humor with a heartfelt focus on found family and friendship as the newly minted trio face impossible odds, both mundane and supernatural... Maeve's drive to eschew marriage and propriety in favor of independence conveys a message of female empowerment."

—*Publishers Weekly*

# Crime and Carpetbags

## ALSO BY JULIE BERRY

*Lovely War*

*The Passion of Dolssa*

*All the Truth That's in Me*

*The Scandalous Sisterhood of Prickwillow Place*

*The Emperor's Ostrich*

## WISHES AND WELLINGTONS SERIES

*Wishes and Wellingtons*

*Crime and Carpetbags*

# CRIME
## AND
# CARPETBAGS

## JULIE BERRY

sourcebooks
young readers

Published by Sourcebooks Young Readers, an imprint of Sourcebooks Kids
P.O. Box 4410, Naperville, Illinois 60567-4410
(630) 961-3900
sourcebookskids.com

Originally published as an Audible Exclusive audio production in 2021 by Audible, a division of Amazon.

Library of Congress Cataloging-in-Publication data is on file with the publisher.

Source of Production: Maple Press, York, Pennsylvania, United States of America
Date of Production: July 2021
Run Number: 5022556

Printed and bound in the United States of America.
MA 10 9 8 7 6 5 4 3 2 1

*For my niece, Rachel Berry, with much affection.*

## CHAPTER

# 1

I f there's one thing I should know better than most, it's to be careful what you wish for. I once commanded an all-powerful djinni, and he turned out to be nothing but trouble. Did I get all my wishes granted? Hardly! Did I nearly die a gruesome death, a dozen times over? Yes, indeed.

(Perhaps not quite a dozen, but after enough near misses, one loses count.)

You would think the experience would've cured me of wishing. You would think, after being, for example, thrown in the cellar at my old girls' school, caught by police, hounded by a ruthless business-man, burgled by a hired criminal, nearly eaten—or worse—by demon beasts, and almost cursed to within an inch of an icy grave by an undead sorcerer, that I would settle down to a quiet life of crocheting lace and planting ferns in flowerpots.

If you thought such things about me, Maeve Merritt, you'd be very much mistaken.

Once word gets about that there's an all-powerful djinni in town, some people will go to any lengths to snatch him from you. The past winter, I'd done battle with enough greedy villains trying to steal my djinni that I could've made a small fortune just by selling them tickets to wait in line for their turn to rob me.

In the end, I parted ways with Mermeros, my ill-tempered, rude, arrogant djinni. Far from curing me of my desire for wishes, this only whetted my appetite for them to a razor-sharp point. Even if it meant I had to earn my wishes myself, without any magical help.

I wished to form a cricket league for girls. I wished to travel the world someday. I wished for a small fortune, as that's what my wishes would cost. I'd need to earn that fortune, now that I had no djinni, so I wished to gain a real education, the kind boys were given, without the silly nonsense of dancing and deportment taught to girls. I didn't just wish it. I *needed* it.

When all the hubbub was over, I no longer had Mermeros. My old school sacked me for my general rottenness. Then, by a pure miracle, I was invited to move into the Bromleys' home and be privately educated along with their granddaughter, Alice. I jumped at the chance. Of course, that's also because I adore Alice. She'd been my roommate at my old girls' school. She was the only good thing about that wretched place. Miss Salamanca's School for Upright Young Ladies. One could hardly say its name without feeling queasy.

With Alice's help, I persuaded Mr. and Mrs. Bromley not to hire us a governess but a real classics tutor, a gentleman out of Oxford who could teach us Greek and Latin. History, too, and literature, geography (my favorite), proper mathematics, and all the subjects one might need to become truly successful.

I'd gotten my wish. I wanted Greek and Latin; now I was saddled with *Greek and Latin*. And with Mr. Abernathy, our very energetic tutor. I rather enjoyed the stories from Homer and Virgil—those naughty, naughty gods!—and the geography bits, but the languages! Conjugations and declensions and definitions until my eyes swam. Symbols that aren't even letters, but pure gibberish. It was a nightmare.

Alice loved it, though, so there was no turning back. I'd created a monster.

Be careful what you wish for.

Scholarly matters aside, 1897 was an extraordinary year. It was Queen Victoria's Diamond Jubilee, celebrating sixty years of her reign. There would be no end of fuss over it, all year long. Much pomp and circumstance.

For me, it was the year I set out to grant wishes for others, so to speak. To weave a web to catch a wish for someone I dearly loved. All the while, someone else was spinning a web to catch Mermeros, the djinni, by any means necessary, and they didn't care if they caught the people I loved best along the way.

Wishes are a dangerous business.

★ ✳ ★

Right at this moment, I was wishing hard for my sister Evangeline's wedding to end.

It was late afternoon on an April Saturday, and the setting sun pouring through wavy glass windows lit up my family's little Luton parish church, filled up with our relatives and neighbors. Men sat in stiff cravats and women in their finest feathered hats. The scent of too many mingled perfumes tickled my nose.

Alice sat beside me in the pew of the bride's family, near the front of the church. She seemed to be enjoying herself, listening to the readings, watching the organist play, even smiling in a sappy sort of way at my sister, who stood next to my soon-to-be brother-in-law, Rudolph, stammering out their vows in turn. As if they were, somehow, a tender picture of sweet romance. Disgusting.

Rudolph looked like a butler, or perhaps, a penguin. My sister looked like someone had taken a thousand lace handkerchiefs and pinned them to a wicker mannequin, with a few orange blossoms thrown in. How, in fact, could Rudolph be sure that was Evangeline under there? One of the better stories from the Bible is about that very problem, when a fellow thought he was marrying one sister, and it turned out he got the other one. I laughed out loud when they read it to us in Sunday school, and got a stern reprimand for it.

To the other side of Evangeline stood my two other sisters, Deborah and Polydora, as bridesmaids, dressed in yellow ruffles and clutching bouquets. Deborah, age eighteen, kept darting coy glances at some young man among the guests, while Polydora, the eldest at twenty-three, made a point of *not* letting her gaze drift to Constable Matthew Hopewood, her not-exactly, not-quite-yet-but-almost-certainly-probably beau. She couldn't, in fact, see him, as Evangeline had put her foot down and insisted that Polydora couldn't, under any circumstances, wear her spectacles during the wedding.

That's Evangeline for you.

There had been talk of me donning the costume and standing there beside them, sneezing into my own bouquet of flowers. One camp in the family said that I must, that it simply wouldn't do for one sister to be absent from the wedding party. The other camp contended that since the sister in question was *me*, I might find six different ways to cause a scene and ruin the blessed occasion.

I don't need to tell you which camp won.

On the other side of me sat my parents. My mother's eyes were pink, and she sniffled through her tears, while my father sat looking silent and stoic. This just goes to show that nothing in this world makes any sense. The way my mother had been carrying on about the wedding for months, you would think all her happiness in life depended on this very moment. She should be grinning like a circus clown, whereas my father, who'd had to put up with all the prewedding folderol in a house full of daughters, and write all the checks for the day's ludicrous expense, ought to have been the one crying, if you ask me.

Nobody asks me.

I fixed my gaze on dear old Polly. If I wasn't much mistaken, that misty look in Polly's eyes had everything to do with her constable and little to do with our sister, the blushing bride.

What, I wondered, was taking that Matthew Hopewood so long to make up his mind?

His reluctance, or whatever it was, was costing my best sister her happiness. The poor thing had even lost some weight, I was sure, pining over that bobby.

No one will accuse me of being romantic without getting a poke in the nose for it, but I do love my sister Polly. She's my favorite. No one who knows Deborah or Evangeline will find this hard to believe.

It was clear Polly had set her heart upon that policeman.

What is it that addles the wits of otherwise intelligent people where love is concerned? *Love*. I can barely stomach the word. In every other respect, Polly is a model of wise judgment and good sense. Then romance had to enter the picture. A case of the Black Plague would be preferable, if you asked me.

Nevertheless, if Polly's happiness was wrapped up in that policeman, then her wish was my command. Wishes were, after all, my forte.

But did Matthew Hopewood deserve my sister?

My father seemed to like him. That was worth something. I'd never had an issue with good old Matthew. My mother found him slightly less than acceptable, but that, in my book, was a mark in his favor.

Polly adored him. That was good enough for me.

Perhaps it was the wedding, casting some of its gooey, pink, romantic spell over me, but I made up my mind. I would make that Matthew Hopewood stop being so reluctant. I'd see my sister with an engagement ring. My other projects—Latin and Greek and girls' cricket—wouldn't suffer any for a brief matchmaking project.

I craned my neck backwards to see Matthew Hopewood's muttonchop whiskers gleaming yellow in the afternoon sun, a bland, sleepy look upon his amiable face.

*Watch out, copper,* I told him silently. *I'm coming for you.*

"Maeve," Alice hissed, "turn around, and stop goggling."

At long last, the vicar managed to accomplish the nearly impossible feat of joining Evangeline and Rudolph in holy matrimony, rings and veil and all, and we were permitted to witness an embarrassing public kiss, then wave them on as they hurried down the aisle, no doubt due to sheer mortification.

As the family of the bride, we filed out after them. I passed by my redheaded friend Tom, dressed in his brand-spanking-new Sunday best, and only barely remembered not to wave at him, for my mother had told me I mustn't, or else. When we reached the vestibule, Alice and I caught sight of Tom's father, also brand-spanking-new, as Tom's adoption had only just been finalized. Mr. Poindexter, the man himself, snapped photographs of the happy couple with his new Kodak camera. The camera was his other pride and joy, after Tom, and he had volunteered to do the honors. I'd orchestrated that arrangement myself, and my father, who likes Mr. Poindexter, and who paid for everything, was only too glad to have his friend take the photographs for free. For my part, it was an excuse to get Tom to the wedding, and even the most ghastly occasion is bearable if Tom's around. If he could help me escape a haunted sorcerer's tomb, he could get me through my sister's dreaded nuptials.

How we'd all come to know each other, Alice and Tom and me, and our families, and in fact to have our lives tangled up together, is a topper of a story, and I recommend it, since it has everything to do with Mermeros, my djinni—my former djinni—but now is not the time.

Rudolph and Evangeline and their families greeted and thanked guests for what felt like hours. I longed to go outside and stretch my legs. Finally, we all left the building and lined up to cheer the couple on as they ran down the steps and into their carriage. My decently jolly Aunt Vera scurried about, handing out handfuls of rice for us to toss at the new Mr. and Mrs. Seymour. I chucked my rice with gusto. I'll be fair and admit it: that part *was* fun. I could've put a ten-pound sack of rice to good use.

The couple drove off. The rest of the throng made its way back to my family's home, which had been scrubbed and decked out with garlands and flowers for the wedding reception. Most people went in carriages that had queued up outside the church, but the day was fine, so Tom, Alice, and I walked.

"What a lovely wedding," Alice said. "Didn't you think so, Tom?"

Tom's eyebrows rose. He spoke as one choosing his words carefully. "I've never been to a wedding before," he admitted. "It seemed a tad...*long*."

"Exactly," I said.

"And feathery," added Tom.

I snickered.

"And flowery."

"Never mind." Alice sighed. "Forget I asked." She turned to me. "Do you think there'll be another wedding in the family before long, Maeve?"

"Why, is Maeve engaged?"

"Bite your tongue, Tom," I told him. "Do you mean Polly, Alice?"

Alice smiled. "It's clear to see she's in love with that constable of hers."

I nodded. "It's true. But he won't say the word."

"What word?" asked Tom.

"Any word." I made a face at Tom, as if he represented all reluctant male suitors. "Poor Polly's practically breaking her heart over him."

"How long have they known each other?"

"Months," I said. "Long enough. They met last Christmas."

Tom blew out his breath. He didn't seem to share my opinion that that was "long enough."

"He came to the wedding, didn't he?" asked Tom. "Doesn't he like Polly?"

"He'd better." I considered. "He stops by sometimes. They see each other at choir practice. I'm not sure what's holding him back."

"Maybe he's shy," suggested Alice.

"Unacceptable," I said. "Shyness can't stand in the way of my sister's happiness."

"Why, what are you going to do about it, Maeve?" Tom grinned. "Badger him until he proposes to her?"

"Maybe," I said, "if a better idea doesn't come along."

"Miss Maeve," cried a man's voice from behind us. I turned to see the man himself, Constable Hopewood, or Matthew as he'd told me to call him, jogging to catch up.

"Talk of the devil," muttered Tom.

"No, thank you," Alice whispered primly.

"Shh!" I hissed. Then: "Hullo, er, Constable. You know my friends? Alice Bromley and Tommy Poindexter?"

"I've had the pleasure of meeting Miss Bromley," he said, holding out a hand. "Pleased to meet you, Tommy." Constable Hopewood shook hands with them both and rose a notch in my estimation, for he didn't treat either of them, nor me, as though we were silly just for being young.

"I thought you'd be riding over to the house in Polly's carriage," I told him, with what I hoped was a very significant air.

His cheeks, surrounded as they were by thick blond whiskers, blushed bright pink. "Your sister rode in the same carriage as the other members of the wedding party, and before I knew it, the other carriages had filled up and gone."

"Walk with us, then," I told him. "We're harmless, despite what my mother says."

He stifled a laugh.

*This is perfect*, I thought. Maybe I could find a way to pump him for information. Carefully.

Another pair of footsteps hurried to catch up to us. Quite the popular party we were this evening.

"Ho there, Dad." I noted the pride in Tommy's voice.

"Hullo, Mr. Poindexter," I said. "Did you get any good photographs?"

Mr. Poindexter patted his red leather Kodak. "Let's hope so. People seem incapable of holding still, but I have great faith in this little beauty." He turned toward the constable and held out a hand. "Siegfried Poindexter, at your service."

"Matthew Hopewood," said he, "at yours."

(To hear them talk, you'd think every person in Britain is constantly in the service of every other, in one great big circle of helpfulness. That, however, hasn't been my experience, or maybe I'm just jaded from years of girls' boarding school.)

"Mr. Hopewood is my sister Polly's..." Too late, I realized my blunder.

"Good friend." Alice came smoothly to my rescue, but it was too late. Poor Matthew now looked like a giant, blond-whiskered tomato.

"I have had the pleasure," he choked out the words, "of forming an acquaintance with Miss Maeve's elder sister."

Mr. Poindexter's eyes twinkled. "Miss Polydora is a charming young woman, with good sense and a lively wit. It must run in the family." He winked at me. "Well, the lively wit, anyway."

What cheek! I laughed all the same. I could never be angry with Mr. Poindexter.

We resumed our stroll in the direction of my home. The sun

was nearly hidden now behind houses and trees. The early evening's soft, dewy air smelled of newly cut grass and Dutch tulips blooming in window boxes. Lights winked on in upstairs windows as little children tidied their nurseries in time for baths and bed.

Mr. Poindexter broke the silence with a question for Matthew Hopewood. "You're an officer in the force, aren't you?"

"Does it show?" Constable Hopewood smiled.

"What's the most sensational crime you've ever worked on?" I asked.

"*Maeve*," scolded Alice.

Perhaps it wasn't polite, as the two men were only just getting acquainted, but I'd been dying to ask Matthew this sometime when they were no female relatives nearby to stop me.

The constable smiled grimly. "I'm afraid it's almost never like the stories in your 'penny dreadfuls,' Miss Maeve," he said. "Real, actual crime is almost never sensational. It's ugly. It's sad. Most crime is just meanness, selfishness, or greed dressed in grown-up shoes."

"Amen," cried Mr. Poindexter. "Well said, sir."

"But aren't there, sometimes, good reasons?" I said. "Times when breaking the law is actually the right thing to do?"

Alice sighed. Tom hid a smile. But Constable Hopewood and Mr. Poindexter both gazed at me in polite horror.

I don't wish to create the impression that I'd led a life of crime, exactly, but I had been known to be somewhat *creative* where laws were concerned, such as laws against breaking and entering, and technically, stealing. But only when I had a very good reason, and only when the thing I was stealing was rightfully mine. Or if the owner had been dead for thousands of years.

Mere technicalities.

"Crime is immoral," Mr. Poindexter said. "There's no excuse for it."

"It's destructive," the constable added. "It ruins the lives of the victim and the criminal."

"Only if the criminal is caught," I pointed out.

"What about a guilty conscience?" Alice *would* ask a thing like that.

"Some people don't have a conscience," I said. "And some people are never punished. The rich and the powerful usually get away with their crimes. Don't they?"

Constable Hopewood winced. It seemed I'd touched a nerve. "Well, we certainly try not to let that happen," he said. "No one is above the law. At least, no one should be. What happens once cases go to court, and barristers take up the matter, is beyond police control."

I'd depressed him, it seemed. He must have felt I'd criticized his profession, though I hadn't meant to. It was a shame, too. Especially after embarrassing him over his relationship with Polly. I was beginning to like the fellow for his own sake, and not just because my sister preferred him. If my plan was to bring the two together, I was off to a terrible start.

The sky's silvery twilight color deepened. We rounded a corner and saw my home up ahead, with bright lights spilling from every window and people milling inside and out. I knew there were marvelous edibles inside, and my hungry stomach grumbled, but I also knew cheek-pinching relatives would ask me booming questions and not listen to the answers.

"Before we go inside, my young friends," said Mr. Poindexter, with a distinct changing-the-subject tone in his voice, "I've been waiting for a chance to tell you all something, and now seems as good a time as any."

We stopped walking and looked up at Mr. Poindexter expectantly.

"It seems I've won a contest for newspaper subscribers to *The Globe and Traveller*," he said. "What would you young ladies say to joining Tommy and me for a day of fun at the Crystal Palace, two weeks from today?"

Cheek-pinching aunts were forgotten. "The Topsy-Turvy Railway!" I cried. "With the upside-down loop!"

Tom was just as surprised as I was. "The Canadian Water Chute!"

"The Handel concerts," Alice said breathlessly.

My turn again. "The dinosaurs!"

Mr. Poindexter smiled. "I'll take that as a yes?"

"I'll have to ask my grandparents," Alice said.

"My parents won't mind," I said. "How many tickets did you get?"

"Six," laughed Mr. Poindexter. "They must think I have quite the family." He rumpled Tom's hair. "And indeed, I do."

Tom grinned in spite of himself.

From the moment Mr. Poindexter adopted Tom, the pair of them had been as happy as two dogs playing tug-o-war with a stick. To watch Mr. Poindexter beam with satisfaction as he took Tommy to the circus, and to ice-cream parlors, and to stores where he outfitted him in all new clothes—just what the fashionable younger gentlemen about town were wearing—would've softened the heart of a hungry shark and brought it to sentimental tears.

"What'll we do with the two extra tickets, Dad?" inquired Tom.

"I don't know," admitted his father. "I hadn't really thought about it."

Out of the corner of my eye, I caught sight of Constable Hopewood, standing with his hands clasped behind his waist as if he'd hardly even heard what was being said.

I saw a glimmer of a plan—*and* my chance to make things right. For Matthew Hopewood's wounded feelings and for my Polly's hopes.

"My parents won't mind," I repeated, "but they'd probably feel easier about it all if Polly came along. Just to keep me out of trouble."

Mr. Poindexter laughed. "That *is* a tall order."

"While *you*," I told Mr. Poindexter, "might enjoy having a, er, gentleman to talk to."

Mr. Poindexter eyed me curiously, while the constable made a careful study of his shoes.

"*Say*," I cried, as if I'd only just thought of it, "why don't you come along, too, Mr. Hopewood?"

The constable stopped in his tracks. "I beg your pardon?"

"A splendid idea!" Mr. Poindexter winked at me. (He and I were, you might say, old partners in crime. In many matters, we understood one another.) "What do you say, Constable? Care to make a day of it with us at the Crystal Palace? Have a little flutter at the games? I'll bet you police chaps are top-notch at marksmanship."

Matthew Hopewood puffed up like a blowfish. "Well, now," he said, as though raising a grave concern, "I'd have to see if I could get the day off from work."

"Absolutely," cried Mr. Poindexter. "Do join us. What a lively party we'll make, eh, Maeve?" He pulled a card from his pocket and handed it to Constable Hopewood. "My card, sir. Drop me a line, or stop by the shop if you're in the city. Do come. I won't take no for an answer."

Just then Polly emerged from the house, finally wearing her spectacles. She saw us, smiled, and made her way toward us. Time for us to disappear and leave her alone for a twilight moment with her constable.

I linked elbows with Tom and Alice, and gave Mr. Poindexter a wink of my own. "Come on, you two," I told my friends. "Let's go find something to eat."

I marched them inside. Mr. Poindexter, I felt sure, would tell Polly of our plans and commit both the bashful lovebirds to joining us at the Crystal Palace, right there on the spot.

Phase One of Project Polly's Romance was already off to a promising start.

It had taken no persuading to get Polly to agree to come on our Crystal Palace outing, once she knew who else would make up the party, and with Polly coming, neither my parents nor Alice's grandparents could object in the slightest. Polly is the essence of respectability. Sensible and kind and good. Essentially my opposite.

Mr. and Mrs. Bromley told Mr. Abernathy, our tutor gentleman from Oxford, that we were to be given that Saturday morning off from our studies. Ordinarily he's as spry as a robin in spring, but all that week he lectured and heard our recitations with a faintly mournful air, as though young ladies *would* be young ladies and go running off to Crystal Palaces, even if it wounded his feelings.

We were too excited to care.

Two weeks was a long time to wait for a day at the Crystal Palace, but at least it was time I could put to use, plotting and scheming ways to entice a reluctant policeman to propose marriage to my sister.

The problem was, I'm the last person in the world anyone should consult on matters of romance. It would be like asking a fish to teach you to fly. The fish might be willing, but it wouldn't do much good. I even considered reading a romantic novel to see if it could teach me something useful. Offer some tips, so to speak. That just goes to show how fond I am of my sister. I would rather read the written records they keep of Parliamentary debates—on, say, methods of agricultural fertilization—than read a gooey, drippy love story.

I found one in the Bromleys' splendid library in their grand home in Grosvenor Square. *Wuthering Heights*, by Miss Emily Brontë. It started off with a suggestion of ghosts, and a bit about an orphan boy and a wildly ill-behaved girl, and lots of jealousy. Great stuff. Perhaps, I thought, romances weren't so bad after all.

I smuggled *Wuthering Heights* into the schoolroom each day and peeped at it under the lid of my desk. On the day before our Crystal Palace outing, a Friday, I was sneaking a read in class while Mr. Abernathy, our tutor, listened to Alice's Latin recitation, when a knock sounded at the schoolroom door.

"Pardon me, Mr. Abernathy," came the deep voice of Mr. Linzey, the Bromleys' tall, portly butler. "There is a...*woman* in the downstairs drawing room, asking to speak with Miss Merritt."

Mr. Abernathy looked as startled by this news as I felt. He stroked his thick gray goatee. "Miss Merritt is engaged in her studies," he informed the butler.

I slid *Wuthering Heights* farther under my desk. No sense in proving him wrong. Especially when he spoke, in his refined Scottish burr, with the tone of one saying, *The Queen is not receiving visiting monarchs at present.*

"Very good, sir." Mr. Linzey looked as excited as a butler *can* look to give an unwanted visitor the old heave-ho.

"Thank you, Mr. Linzey," said Mr. Abernathy, with an air of *you may go now.* Mr. Abernathy, I've noticed, says quite a bit without saying any of it. Perhaps that's a skill they teach you at Oxford.

"I beg your pardon, Mr. Linzey," I called after the butler. "Was it my sister Polly? My aunt Vera?" I paused. "Surely it wasn't my mother..."

Mr. Linzey coughed politely. "I seriously doubt," he said, "that you and your visitor are at all related."

Then who could it be?

As if reading my mind, Mr. Linzey added, "Your visitor claims a connection with you from your boarding-school days."

Alice and I gazed at each other in astonishment. Not Miss Salamanca! Not the dreaded old gargoyle of a headmistress at our old school!

"Mr. Linzey," Alice Bromley, that excellent soul, said gently, "did the visitor state her name?"

The butler wore the expression of one sucking on a pickle. "The...*person*," he said, "ascertained herself to be a baroness, but I—"

"A *baroness!*" Alice cried.

We knew only one baroness, but then, she was no baroness at all.

The Bromleys' grave, ever-proper butler looked ready to pop. "My sentiments precisely," he said. "To my knowledge, your grandparents aren't acquainted with any baronesses." He swallowed. "I took the liberty," he confessed, "of searching for her name in *Burke's Peerage*, before coming upstairs to find you. *It was not there.*"

Of course it wasn't. I could've saved him the trouble. This phony baroness could only be one person: Mrs. Gruboil, the meanest red-faced cook ever to burn a girl's breakfast eggs at boarding school. Mean enough to steal a tin of sardines from my dormitory bedroom so *she* could eat them as a snack. When she opened that tin, she got a whole lot more than she bargained for. She got Mermeros, my great, green djinni of fantastical power. That's how she "became" "Baroness Gabrielle." With the pots and pots of money she wished for, she bought a derelict old mansion near the school, fixed it up, and poured it full of luxuries and servants, all ready to enjoy a life of stolen ease.

Until Tommy and I stole Mermeros back.

"Mr. Linzey." Alice's voice disturbed my recollections of that conniving cook. "Are my grandparents aware of this visitor?"

"No, miss," the butler said gravely. "They've gone out."

"Of course." Alice sighed. "The Orphans' Charity luncheon."

Alice was still frowning over the dilemma of Baroness Gabrielle, formerly and forever Mrs. Gruboil. "I wouldn't dream of meeting with her without Grandmother or Papa present," she said. "Yet I have no wish for them to meet her. She's..." Alice blushed. "She's not *nice*. I suppose you'd better tell her we can't meet with her now."

Mr. Linzey was only too eager. "Very good, miss."

"She'll be sure to come back," I pointed out. "If she's tracked me here, there'll be no getting rid of her."

"*Tracked* you *here*?" repeated Mr. Abernathy. "Good heavens. Who is this visitor, some sort of lady Sherlock Holmes?"

I pictured Mrs. Gruboil in a deerstalker hat and a pipe. I would've laughed, but somehow her visit today didn't feel very amusing.

Mr. Abernathy heaved an exaggerated sigh. "As it seems my pupils will be completely incapable of resuming their studies until this matter is laid to rest," he told the butler, "*I* will accompany the young ladies downstairs to the dining room and guard them from this baroness-that-isn't. Come along."

He stoppered his inkwell, tugged at his checkered waistcoat, and dusted chalk powder from his fingertips. We followed him as he trotted out the door and down the stairs. Mr. Abernathy was a dapper man, neat and fussy in his appearance, and always bristling with energy. Whenever he took us anywhere—and he was a great believer in field trips—it felt like an occasion. Almost a military march, brass band and all. Mrs. Gruboil had no idea what was about to hit her.

The butler ushered us into the drawing room to announce us, but Mr. Abernathy beat him to it.

"Hamish Abernathy," our tutor told Mrs. Gruboil briskly, "at your service."

"Baroness Gabrielle," stammered our former boarding-school cook.

Alice and I curtsied, because we must.

It was Mrs. Gruboil, all right, but instead of a cook's apron and cap, she wore a ludicrous hat, weighed down with wax cherries, and a dress of purpled silk trimmed with velvet and elegant buttons. Elegant, but in a faded way, muddied way. Several buttons were missing, and the dress was rumpled and soiled. Her white gloves were brown with dirt. In her guise as baroness, I'd only ever seen her previously in her nightclothes, and certainly not by my choice. It was an image I would rather forget.

Mr. Abernathy played host. "Won't you sit down?"

Mrs. Gruboil sat. She was a pestilential person even on her sunniest of days, yet I was surprised by the baleful look she now cast my way. If malice could bite, hers had sharks' teeth.

She glanced around the elegant sitting room. "Living very fine now, aren't we, Miss Maeve?"

Alice blushed scarlet. She hated it when people drew attention to how well-off her family was.

"The Bromleys' home is quite comfortable," I said, "though I'm sure it's nothing to what a *baroness* enjoys."

"Even a baroness," Mrs. Gruboil practically hissed, "can fall upon hard times, when she's the victim of a *wicked crime*."

"Even when her wealth is the result of her own crimes?" I replied.

Mr. Abernathy shot me a look. I could smell a lecture on propriety brewing. I didn't care.

"Surely, Baroness," I said, "you had enough for a dozen lifetimes."

She gazed down ruefully upon her soiled clothing. Not anymore, it seemed.

"You can't have lost it all," I added.

"Miss Maeve," Mr. Abernathy said in a warning tone, "I'm surprised at you. This hardly seems necessary, or kind."

I stewed in my seat. Was I supposed to be kind to cruel, vindictive cooks who'd robbed me of my djinni, and called the constables on me when I went to fetch it back?

"Er, Baroness. How have you passed the winter, pray tell?" Alice was clearly trying to rescue me from disaster.

"Kind of you to inquire." Mrs. Gruboil's wounded pride was on full display. Alice was the good girl, and I was the bad. I was used to this. "I passed it pleasantly on the French Riviera. Until I...had to leave."

Because she'd gambled away all her wish-begotten money at the casinos. The puzzle pieces began to fit. She'd probably gone there hoping she could earn more at the roulette table, since she no longer had the goose that laid the golden egg in her pocket. Not that a goose would fit in a pocket, but a sardine tin would.

Conversation had ground to an awkward halt. Mrs. Gruboil turned to Mr. Abernathy. "Pardon me, sir," she said tartly. "Are you Miss Alice's father?"

His brows rose. "I have not that privilege," he said slowly. "I am her tutor. Why do you ask?"

The so-called baroness cast another hateful glance at me. "Miss Alice's parents need to know they've welcomed a serpent into their home," she said. "This one. Maeve. She's a snake in the grass. A liar and a thief."

"You waste no time in coming to the point," my tutor said coolly. "How, may I ask, did you come to this conclusion?"

"She robbed me blind," Mrs. Gruboil panted. "Broke into my very bedroom while I was sleeping! Stole from me my most precious treasure." She nodded toward Alice. "Miss Alice's parents have been deceived if they think she's a proper companion for their lovely girl."

"Well, now." Mr. Abernathy folded his hands over one knee. "I've known Miss Maeve for some months now, and while she does tend to prefer frivolous novels over the classics, and even sneaks them under her desk cover when she thinks I'm not looking, I would not otherwise say she has a dishonest character." He gave me a sly look. "A stubborn, outspoken character—outspoken to a fault, it seems— but a clever one."

How red did my face grow? He'd seen me reading *Wuthering Heights*? And here I thought I'd been...well, *clever* about it.

"She *thinks* she's clever." A snarling Mrs. Gruboil accidentally read my thoughts. "She's not clever enough by half."

"We are forced to view that as a matter of opinion," said Mr. Abernathy. "What perplexes me is why you took the trouble to come here simply to insult a young girl." He gave me a stern look. "Even if she is rather prone to return the insults that come her way."

His words hung in the air.

"I told you," she said. "I've come to warn Miss Alice's parents."

Alice's parents had died of influenza when she was little more than a baby, but if my friend saw no reason to correct Mrs. Gruboil's false assumptions, neither did I.

"I will relay your message," replied Mr. Abernathy. "Is there anything else?"

Mrs. Gruboil's eyes narrowed. "As for this Maeve," she said, "I'd insult her again tomorrow, and the day after that. She deserves it."

"Please don't," said Mr. Abernathy. "One interruption to her studies is already one too many." He turned to me. "Miss Maeve, what do you say to the, er, baroness's charge that you burgled a valuable object from her bedroom?"

I held my head high. "I say nothing at all."

The corners of his mouth twitched.

"It wasn't just a valuable object." Mrs. Gruboil spat her reply. "It was a magical *djinni*." She clapped a hand over her mouth in horror.

*Too late, Baroness. You can't unsay it now.*

Mr. Abernathy's eyes, on the other hand, sparkled with delight.

"A djinni," he said. "In a bottle, I suppose. Or a lamp, is it?"

She shook her head. "In a tin of fish."

"A tin of *fish*." I could see him press his lips together, trying hard not to laugh. "Are you sure it wasn't potted shrimps?"

Mrs. Gruboil's face reddened. "Some gentleman you are," she snapped, "to sneer and mock and disbelieve a lady. Potted shrimps indeed!"

Mr. Abernathy controlled his face with an effort. "I do beg your pardon, then, madam," he said, "though you must admit, it does rather sound unbelievable."

"No, I mustn't admit any such thing," she cried.

"As you please."

Mrs. Gruboil sputtered and fumed, for once at a loss for words. I might've laughed at the cool, skillful way in which my tutor was managing the problem of "the baroness," except that something tugged at my worries. Something didn't feel right. Mrs. Gruboil finding me here was very bad news.

Alice's voice broke the silence. "Mrs. Gruboil."

The former cook's gaze rose to meet Alice's in a silent but unmistakable reply.

"How did you know to look for Maeve here?" asked Alice.

"I asked one of the kitch—" Mrs. Gruboil stopped. She'd realized her mistake. "I...I had one of my *many* servants make, er, discreet inquiries."

She'd asked one of the kitchen staff at our old school. Of course. The servants would know where we'd gone when we unenrolled.

"Aha," cried Mr. Abernathy. "Is that so, *Mrs. Gruboil*?"

"What d'you mean?" gasped the former cook. "Why d'you call me that?"

"It's your name, isn't it?" pressed Mr. Abernathy. "You just answered to it when Miss Alice called you by that name. You're no baroness at all, are you?"

Her face paled. For once, she had nothing to say.

Mr. Abernathy waited a moment longer, then called for Mr. Linzey. The door opened so fast, I knew the butler had stood by with an ear pressed to it, eavesdropping.

"Yes, sir?"

Mr. Abernathy gestured toward Mrs. Gruboil. "Would you be

so good as to fetch our visitor's things? She is just leaving. Ah. You already brought them. How thoughtful of you."

Mr. Linzey thrust a once-fine shawl at the disgraced cook. She snatched it away from him and made her way toward the door.

"You can throw me out," she cried, "but I'll be back. Remember that, Maeve. I'll get Mermeros back. No matter where you hid him, you rotten girl, I'll find him."

"Mrs. Gruboil," Alice called in some distress. "Maeve hasn't got him." She glanced nervously at our tutor. "Erm, *it*. She hasn't got *it*. So there's no point in coming here to search. You'll never find it."

"Find what?" inquired Mr. Abernathy. "The potted shrimps?"

Mrs. Gruboil ignored him. "You wouldn't lie to me, I don't believe, Miss Alice." A thought struck her. "It's that boy, isn't it? With the red hair?"

She caught me off guard. My face... Well, I don't know what it looked like, but from the look of triumph in Mrs. Gruboil's eye, she was certain she'd found the truth. In fact, she'd come pretty close.

Mr. Abernathy turned to me. "Does she mean your friend, young Tommy Poindexter, Miss Maeve?"

Oh, *no*.

How I wished he hadn't said that. Naming my friend aloud was the worst thing he could've done.

"Tommy Poindexter, eh?" echoed Mrs. Gruboil. "Is that him? That red-haired orphan boy that's got my djinni?"

My heart sank.

"No," I said quickly. "Tommy hasn't got it."

Which was, technically, true. But also, technically, a bit misleading, since unbeknownst to Tom, his new adoptive father, Mr. Siegfried Poindexter, did have it.

"You think I can't tell when you're lying?" crowed Mrs. Gruboil. "Many thanks, indeed, sir," she told our tutor. "You've told me just what I needed to know. *Tommy Poindexter...*"

Mr. Abernathy saw my despairing look. "Come along, Miss Alice, Miss Maeve," he said. "Virgil won't keep."

As the dead Roman poet had "kept" for nearly nineteen hundred years, I didn't see how a few minutes more would matter, but I wanted to get out of there, too.

"Good *day*, Mrs. Gruboil," Mr. Abernathy told the would-be baroness.

"Oh, don't worry," she cackled. "I'm leaving. You've been *most* helpful."

We heard her footsteps trip-trapping down the marble-tiled foyer, and then sound of the door shutting. Mr. Linzey trotted after her to make sure she had really gone.

My head spun. A world in which Mrs. Gruboil knew where the

sardine tin containing Mermeros the djinni was wasn't a world that suited me at all. All I could smell was danger on every side. I would need to warn Mr. Poindexter. And somehow, I'd need to make sure Tom never heard about this.

Mr. Abernathy turned to me. "Miss Maeve," he said quietly, "it appears I said more than I should have. I am sorry."

I was so taken aback by his apology, I didn't know what to say.

"Do you worry that this person might try to burgle the Poindexters?" he asked. "In search of a *magical tin of fish*?" He ran his fingers through his thick shock of gray hair. "She's clearly a person who could be a nuisance. Can I do anything to set matters to rights?"

If only!

"No," I said. "There's nothing more. But thank you for asking."

He nodded in relief. "*Mermeros*," he echoed. "What a curious name. Did you borrow from French, *la mer*, or Spanish, *el mar*? All deriving, of course, from the Latin, *mare*, for the sea."

The man could not resist teaching. If the executioner were about to chop off his head, Mr. Abernathy would first pause to point out that "execute" derived from the Latin *exsequi*, which means "to follow out," or even "to follow one out to the grave."

How do I know this? Because he made me look it up.

"Or was it, perhaps, the Italian, *il mare*, that inspired you?"

"I didn't make the name up, Mr. Abernathy," I told him.

"Then who did? Your friend Tom?"

Alice watched me anxiously. For my part, my djinni—my former djinni—wasn't something I wanted to talk about with anyone. No one, that is, who hadn't been part of the commotion Mermeros had caused last winter.

I looked back at Mr. Abernathy as calmly as he looked at me, and said nothing at all.

Mr. Abernathy turned to Alice. "Who was she really?"

My friend sighed. "She used to be the cook at our old school."

Mr. Abernathy nodded thoughtfully. He left the room, beckoning us to follow him back up the stairs. We reached the schoolroom and returned to our desks. I crawled my fingertips under my desk lid and slid *Wuthering Heights* farther from view.

"The cook," Mr. Abernathy mused. "Miss Maeve," he said abruptly, "do you fill the servants' heads full of cotton fluff about djinnis and whatnot here at this house, too?"

"Mr. Abernathy," I said sweetly, "do you believe the tales told about me by a former cook who calls herself a baroness?"

Mr. Abernathy's goateed face broke into a grin. "Touché, Miss Maeve, touché. I *told* that unpleasant woman you were clever. Now, *touché*, as you know, is French, meaning 'touch,' and we use the term in fencing. It comes to us from the Latin *toccare*, meaning 'to strike' or 'to knock,' and likewise, 'to ring a bell'..."

★ ✸ ★

What to do? Would Mrs. Gruboil be able to figure out, in all of London, that 'Tommy Poindexter' was the son of Siegfried Poindexter, owner of the Oddity Shop, on Mantlebury Way in London? How many Poindexters could London hold? Not enough, I was afraid.

Afternoon lessons were nearly done. Polly would arrive in time for tea that night, and sleep over, to accompany us in the morning to the Crystal Palace. In between nudges to make sure Matthew Hopewood fell in love with Polly, I would find a way to speak privately to Mr. Poindexter and warn him about Mrs. Gruboil.

He was an adult, and a resourceful one. Mrs. Gruboil was an adult, but a disgraceful one. Surely Mr. Poindexter could outwit "Baroness Gabrielle" Gruboil any day. He would know what to do. She couldn't be much of a threat. She'd tracked me here, but everything would be all right. Of course it would.

Friday evening came, and Polly arrived at the Bromleys' house in Grosvenor Square to spend the night with us. We had a festive time. Alice, in particular, loved having Polly sleep over. I was used to having a houseful of girls, but for Alice, an older sister must've seemed a real treat.

That Saturday dawned especially bright and fair, with breezes off the Thames blowing much of the fog and smoke of London elsewhere. Just the sort of day I would've wished for if I still had Mermeros, my djinni, and asked him to arrange a perfect outing for Polly. (In truth, I never would've squandered a wish on weather.) Polly was up before either Alice or me, tending to her toilette with special care. I managed to get all three of us downstairs ready to meet Mr. Poindexter and Tom when they arrived.

We took a cab to the London Bridge train station and boarded the Brighton Line. Onboard our train, we all squeezed into a compartment and discussed our plans for the day. This day, Saturday, the first of May, kicked off the Imperial Victorian Exhibition in honor of Queen Victoria's Diamond Jubilee. Sixty years, she'd been our queen! The nation would celebrate all year long. The Crystal Palace would be jam-packed with performances, music, and festivity. I didn't want to miss a minute of it.

"What do we do first?" I asked Alice and Tom. "The Topsy-Turvey Railway? Or the Canadian Water Chute?"

"Will we get quite soaked on the water chute, do you think?" asked Alice.

"I hope so," cried Tom. "It'll be marvelous."

"Maybe we should do that later on in the day," Alice suggested timidly. "After we've seen the sights."

"I think we should get in line for the roller coaster first of all," I said. "I'll bet everyone wants to ride that."

"I'm not sure I want to," Alice said. "It loops upside down!"

"You'll be safely buckled in," Tom pointed out.

"I've seen enough luggage and shoe buckles break," Alice said, "to place much faith in that."

We transferred to the Crystal Palace Line. This train was even more crowded. All of Britain, it seemed, wanted to celebrate the Imperial Victorian Exhibition's opening day.

Polly pulled her watch and chain from her handbag for about the dozenth time.

"Is the train running on time, do you think?" she asked Mr. Poindexter.

"I expect so," was his reply.

A pause.

"What time did Constable Hopewood say he would arrive at the Crystal Palace stop?"

"Nine o'clock sharp." Mr. Poindexter suppressed a smile. "I imagine we'll find him there when we arrive."

And sure enough, we did.

He wasn't easy to find. The station was mobbed. Families upon families. Swarms of children. Boy Scouting troops and Sunday school outing groups. Women with bright parasols, and men toting picnic baskets. Many, Mr. Poindexter included, with camera cases. Mothers and nannies counting children's heads. Finally Polly caught sight of him.

"Matthew!" she cried. "Matthew Hopewood!"

He saw Polly and pushed his way through the throng to reach her. Her face flushed pink with pleasure. Alice and I shared a secret grin.

Constable Hopewood wore a light-colored summer suit and a straw boater hat. Even so, he still had the air of one who might put a miscreant under arrest. He wore an invisible helmet, so to speak. Once an officer, always an officer. He shook hands with Mr.

Poindexter, and with us, then offered Polly his arm as we forged our way through the crowd.

We followed the herd up the stairs to the glassed-in walkway to the Crystal Palace, called the Crystal Colonnade, and jostled our way forward. The walkway was long and wide, humid with the scent of people. I didn't care, for when we turned a corner, the marvelous Crystal Palace came into sight atop Sydenham Hill.

"Blimey," whispered Tom, and he was right.

The morning sun, glinting off the Crystal Palace's thousands of panes of glass, nearly blinded me. The building was absolutely massive, yet it looked light as a bubble, carved from spun sugar. Fountains, pools, and pleasure gardens spread all around it for hundreds of acres. Off in the distance I saw the great curved loop of the Topsy-Turvy Railway tracks, and my stomach flopped in a happy little lurch of dread. Signs pointed to the dinosaur gardens and all the games along the fairway. As for the palace itself, music drifted out from the building, while balloons, clowns, stilt-walkers, and acrobats bobbed about before the great building, welcoming the throng.

Other visitors to the palace, coming from the street instead of the trains, climbed the granite steps, passing between massive, bloodred sphinxes, and entered the palace itself. For those of us coming from the trains, our glass-covered colonnade brought us right inside the building. We'd decided to begin indoors, to see some of the famous exhibits. Alice was determined not to miss the choral concert of music by Handel. I wanted to see the animals. The amusement rides, we decided, should come later.

The building felt even more huge inside than it had from outside. We came through the vestibule and marveled at all the indoor palm trees and ferns, growing in the lush, almost tropical warm air inside the glass-domed building. Water lilies swam in water fountains. Mighty statues of Greek gods and ancient warriors on horseback stood proudly at every turn. Signs pointed to the galleries of artwork, and to the Pompeii exhibit, the Medieval exhibit, the Byzantine, the Renaissance. Red and green parrots swooped through the air along with blue macaws and yellow parakeets. From one end of the grand nave we heard the distant screech and chatter of dozens of monkeys.

It was going to be quite a day.

"It's like reliving the history of the entire globe," Tom said, gazing about in wonder. "Starting with the dinosaurs."

"Not quite," Mr. Poindexter said with a smile. "But it's pretty spectacular, all the same."

We moved along the nave. The blue sky overhead gave a lightness to the whole space. A mezzanine level of walkways encircled the upper story of the building, crowded with people heading into different gallery and exhibit rooms, while on the lower level, vendors plied their wares of souvenirs, lemonade, and lobster salad.

I could have stared forever. Fountains and pools bobbing with lily pads. Colors and sounds, sizzling smells, throngs coming and going. The vastness, the sheer, staggering height of it all. Like a great cathedral filled with color and delight, and all of it glowing in the light pouring through millions of panes of glass.

Alice prodded my arm and startled me out of my reverie. "I'm going with Polly and Mr. Hopewood to find a seat at the Handel performance," she said. "I'll see you later."

I watched them leave. So far, my plans for Polly's romance with the reluctant constable were swimming along nicely. Sitting side by side at a concert for an hour would be just the thing. For them, that is. It wouldn't work any kind of a spell on me.

Tommy, Mr. Poindexter, and I spent a marvelous hour exploring one exhibit after another. Merchants displayed their most exciting new products. Ladies in aprons tried to dab me with French perfume. They clearly couldn't tell what kind of girl I was, but I felt too festive to be irked by it. Vast chambers were decorated in the rugs, drapes, and tapestries of periods gone by, with replicas of classic works of art. It really did feel as though we were visiting the great cities of long ago. As if we were really and truly there.

After a while, we passed by an area, shaded by leafy potted trees, where weary adults sat fanning their foreheads with their hats. Mr. Poindexter found an empty bench and sat down. I joined him. Before

Tom could, Mr. Poindexter thrust two shillings at him. "Go and buy us ginger ales, will you, my lad?"

Tom headed over to the nearest vendor and took a spot at the rear of a long queue. Musical strains from the Handel concert filtered along the length of the building over the voices of Palace attendees.

"This is wonderful, Mr. Poindexter," I told him. "Thanks for bringing us here for such a treat."

"The day wouldn't be complete without Tom's best chums." He leaned back on the bench and loosened his shirt collar. "Getting warm in here. The sun beating down through all that glass makes it a greenhouse."

"All the better reason to visit the Canadian Water Chute."

"I intend to be laughing from the sidelines," said Mr. Poindexter, "while the three of you get drenched."

I smiled at this image.

"And taking pictures." He pulled his camera from his case and peered through it. "Lighting's not bad," he murmured. "With the glass ceilings. Maybe I could attempt some indoor photographs, just for the sake of experiment."

I glanced over at Tom. The line at the refreshment bar didn't seem to have budged an inch. It seemed a safe enough time to ask Mr. Poindexter a question I'd been dying to ask for months, but no opportunity had arisen. And now I had a double reason for asking it.

"Mr. Poindexter," I began. "Have you, er, used it?" I knew he would know what I meant.

He peered through the camera. "Of course I have."

My heart sped up. *He'd used the djinni.* He'd already spent one of his wishes with Mermeros!

I was dying to know. "What did you do?" I inquired. "Did you go somewhere?"

He paused and turned a curious look my way. "I took it to your sister's wedding."

My jaw dropped. "You brought a *djinni* to Evangeline's wedding?"

His eyes grew wide. "Shh!" he hissed. He glanced around, apparently checking for signs of listening ears. The only person within possible range was a snoozing older gentleman. Satisfied, Mr. Poindexter turned back to me.

"Of course I didn't. *That's* what you thought I meant?"

"Well, what else could you mean?" I demanded. I checked once more on Tom's spot in line. Moving along, though slowly. "I asked you if you'd used '*it.*' What other 'it' could I mean?"

He chuckled. "*I* meant my new camera." He shook his head and lowered his voice to a whisper. "Not our, er, green friend."

I'd better pause to set things straight. I've mentioned that Mermeros, my djinni—my former djinni—whose rather fishy skin was green—was now in Mr. Poindexter's possession, but what I never explained is why. I gave him away, in fact. To Mr. Poindexter, in a trade for something very important to me. More important, even, than a third and final wish.

I now matched his low tone of voice. "You've had him, then, for months," I whispered, "and you still haven't used him?"

He shook his head. "I admit I've, er, brought him out of the tin for a bit of a talk, once or twice." He grinned. "He's quite a character, that Mer—"

"I know." Now I was the one glancing around suspiciously. "I wish I'd had your self-control. I'd be a rich girl today, if I hadn't been so foolish in my wishing."

"Come, now," he said. "That's hardly fair to yourself. I'd say you made excellent choices with your wishes."

"What do you think you will wish for, Mr. Poindexter?" I whispered. "I won't tell anyone. Your secret will be safe with me."

He turned and watched Tom across the wide nave of the Crystal Palace. "I already have everything I could wish for," he said simply. "I'm saving Mermeros for Tom."

I came very close then to jumping up and planting a kiss on Mr. Poindexter's shiny, bald head. Which is saying a lot, since the only thing I ever plan to kiss is a collie, someday, when I can have a dog of my own.

I managed to restrain myself. But oh, how it made me glad. I knew well how the greed for money and lust for power could take hold of someone, once a mighty djinni enters the picture. More than ever, I knew Tom had found one father in a million. He deserved him.

"You won't tell him, will you?" Mr. Poindexter's face had taken on a worried look.

"I won't," I told him solemnly. "I swear it."

Finally, Tom had reached the food counter and proffered payment for three ice-cold bottles of ginger ale. Even the sight of them from this far off made me thirsty.

I had just enough time to say what I must.

"Mr. Poindexter," I said softly, as though even the leafy potted palm trees had ears, "a woman came to Alice's house yesterday. She was the cook at our old school. She's been looking for me. Looking for—"

"*Shh.*" Mr. Poindexter let the soft sound escape his lips.

I nodded. I understood.

"She wouldn't have any reason to know where, er, he is now, would she?"

"I'm afraid she does know," I said faintly, "or will soon figure it out."

Tom headed back toward us with the cold drinks. Time was up.

Mr. Poindexter's expression grew grave for a moment. Then he straightened up tall. "I'm not worried about boarding-school cooks," he said. "Let her try. I've taken care that no one will ever find it."

My worries lifted. Mr. Poindexter was a brave man, and a wise one. If Mrs. Gruboil ever came hunting for Mermeros, he'd be ready. Mr. Poindexter was a thoroughly good egg, and a clever one, too.

★ ✳ ★

Tom appeared with three fizzing Schweppes ginger ales. The shopkeeper had already popped off the bottle caps. Tom handed his father the change, which Mr. Poindexter dropped into his coin purse. As he clasped it shut, the purse slipped through his fingers, and Tom and I spent a comical minute rounding up runaway coins and calling cards that had scattered on the wooden slat floors.

"Clumsy me," said Mr. Poindexter.

"What have you two been talking about all this time?" Tom asked.

"The water chute," I told him.

"And cameras," added Mr. Poindexter.

"Oh," said Tom, clearly unimpressed. He took a swig of ginger ale.

I took a drink of mine and glanced over at Mr. Poindexter. Behind Tom's back, he raised his bottle to me. A toast, so to speak. To our magical secret and to keeping it hidden, Mrs. Gruboil or no Mrs. Gruboil.

Partners in crime, all right.

S peaking of cameras, which we hadn't *exactly* been doing, but I won't split hairs, Mr. Poindexter was a child in a toy shop when we came upon the Photography and Motion Picture exhibit.

*Motion pictures!*

Mr. Poindexter could have more easily persuaded me that magic was the cause, and not science. For a sixpence, we each took a turn peeking into the hole in the Kinetoscope and watched a man doff his hat and wave hello, then watched another man sneeze, and then watched pair of prizefighters box in the ring.

It was incredible. It was so *real!* Somehow a photograph in a frame had come alive. As though miniature boxers and sneezing gentlemen in hats actually lived inside the tall wooden box.

Mr. Poindexter explained that a special camera, called the Kinetograph, took many pictures, one after another, and that if one looked at the pictures in rapid succession through a special light, it seemed as though the people were really moving, though they weren't. I wasn't sure I believed it. How could anyone ever take so many photographs so quickly?

The Kinetoscope and Kinetograph, Mr. Poindexter explained, were the inventions of an American, Mr. Thomas Edison, and a Briton, Mr. William Dickson. We also saw the Cinématographe, another moving picture machine by a Frenchman, Monsieur Louis Lumière. These tools were brand new and constantly changing.

"We live in a wondrous age," Mr. Poindexter declared. "Science will make anything possible. Someday we'll take trains across the oceans, and sail through the stars."

We toured the latest innovations in photography, cameras, lenses. A gentleman showed us a stereoscope, which we peered into much as one would a pair of opera glasses or field glasses, with a hole for each eye. Inside we saw a single picture, but instead of looking flat, it had *depth* to it. It was the most astonishing thing! The skier coming down the mountain was really coming straight at me. It made me dizzy. I backed away, as though the skier was going to hit me. Mr. Poindexter laughed.

These were, indeed, marvelous contraptions, but I was beginning to grow itchy and restless, anxious to go see the Monkey House, when Alice, Polly, and Constable Hopewood found us. We headed for the main corridor to swap details of our morning's adventures.

They began immediately, gushing about the Handel concert,

overflowing with rapturous praise. Which just goes to show that it takes all sorts to make a world. They might keep their Handel, and I'd keep my monkeys. To each, their own.

I pulled Alice aside and quizzed her.

"How was it?"

"Wonderful," she sighed. "The choir had *three thousand* singers, and—"

"I don't mean the music," I said. "I mean the romance."

Alice nodded thoughtfully. "Not much could happen with me there," she said, "but they did a fair bit of whispering back and forth between musical selections."

"Excellent." I chewed on my lip. "We need to get them alone together as much as possible."

"But Polly thinks she's here to chaperone us," Alice pointed out.

"We'll just have to show her we don't need that."

We returned to the rest of the group, who were beginning to discuss possibilities for the midday meal.

"Polly," I said, "why don't you go take a look at the Picture Gallery?"

"What a lovely idea," Polly said. "You'll come, won't you, Maeve?"

I hesitated. "I know how much you love artwork," I said. "I might spoil it for you with my, er, ignorance. You go. Tom and I need to plan our outdoor schedule. The rides, and things."

"Will you come, Alice?" asked Polly.

Alice would like nothing better, but I had to intervene.

"We need Alice to help make our plans," I said. "You go on without us. Mr. Hopewood, you enjoy picture galleries, don't you?"

"Well," he stammered, "that is to say…"

"Wonderful," I said. "Have a good time. Meet us afterward— after dinner, I mean. There are some lovely tea shops and cafés to choose from. Look for us outside after you've eaten."

"But, Maeve," cried Polly. "I promised I'd keep a close eye upon you girls."

"Mr. Poindexter will do just fine," I said. "We'll stay right with him. Run along now, Polly, Constable. Admission to the Picture Gallery is free, so no doubt the queue will be long. Have fun!"

I tugged Alice away and pretended to show her a carving of a satyr, spying all the while to make sure Polly and Mr. Hopewood left for the Picture Gallery.

"Your methods are fairly obvious," said a voice behind me.

I turned to see Mr. Poindexter gazing down at me with a faint smile on his lips.

"I don't know how to be subtle," I admitted, "but I'm determined to help Polly get what she wants."

"To grant her wishes, so to speak?" asked Mr. Poindexter.

"Something like that."

"Meaning," he said, "Mr. Hopewood?"

I nodded.

Mr. Poindexter pulled a monogrammed handkerchief from his pocket and used it to polish his spectacles. "Of course, I'm only a bachelor," he said, "so perhaps I wouldn't know, but I don't think such things can be rushed, or forced."

I ignored this. "Have they gone yet?"

He nodded. "Just left."

"Then, subtle or not," I told him, "my methods work."

Tom appeared at his father's side. "What methods?"

"Methods of matchmaking," I said.

He groaned.

I pulled two pence from my pocket and purchased a Crystal Palace programme book from an aproned young lady selling them. Sponsored, so the bold, black letters at the top declared, by "Epps's (Grateful, Comforting) Cocoa." Grateful cocoa? What did cocoa have to be grateful for?

I waved the programme book at them. "This tells what's going on today at the Crystal Palace. We can use it to make plans." I began leafing through the pages. "We need to keep Polly and her constable together as much as possible. Just the two of them."

"Do it too much, and they'll become suspicious," Mr. Poindexter pointed out.

"Welcome to the team," I told him. "I see you've joined the cause."

Tom looked over my shoulder at the programme book. "Roller skating?" he suggested.

"If it were me, I'd love it, but Polly's not the most coordinated person I know," I told him. "I'm not sure smashed knees and black eyes are very romantic."

"Aha," said Tom, "but if she's clumsy, all the better reason to hold on tight to the constable, to stay upright." He waggled his eyebrows.

Tom was beginning to surprise me. Mr. Poindexter had to look away to hide a smile.

"They'll have a nice luncheon," Alice said. "Maybe next they might enjoy boating on the lake?"

"How about the Royal Exhibition of Working Ants?" suggested Tom. He read from the programme: "'Glass Nests of Living Animals at Work, Illuminated and Magnified.'"

Alice stared at him.

"What?" demanded Tom. "No ants? All right. How about the New American Bowling Saloon?"

I turned to see Mr. Poindexter shaking with laughter. "Son," he said, "if the day ever comes that you decide to go a-courting—"

"*Dad!*" groaned Tom.

"Then you and I will need to have a talk."

I personally didn't think Tom's ideas were half-bad, but I could see at a glance that they wouldn't do at all for Polly and her precious Matthew.

"You three need help, it's plain." Mr. Poindexter relieved Tom of the programme book and leafed through it. "Alice's idea of boating on the lake is very sound. And the fireworks show at dusk should be exciting. Romantic, even."

"What about this comic play at three o'clock?" I asked. "It's called *The New Baby*."

"Good heavens!" Alice, in a rare display of firmness, folded her arms across her chest. "I think we should leave them to their own devices," she said. "Let them choose what they enjoy. You can't control this, Maeve."

"I'm not trying to," I said. "I just know Polly will feel she needs to stick with us, so I thought we should plan our day around romantic activities for them."

"Just please promise me you'll never try to arrange a romance for me," Alice said.

Tom scowled. "*I* didn't come here for romance," he said. "This is rubbish."

"Why don't we take ourselves out of the picture?" suggested Alice. "We'll go outside and ride the rides you've been going on about. They'll find ways to amuse themselves without us, I'm sure."

"Hear, hear," cried Mr. Poindexter. "A very sensible proposal.

Let's go find your Topsy-Turvy Train or whatever it is. We'll find
something to eat at one of the outdoor stands."

This arrangement suited everyone, so we made our way outside.
The sun was hot, yet the breeze felt cooler than the air inside the
hothouse atmosphere of the Crystal Palace. We hurried over to the
queue for the Topsy Turvy Railway. Mr. Poindexter declined to ride
the roller coaster, but held our hats and promised to try to get a
photograph of us.

We climbed into the open train carriages and let the attendant
buckle us in. I confess I tugged hard on my straps to make sure they
were tight. That strap was all that stood between me and a long fall
to my death. Tom and I sat side by side in the front seats of the first
carriage in the train. We would have the best view of all. Or worst
view, depending on how you felt about it. Alice wanted no part of the
front seat. She sat behind us.

Once everyone was secured, the operator cranked the great lever,
and we were off.

I like to think I'm brave, but this roller coaster was like nothing
I'd ever experienced. And I'd flown from London to Persia on a
magical journey, carried aloft by a djinni's power. This rackety ride
was awful and wonderful, both together. Our stomachs flopped as
we tipped downward over the first descent. How we screamed! How
the wind rushed through our hair! How the clacking wheels on the

wooden tracks sounded determined to fly apart! How time stood still, right at the upside-down peak of the loop-de-loop!

And to think it needed no magic.

Finally the marvelous terror came to an end. Our carriage coasted to a stop. We clambered out on shaky legs.

"I will never, ever do that again," moaned Alice.

"Maeve," cried Tom, "let's get back in line."

We saw Mr. Poindexter waving at us from beyond the rope cordoning off the ride from curious onlookers, so we hurried over to him.

"How was it?" Mr. Poindexter's eyes twinkled. "As much fun as you imagined, Tom?"

"More," said he. "Did you get any good photographs, Dad?"

"Sadly, no," confessed Mr. Poindexter. "I kept hunting for a good spot. Finally I found one, but before I could get my Kodak focused, a uniformed chap told me photographs weren't permitted in the Palace or on the grounds. Only their authorized photographer is allowed to take pictures. Negretti and Zambra, I think he said their names were. You can bet they'll charge a mint." He patted his camera case despondently. "I'll be carrying this all day for nothing. Other chaps managed to get some photographs in before they came over and stopped me, confound them."

The rest of the day unfolded like a grand game of hide-and-seek.

We were the seekers, trying to spot Polly and her constable without being seen. We spied them eating ice cream cones and strolling through gardens while we watched the steeplechase pony races, which were tremendously exciting. We saw them pause to watch a gigantic strong man swing a long-handled hammer to strike the strength tester. The man was impossibly huge, positively bulging with muscles, and his mighty swing rang the bell at the top of the pole. Polly clapped and clapped. As they walked away, Constable Hopewood somehow inflated himself to a full swagger, as if to show that he had muscles, too. It was a good thing I was far enough away to howl with laughter without being heard.

The clincher came while waiting in line for the water chute. We saw Constable Hopewood pulling at the oars of a rowboat, sculling Polly around on the quiet lake. Polly reclined under her parasol like some lady in a painting. It would probably give me hives—I'd much rather have a go at the oars myself, and no gentleman required—but she looked like she couldn't possibly be happier.

We saw them so many times that I began to wonder how they hadn't seen us. Perhaps they were lost in romance. More likely, Polly was pretending not to see us. What had come over my sister, the queen of propriety?

As for our party, Mr. Poindexter was vexed by the no-camera policy. He ground his teeth every time he saw people taking unauthorized photographs. He was too law-abiding by nature to break the rules, but that didn't stop him from grumbling when others did. It was a shame, too. We would've gotten some topping photographs out of our grand day out. We crammed a month of fun into a single day. We rode the roller coaster two more times (minus Alice) and took two soaking trips down the Canadian Water Chute. To her credit, Alice didn't complain when the splashes soaked her right through.

The late afternoon air began to cool. It smelled of sugary dough-nuts and frying potato chips. As the sun sank beneath the distant rooftops, lights winked on all over the Palace grounds. Lighted signs in their many colors, and lighted rides spinning through the sky, mingled with strains of festive music and cries of laughter from every corner gave the place a truly magical, carnival air.

Mr. Poindexter, Alice, Tom, and I were sitting eating candied apples when we spotted Constable Hopewood and Polly stepping up to the opulent carousel. Polly shyly accepted her companion's help to sit atop her painted horse.

"Feeling pleased with yourself, Miss Maeve?" inquired Mr. Poindexter.

"I can't take any credit," I told him. "It was Alice who said we should leave them alone."

"Do you think he'll propose to her?" Alice's eyes shone.

"Probably not here, today," Mr. Poindexter said. "Let's just hope they've been having a good time."

Families with younger children began to make their way toward the exits. Children protested that they weren't tired, not even a little, even as they rubbed their eyes and tugged their fathers' sleeves, asking to be carried. Hawkers, vendors, and ride operators began bawling their cries of "Last call! Closing soon! Have a final go!"

"Fireworks in ten minutes," criers bellowed. "Gather at the amphitheater!"

We gathered up our things—Tom and I had both won prizes at game stalls—and followed the throng toward the amphitheater, where the best views of the fireworks could be had.

The show began, you might say, with a bang. One rocket after another whined as it raced into the sky, then exploded with a boom that set our teeth rattling. Rockets of every color burst overhead, ever faster, one after another. The popping of bombs rattled with the staccato burst of a military drumroll.

I turned to Mr. Poindexter.

"Thank you again," I said, "for a magical day."

"What'd you say?" he cried.

"Thank you again," I repeated loudly, "for a magical day."

He held up a hand to his ear. "Sorry," he roared. "Can't hear a thing."

I shook my head. "Forget it," I bellowed. "Tell you later."

Overhead, the pyrotechnic finale roared, lighting the sky with explosive showers of glittering colored light. I watched, feeling like a tiny little thing perched atop my dad's shoulder on Guy Fawkes's Night. Some wonders never grow old. I hope they never will.

I felt a tap on my shoulder. Looking up, I saw Mr. Poindexter's sly expression as he pointed surreptitiously over his shoulder to something behind him and uphill.

There, standing at the very rim of the amphitheater, where there was nobody behind them to see, stood Matthew Hopewood, spangled in swimming dots of firework light, leaning down to kiss my sister.

She certainly did *not* seem to mind.

*Well.*

I couldn't look, and I couldn't not look.

As I say, kissing is not a subject that interests me. The less of it I need to witness in my lifetime, the better. (Collies excepted.) But this kiss—unlike, say, Evangeline's wedding performance—left me with a glow all my own. Good old Polly. May Matthew Hopewood come, in time, to deserve her. If Polly felt he would, who was I to say nay?

Mr. Poindexter's eyes twinkled. He held out a solemn hand, and I shook it. A scheme well executed. A job well done.

Partners in crime to the last.

I 'll say this for Polly. When we rejoined her and her constable after the fireworks show—"Fancy finding you here!"—and made our way together back to the Crystal Palace train station, she was as cool as a cucumber. I expected her to be a fluttery mess, given what had just happened. Not she. (Perhaps I momentarily confused her for one of our other sisters.)

"We've been looking for you all day long," she told us. "I've been worried sick."

*Ha!* Worried sick, was she? Not lounging in her lake boat like Cleopatra? It seemed even Polydora had a sneaky side. I liked her better for it.

I glared at Tom to make sure he didn't produce any saucy replies to her statement. He only laughed silently at me. I nearly burst into laughter myself, just by looking at him.

"We stayed right with Mr. Poindexter all day," Alice said sweetly. "He was very obliging about visiting the rides and things we wanted to see."

We said our goodbyes on the train, and Mr. Hopewood shook

hands with us all. Polly's hand he shook so seriously, I nearly laughed aloud. It was all I could do not to crow, "I saw you kiss my sister!" But I managed to stay quiet.

Mr. Poindexter and Tom deposited us at the Bromleys' home late at night, then made their way home.

Polly slept over once more, and left for home early Sunday morning. She never said a word about Mr. Hopewood. But surely, I thought, wheels were in motion. My web-spinning had indeed caught her the constable of her dreams. I was certain of it.

Sunday afternoon brought more sunny weather, so Alice and I took a walk through the park at Grosvenor Square. We were just returning to the Bromleys' front door when a cab drove up and disgorged Tommy and Mr. Poindexter, looking grim.

"The shop's been robbed!" cried Tom. "While we were at the Crystal Palace, someone broke in!"

"Oh, no," cried Alice. "How awful!"

I turned to Mr. Poindexter. He gave a short, grim shake of the head. She hadn't gotten Mermeros.

*Mrs. Gruboil.* It had to be. Oh, I would find her and make her sorry she ever laid a finger on the door to the Oddity Shop.

"What was stolen?" I asked. "How much is lost?"

Mr. Poindexter looked both dejected and furious. I'd never seen him this way before. He opened his mouth to answer, then shook his head.

"Won't you come in?" Alice beckoned our visitors up the stairs. Mr. Linzey welcomed us in, relieved us of our coats, and brought us to the drawing room.

When he pulled the door shut behind him, Tom answered my question. "The thief took loads of things," he said. "Vases, old bottles. A few lamps, and a very precious Chinese urn."

Alice glanced at me nervously. "Are those, er, the most valuable things in the shop?"

Mr. Poindexter shook his head. "The thief was a bumbler," he growled. "Didn't know the first thing about antiquities. Left the most valuable items untouched. Passed right over the jade hair clips, the ivory combs, and several fine items of Egyptian jewelry."

Vases, bottles, lamps, and an urn? It certainly sounded like someone searching for a djinni. But the only person who would have even a suspicion of finding Mermeros at the Oddity Shop knew full well that Mermeros made his home in a sardine tin.

Why would Mrs. Gruboil steal lamps and bottles?

"We've just come from the police," said Tom. "Scotland Yard. They've got a detective on the case."

Mr. Poindexter's gaze kept glancing my way, then at Tom, then at the floor. I realized he wanted to speak to me alone, but didn't know what to do about Tom.

"Say, Alice," I said, "remember those new Robert Louis Stevenson novels you were saying you wanted to show to Tom?"

Alice blinked. She'd said no such thing to me, ever.

"I—"

"The ones in the library, on that shelf to the left of the fireplace," I prompted. "Remember how you said they'd be just the thing for Tom?"

Tom scratched his head. "I'm not really thinking about books right now, Maeve."

I gave Alice a bit of a waggle to my eyebrows.

"Yes," Alice said slowly, "but it will only take a moment, Tom. Come with me, won't you?"

Looking rather bewildered, Tom followed Alice out of the room.

"Miss Maeve," Mr. Poindexter whispered, "what can you tell me about this cook you mentioned? From your school? Where she lives, and so on? Could you describe her?"

I gulped. "I could describe her," I said. "Last I knew, she lived at that grand old house near Miss Salamanca's School." I searched my memory. What was it called? "Darvill House," I said. "That's the name of the place. But perhaps she doesn't live there anymore."

"And her name?"

"Mrs. Gruboil."

He rubbed a hand over his bald head. "Do you know her given name?"

The thought that someone as unpleasant as Mrs. Gruboil might once have been a little Charlotte or Vivian was too strange to contemplate.

I shook my head.

"Is there a *Mr.* Gruboil?"

"Not that I've ever heard of," I replied, "though I suppose there must have been, once."

He sank back into his chair and gazed helplessly at the embers on the grate. "What to do, what to do…"

I leaned in closer. "But she didn't get Mermeros, did she?"

He shook his head distractedly. "No one would ever know how to find him. But that's not my chief concern. I can't run a business, nor raise a boy, in a home that's being broken into every night. What must I do? Move away? Never leave the shop? Sleep downstairs with my pistols in hand? Get a guard dog?"

I thought the last idea was a splendid one, but not necessarily a solution to his problem.

"It's only Mrs. Gruboil," I said. "How dangerous can she be?"

At this, Mr. Poindexter roused somewhat. "Whoever did this," he said, "was powerful. The rear door to the shop was shattered, Maeve. Glass broken everywhere. Cabinets turned on end."

I rubbed the goose pimples on my arms.

"She must have brought someone along," he said. "Must be, she was the diver, and she brought along a cracksman."

"I beg your pardon?"

He glanced up at me. "Oh. A diver is a thief who breaks in and keeps watch. The cracksman is the one who does the actual stealing. They work in pairs."

Nobody'd ever taught me this at Miss Salamanca's School for Upright Young Ladies, to say the least.

"Mr. Poindexter," I said, "what will you do?"

He blew out his breath. "I don't know, Maeve," he admitted, "but I plan to treat this as nothing more, and nothing less, than a simple robbery. I don't want Tom to get any idea of what Mrs.... Whatever-her-name is after."

I nodded. "I understand."

A moment later, Tom and Alice returned from the library. Tom held two books in his hands. Mr. and Mrs. Bromley joined us, too, and for the remainder of their visit, Tommy and his dad spoke of the robbery in worried tones and munched on the sandwiches Mrs. Harding, the housekeeper, brought, without another mention of Mrs. Gruboil, and certainly no mentions of djinnis hidden away in sardine tins.

Hidden *where*? I wondered. If I knew where Mermeros was, could I...

*Stop that, Maeve*, I told myself sternly, *or you'll turn into a Mrs. Gruboil yourself.*

Two days later, on Tuesday afternoon, Alice and I were hard at work in the schoolroom with Mr. Abernathy, our tutor, copying passages in Greek from the *Iliad* and translating them into English. Achilles was just then chasing Hector around the walls of Troy, and I'd been waiting *weeks* for these two to finally start fighting, so for once, I didn't welcome the interruption when Mr. Linzey, the butler, appeared at the schoolroom door.

"A telephone call," he announced in his deep, respectable, buttling voice, "for Miss Maeve."

Alice and Mr. Abernathy both stared at me. I'd never received a telephone call in my life. I'd never even spoken into a telephone before. Our family didn't have one, and who else would I have to call?

"I'm not sure that our classroom can endure these continued interruptions due to Maeve's busy social calendar," Mr. Abernathy said drily. But he winked at me as I rose from my desk.

I followed Mr. Linzey downstairs to the receiver in Mr. Bromley's office. Fortunately, he wasn't in. I held the handset up to my ear and leaned in toward the speaker mounted to the wooden box, feeling more than a little bit silly.

Was this how it was done? What did one say?

"Maeve Merritt speaking," I said. Too loud? Too soft? I had no idea.

"Maeve!"

A voice came crackling over the wire and into my ear, so loud I almost dropped the handset.

"This is she," I said. "Who is this?"

"Can't you tell? It's Poindexter. Tommy's dad."

For heaven's sake. How many Poindexters did he think I knew?

"Good afternoon, Mr. Poindexter."

That was him, all right. His voice, crackly and fuzzy though it sounded, coming magically across the wires. There he was, far across town, and here was I, and yet we spoke to each other as if face-to-face. Of course, I knew that was how it worked, yet still it was extraordinary, when you stopped to think about it. Over all the noise and clamor of London between us, we could talk to each other privately.

"Where are you, Mr. Poindexter?" I knew his store, the Oddity Shop, didn't have a telephone.

"At the post office."

Then I began to worry. Had he not yet received my thank-you note? Did he think I was being rude?

"Maeve, which newspapers do the Bromleys take?"

How would I know?

Fortunately, I was in the right place. The day's papers were stacked in a neat pile atop Mr. Bromley's desk. "Hold a moment," I told him. I set down the handset and fetched the papers. "*The Daily News,*" I told him. "*The Morning Post, The Times, The Daily Telegraph, The Financial News—*"

"Confound it," he cried. "They can't possibly read all those."

*They employ a dozen household servants who like to read the paper in their leisure hours*, I thought, but I said nothing.

"*The Globe and Traveller,*" I continued, "*The Westminster Gazette.*"

"*Globe and Traveller,*" he cried. "That's my paper. Do you have today's edition?"

I checked the date. "Yes," I told him. "Tuesday, May 4."

"Good," he said. "Now, turn to the very back page. The advertisements column."

I set the other papers down on a window seat and turned to the back page of *The Globe and Traveller.*

"Are you there? Good. How many telephone receivers are in the Bromleys' house?"

How *many*? What would a household need with more than one telephone? "Just the one."

"Now," he said, "listen carefully. The second to the last column, about two or three inches down. Tell me when you see it."

"See what?" I asked.

"You'll know," he said ominously. "But, Maeve, listen. Don't read it out loud. Just read it to yourself. All right?"

Curiouser and curiouser.

I scanned my finger down the column, and then I saw it.

*Reward given for verifiable information about recent djinni sightings in London. Write to Box 927, in care of this paper.*

Silence crackled over the line.

Mr. Poindexter's voice broke it. "You've read it?"

I nodded. Then I remembered he couldn't see me. "Yes, sir."

More silence. I writhed in my shoes.

"Is there anything you want to tell me, Maeve?"

My mouth was dry. "No, sir. Nothing."

"Do you know anything, anything at all about this?"

I swallowed. "Nothing," I said. "Nothing at all."

"Do you think it was the boarding-school cook who stole Mermeros from you? What was her name—Mrs. Gargoyle?"

"Gruboil," I said. "If she's really squandered or lost all her money, she couldn't give a reward. And it doesn't sound like her, though maybe she had help in writing it."

I waited a moment for Mr. Poindexter's reply.

"Now, Maeve," he said. "I want you to think. Of all the people who knew about, or had heard about, you having, er, *it*, would any of them have cause to know...who has it now?"

I ticked through the people in my mind, the cast of nasties who'd tangled with me last winter.

"Only my father," I said at length, "and he would never betray a secret like that."

"No," said Mr. Poindexter after a pause, "I don't believe he would. I've been running through, in my mind, all that you've told me about your past, er, escapades. It got me thinking. What about the fellow who had burgled you? You called him 'the ginger-whiskered man.'"

Ah. Him. Back when I had Mermeros, my chief nemesis, Mr. Alfred P. Treazleton, had sent his hired secretary after me, wearing false ginger whiskers as a disguise, first following me all about London, then breaking into my home and my dormitory room to steal Mermeros from me. The monster.

"His name was Mr. Rooch," I said, "but I can't see any reason why he would know that you now have—"

Mr. Poindexter cut me off before I could say too much. "I understand," he said. "I had to be sure."

"Mr. Poindexter," I said, "would you mind waiting for just a
moment?"

He consented. I set the handset down and leafed through the
other newspapers on Mr. Bromley's desk. It didn't take long to
locate their advertisement pages, toward the back. I began scanning
through the columns, one paper after the other. Finally I returned to
the telephone, though my feet felt made of lead.

"Mr. Poindexter," I told him, "the advertisement is in all the
newspapers."

His moan sounded in my ear.

"Do you have, er, it safely hidden?" I asked in a low voice.

"Yes," he said. "I'd better go. If you hear anything, or think of
anything, you will send me word, won't you?"

I nodded, then caught myself once again. *He can't see you.* "I will.
I promise."

"Thank you," he said. "I don't like this, but it's likely to come to
nothing. Good afternoon, Maeve."

"Good afternoon."

I hung the handset back in its cradle, and walked slowly back to
the schoolroom, the *Iliad*, and my very puzzled thoughts.

CHAPTER

6

The baffling advertisements appeared in Wednesday's papers also, but by Thursday they'd vanished. They weren't the only bizarre and ludicrous advertisements in the column, to be sure. People offered their services bleeding the sick with leeches, and speaking with the departed souls of one's dead relatives. Dozens upon dozens advertised things like "Active woman (30) with £2000 seeks mature gentleman, matrimonially inclined." *Egads.*

As days passed, and I heard nothing more from Mr. Poindexter, my worries faded into the distance. In a metropolis the size of London, burglaries were bound to happen. It could well have been a fluke. It might have had nothing to do with Mrs. Gruboil and the djinni. The police were investigating things. I had much more pressing things to think about: Polly's romantic developments, or rather, the lack thereof.

I wrote Polly several letters, never mentioning Matthew Hopewood directly, but often reminiscing about what a grand time we'd all had at the Crystal Palace, asking her what she'd been doing lately, and if there was anything new. Her replies were Classic Polydora—warm, friendly, conversational, affectionate, and 100 percent free of any glimpses into her romance whatsoever.

A lesser girl might surrender. A lesser girl might say to her immortal soul, "Leave off, then. It's out of my hands. I can't make this union come about, try as I might to employ tricks and strategies." A lesser girl might say all this, and more.

I am no lesser girl.

"Very well, Polly," I told my soul—as to its immortality or otherwise, I can't be sure. "You may keep your secrets. I know I keep mine. But I won't back down until I've secured your happiness for you. So there."

If I couldn't pry information from Polly, I needed another source. I made a list of possibilities:

1.   Father.

A good sport, but probably oblivious to romantic matters. Would grow suspicious if I asked him questions.

2.   Mother.

Very funny. I crossed her off.

3.   Deborah.

Good heavens. Too self-absorbed by half to take any interest in Polly.

I nearly stopped there. Then one more idea crossed my mind. I took pencil in hand once more.

4. Evangeline.

The new bride herself. Now back from her honeymoon trip and setting up housekeeping. With her own wedding behind her, might she take an interest in the marital hopes of her eldest sister?

She just might.

I wrote her a letter.

Dear Evangeline,

I hear you are back now from your trip to the Isle of Wight. Did you have a good time? Did you see any seals? Congratulations again on your marriage. I had thought I would find the wedding day dreadfully dull, but it wasn't too bad. The cream puffs were a treat. How is Rudolph? Do you like your new home? Have you seen much of the family yet? How is Polly? I saw her when she came with me to the Crystal Palace last weekend. With the wedding over, I wonder what

Polly will do with herself these days. She talks about her flower beds in her letters, but I think she needs more than that to occupy her time. Don't you?

    Write soon.

                    Your sister,
                    Maeve

I posted the letter, and waited.

Evangeline's reply came quickly.

Dear Maeve,

Well! Fancy getting a letter from you. Dad may be right; perhaps you are growing up.

The Isle of Wight was lovely. Thank you for asking. Rudolph and I had a wonderful time. We met some charming people. No, I didn't see any seals. Why on earth should I want to?

It is good to be back home and to set up housekeeping with all our new things. We received some lovely presents, and some odd ones. A silver creamer, shaped like a cow. I won't say who gave it to us. It's hideous.

Funny, you mentioning Polly. Do you know, between the two of us, I do believe she's in love. That policeman of hers, the one who came to the wedding. Deborah tells me he's been to the house more lately. Mother and Dad have invited him to come for dinner this Sunday. Rudolph and I will be there, too, and Mother is ordering up quite a menu for the occasion. Don't tell Deborah, she'll have fits, but I shouldn't wonder if that policeman doesn't ask Dad for Polly's hand Sunday evening. I do hope so, for I now know loads and loads about how to plan a wedding, and I can tell Polly where to find all the best bargains on chiffon and lace.

Well, behave yourself if you can, and do write again.

Your loving sister,
Mrs. Rudolph Seymour

Mrs. *Rudolph* Seymour! She must've felt quite fancy and all grown up, calling herself that. As for me, if I were ever to marry, which I never, ever, ever shall, you wouldn't catch me calling myself Mrs. What's-*his*-name for all the gold in the Tower. *Mrs. Rudolph Seymour* indeed!

But my plan had worked. Evangeline would tell me what I needed to know. And, I had to admit, it was fun to get a letter from her. Maybe now that she was settled down, I would learn what else went on between her ears besides romance. Prior to now, I would have sworn there wasn't much. I resolved to write back and keep the correspondence going.

But before I had a chance to reply, something happened that drove all thoughts of letters, and of matchmaking, far, far from my mind.

A long, eye-splitting day of trying to decode a paragraph in Greek left me cross and droopy, so, along with the rest of the household, I went to bed early that Thursday evening, nearly two weeks after our Crystal Palace outing.

The night was chilly for late spring, but I'd just begun to feel that warm, melting feeling underneath the eiderdown, not long after tucking myself in and cracking open *The Count of Monte Cristo* (I'd finished *Wuthering Heights*), when the quiet of the Bromleys' Grosvenor Square town home was shattered by an urgent pull on the downstairs bell.

Alice sat up in her bed and dropped her copy of *David Copperfield*. "What on earth?"

We reached for our housecoats and slippers. A ring at this late after dark, on a cold night, could only mean something interesting. Possibly tragic and terrible. I wasn't about to miss it.

We hadn't climbed down many stairs when a familiar voice

reached my ears. What could bring Tom here at this hour? I scrambled down the remaining flights and slid down the banister.

Mrs. Harding, the housekeeper, was too startled by the late visitor, and probably too embarrassed by being seen in her nightcap by Mr. Linzey, to scold me about my disgraceful conduct.

"Maeve," Tommy said vacantly. His face was pale and pinched with cold.

"What's the matter, Tom?" The sight of him alarmed me. He shivered as if he'd seen a ghost.

"Mr. Linzey, is there a fire lit anywhere?" Alice asked. "Tom's freezing."

Mrs. Harding pointed to a door at the rear of the foyer. "Bring him into the kitchen," she said. "We'll warm him up."

Mr. and Mrs. Bromley appeared one floor above, peering down over the railings. When they saw Tommy, they descended quickly and followed us in.

In short order, Mrs. Harding turned up the gas lamps, lit the kitchen stove, and put the kettle on. She set slices of bread and a dish of butter before Tom, but he didn't even look at the food. That's when I knew something was really wrong.

"Did you take a cab to get here, Tom?" asked Alice.

He shook his head. "Ran."

"Good gracious," gasped Alice.

"Tom, what is it?" I asked him. I took him by the shoulders and made him face me. "What's happened?"

"Have some tea, my dear," urged Mrs. Bromley, offering him a cup. "It will do you good."

Tommy took the tea obediently but seemed not to know what to do with the cup. It wobbled in his grip. I took it from him and set it down again.

"Papa," Alice said, addressing her grandfather, "hadn't we ought to find a way to ring Mr. Poindexter? Send him a message? He must be worried sick."

"He's not there." Tommy's voice sounded hoarse.

"What do you mean, he's not there, young man?" inquired Mr. Bromley. "Has he gone out for the evening?"

Tom shook his head. "He's been gone for three days."

Cold of another kind swept over me. Mr. Poindexter? Missing?

"Three days?" gasped Mrs. Bromley. "But where?"

"Dunno." Tommy replied. "Begging your pardon, ma'am. I don't know. He never said anything about going anywhere. Tuesday morning, I woke up, and he was gone."

Alice's hand flew up over her mouth. "What did you do then?"

"Nothing," Tom said. "Opened the shop and ran it as usual. At first I thought he must've just gone out early in the morning. I kept on waiting, thinking any moment he'd come back. All day long, I thought up new reasons why he might've gone away. When he didn't come back by night, I thought, well, maybe a coach or train was held up. When he didn't come back the second night, I thought, maybe he's taken ill somewhere. When he didn't come back today, I went out and started asking at hospitals and—" Tom's voice broke off.

"But surely," protested Mrs. Bromley, "if he'd fallen upon some misfortune, he would have sent a message. He can't have gone far. Word would have reached you by now. I feel certain of it."

"I didn't find him," Tom said. "Not in any of the hospitals or... other places I looked."

*Mortuaries.*

"That's not all," he went on. "An inspector from the Orphans' Committee, or something like that, came by today to see how Dad was treating me." He gulped. "She said she'd heard reports that he wasn't treating me right."

"*What?*" cried Alice.

"Who would ever say that?" I demanded.

"It's not true," Tommy declared angrily. "My dad's the kindest, friendliest—"

His face crumpled. He buried it in his napkin.

Alice and I gazed at each other in dismay. Mr. and Mrs. Bromley stood holding on tightly to each other, watching Tom with compassion and concern.

Poor Tom. I wanted to sock whoever had done this to him. Right in the nose, with two black eyes for good measure. But no amount of pummeling anyone would solve the mess Tom was in.

Finally he set down his napkin.

"The woman waited for two hours," he said quietly. "Asked me all sorts of questions. When he never came back, she looked ready to boil." His head drooped. "I'm afraid they're going to try to take me back to the home."

It broke my heart to see Tom looking so frightened. And no wonder. To be sent back to that dreadful Mission Industrial School and Home for Working Boys would feel to him like a fate worse than death. Especially in his case. An orphan boy his age would be sent directly to the cotton mills up north and put to work.

But Tom! This wasn't anything like the brave, brash lad I knew, the one who had terrorized me so when I first found my djinni in a sardine tin last winter. He saw Mermeros, too, and until we'd finally made a pact, of sorts, and became friends, he never let up in his attempts to steal him from me.

Tom was always fearless. But not tonight. Not now that he had a home and a father and a place to belong. Perhaps it's easier to be fearless when you have nothing to lose.

"Eat something, Tom." I buttered him a piece of bread. "You're not going back to that horrid orphanage. We'll find your dad. But you'll be no use to Mr. Poindexter if you haven't any strength." I practically shoved the bread into his mouth, and watched to make sure he chewed and swallowed it.

"Come, now, young Thomas," Mr. Bromley said. "It's late, and you need sleep. If Mr. Poindexter has been gone three days, it's doubtful that searching anywhere for him tonight will amount to much. You shall sleep here tonight, and in the morning we'll decide what to do. Mrs. Harding is lighting a fire and preparing a bed for you right now."

Mr. and Mrs. Bromley left the kitchen, beckoning for Tommy to follow them upstairs. Alice and I brought up the rear, but as Tom began to climb the stairs, I tugged at his sleeve.

"Tom," I whispered, "had your dad said anything about going anywhere? Mentioned any place he needed to visit? Anything like that?"

Tommy's face fell. "Nowhere at all," he said. "I mean, we talk all the time about grand trips we want to take, all over the world. Imagining. Not making any real plans." He chewed his lip. "Just Sunday night, he said we were going to dust and organize the shop's Chinese curio cabinet this week. I'm sure he hadn't intended on leaving."

Alice's grandparents turned to see why we weren't following them, so we hurried to catch up.

"He's been on edge, though," Tom added, "ever since the burglary."

And the advertisements in the papers, too, no doubt, though

Tom would have known nothing about them. I bit my lip. Was there a connection? Surely *Mrs. Gruboil* couldn't have kidnapped Mr. Poindexter. I couldn't believe anyone could. Wherever he went, I felt certain, he'd gone of his own choice.

"Had he any telegrams or strange letters lately?" whispered Alice.

Tommy shook his head. "Not that I know of."

We reached the landing, and Mrs. Bromley led Tommy into a guest room, where a clean nightshirt and a pair of pajama trousers lay waiting for him on his bed. We bid him good night and left him to Alice's grandparents' care, trudging up the next flight of stairs to our own room.

As soon as we were inside, I shut the door behind us.

"Alice," I whispered, "do you realize what's happened?"

She looked startled. "How could I? I can't imagine what horrible thing has happened to Mr. Poindexter—"

I cut her off. "Nothing horrible happened," I said. "Well, something horrible has probably happened by now. But he's not gone because—oh, don't you see? He went somewhere. Expecting to come straight back. In a few hours, tops. But something went wrong."

Alice's eyes grew round. "You mean, Mermeros?"

I nodded. "It has to be. There's no other explanation. Mr. Poindexter took a magical journey with the djinni. And somehow, wherever he went, he's gotten stuck there, and he can't come back."

CHAPTER
8

Alice sank onto her bed in a state of shock. "That means he could be anywhere in the world, and in heaven knows what sort of danger."

I nodded.

"Or even..." Alice paused.

"Don't say it," I told her. "He's in some sort of trouble, but he's alive. I'm sure of it."

Alice's look said she was anything but sure of it. "I hope you're right." She took off her slippers and hung her housecoat on its hook. "Do you think Mrs. Gruboil has anything to do with it?"

I frowned. "I couldn't imagine her kidnapping Mr. Poindexter."

"But what if she didn't act alone?" pressed Alice. "What if she had some kind of help? Or had hired someone?"

"I wouldn't have thought her capable of pulling it off," I said. "She's neither clever nor brave."

Alice shook her head. "I don't know about that," she said. "When she came here to the house, she seemed quite desperate. Perhaps greed brings out someone's cunning." She smiled ruefully. "It did for you."

I ignored her little jab. It *couldn't* be Mrs. Gruboil. All the same, who else but she had an inkling that Mr. Poindexter had Mermeros? It must have been she who robbed the shop, though Mr. Poindexter believed it had to have been a strong man who did it.

Maybe she did have an accomplice. Maybe it was Mrs. Gruboil after all.

"How will we ever find him, Maeve?"

Alice's words interrupted my thought. I had no idea how to answer. But I couldn't let Alice see my doubts or fears. "We'll find him," I insisted. "We'll find a way."

Alice was quiet for a moment. Finally she spoke. "Tom still doesn't know, does he?"

I shook my head. "I'm sure he doesn't. If he knew his father had Mermeros, he'd have said something."

"And when he finds out...?"

I went to the window and gazed at the twinkling lights of a nighttime London sky.

"I can't predict what he'll say," I said slowly. "He may never forgive me. But finding Mr. Poindexter matters more than worrying what Tom thinks, now."

When I showed the djinni to Mr. Poindexter to prove Tommy wasn't out of touch with reality for believing in djinnis, and then bartered Mermeros in return for the shopkeeper making Tommy his apprentice, I had no idea that Mr. Poindexter would actually adopt Tommy and become his father. That had been his plan all along, until he began to question whether Tommy's "delusions" about djinnis might mean he needed more care than a bachelor shopkeeper could provide. I only wanted Tommy safe from the orphanage, where boys his age were bound for a miserable life in the cotton mills up north. A full life for him, I finally decided (though not without dragging my heels, I'm ashamed to say), was worth far more than a third wish for me.

I knew if Tommy realized I'd helped bring his new circumstances about, he'd feel he owed me something. Worse, he might feel that Mr. Poindexter wasn't, truly, his loving father, but had somehow been bought, persuaded, or coerced into adopting him. That wasn't true, not in the slightest. But I could see how it could look that way. Especially to someone as proud and independent as Tom.

So I'd sworn Mr. Poindexter to secrecy. I was certain he'd kept that promise.

Then, suddenly, he'd used the djinni. I didn't know why.

*I'm saving Mermeros for Tom.*

I believed Mr. Poindexter when he told me that at the Crystal

Palace. I believed him still. So something must have been sorely tempting. Urgent, maybe. An emergency.

Or, could I be all wrong? Could Mr. Poindexter have simply been, let's say, kidnapped? Or been a victim of some other misfortune?

I couldn't prove he hadn't been. But neither did I believe it. Tommy was no fool. If someone had broken into their house and shop again, Tom would've found evidence. They'd only just finished repairing all the damage caused by the last burglar. If Mr. Poindexter had been a victim of a crime, and been wounded or killed—my mouth went dry at the thought—he would've been found, dead or alive, and Tommy's inquiries would almost certainly have led to some answers.

Mr. Poindexter had slipped away magically, intending to come back. Wherever he was now, he was probably frantic with worry for Tom. If he was alive. I shuddered.

And what about Tom? To gain a father, after being an orphan for so long, only to lose him again? It was too cruel. Was this miracle, this first solid piece of happiness and security to come into Tom's life since infancy, to be snatched away from him now? I couldn't stand the thought.

Tommy and Mr. Poindexter would never have found each other if it weren't for Alice and me. They never would've become a family if I hadn't helped nudge things along.

We were responsible, then, for this little family. It was as simple as that. We had to find Mr. Poindexter before he came to real harm, and before the Mission Industrial School, or whoever that lady from the Orphans' Committee was, forced Tommy to go back to the only other home he'd ever had, and hated.

I came away from the window and returned to my bed. The Count of Monte Cristo would have to escape his prison fortress at Chateau d'If another day to take revenge on his enemies. Alice lay quietly, so I slid between my sheets and turned out the gas lamp beside my bed.

Alice's voice startled me. "Where do we even begin, Maeve?"

"At the Oddity Shop," I told the darkness. "Tomorrow morning, we go hunt for clues."

W e climbed down the three steps to the garden-level shop the following day—me, Tommy, Alice, and her grandfather, Mr. Bromley. THE ODDITY SHOP, the familiar sign overhead announced. MYSTERIES, MARVELS, AND WONDERS FROM BEYOND THE SEVEN SEAS. WE BUY AND SELL RARE AND WONDROUS THINGS. MR. SIEGFRIED POINDEXTER, WORLD TRAVELER, CHIEF BUYER, PROPRIETOR. I'd always found the sign, and the images it conjured, wondrous and bold. Now, knowing Mr. Poindexter was out there somewhere, trapped, the sign made me feel dismal.

But we would find him.

Morris the owl hooted softly as the jingling bell on the door announced our entry. Good old Morris. He and I shared a bond. We understood each other, you might say. Twice, he'd saved me from a heap of trouble. Once when a rat stole the sardine tin that held my djinni, and the other time was too horrible to speak of now.

The shop lay dark, shrouded in shadow. Tommy pulled back the curtains to let a bit of London's gray light in, then went and tended to Morris's food and water. Velvet drapes lay over the tops of the glass cases showcasing artifacts and curios from around the world. Above the counter where the proprietor of the Oddity Shop waited upon customers hung a framed photograph of Tom and Mr. Poindexter, smiling together, with an old castle behind them, on one of their weekend sightseeing trips into the country. It pricked my heart to see the two of them together, grinning as though they hadn't a care in the world. Stocky, strong, balding Mr. Poindexter, and tall, skinny Tom.

"*Yoo*-hoo," called a voice that made us jump in our boots.

We turned to see a woman poking her head in the door.

"That's her," Tom hissed softly. "The orphan lady."

"Good morning, good morning." The newcomer's voice had a singsong quality, as if she were speaking to tiny infants. "Ah. I see Master Thomas has returned. Would you, sir, be Mr. Poindexter?"

She ventured forward, winding her way around the shop's display cabinets. She was short and middle-aged, with thick, graying hair pulled back into a soft bun underneath a fancy hat. Hers was a round, matronly, dimpled face—the kind that at first glance seems warm and welcoming, but on second glance may contain a hidden edge.

She reached us and held out a gloved hand to Mr. Bromley. "Pearl Fletcher. From the Committee on Adopted Children's Welfare."

"Good morning, madam," replied Alice's grandfather with a courtly bow. "I am not Mr. Poindexter. I am Theodore Bromley. A friend of the family."

"Bromley?" Mrs. Fletcher began shuffling through a sheaf of papers clutched against her bosom. "I don't see any Bromleys listed among the references of friends and acquaintances Mr. Poindexter provided in his application materials."

My goodness.

"I did not yet have the pleasure of Mr. Poindexter's acquaintance," replied Mr. Bromley smoothly, "when he began his adoption process. I knew him as a merchant, that is to say, but not as a friend. But as young Thomas is a good friend to my granddaughter, and my, er, charge, Miss Maeve Merritt, our families have grown close."

"And has Mr. Poindexter returned?" demanded Mrs. Pearl Fletcher. "Yesterday I waited here for over two hours for his return to a newly adopted son who had no idea where he had gone. Does that sound like responsible parenting to you?"

Tom swelled with wrath. Mr. Bromley saw it, too.

"Well, now," he said gently, "I don't know that I'd go so far as to say that. A strapping lad like young Thomas, at—how old are you now, Tom? Fifteen?—hardly needs a hovering parent. When I was his age, I was already working a job at a button factory."

He would go on to own that factory by the time he was twenty.

"Work builds character." Mrs. Fletcher nodded her agreement. "We at the Committee on Adopted Children's Welfare believe strongly in the value of work. Which is why we feel the best placements for orphaned lads are with Britain's thriving, industrious factories."

"But surely," protested Mr. Bromley, "a factory is no substitute for a home. The best place for any child is with a loving parent or parents."

"Loving parents who aren't around?" demanded Mrs. Fletcher.

"Did you have an appointment when you came by yesterday?" parried Mr. Bromley.

She sniffed. "We find it best to drop by unannounced. Anyone can put on a good show when they know you're coming."

Tom swelled like a fighting rooster. "My dad doesn't 'put on a show.'"

"Really?" It was hardly a question. "The man who sells so-called 'magical' oddities?"

This woman was scribbling her name fast upon my list of adults I'd like to take a poke at. And not just me. Mr. Bromley rested a hand on Tom's shoulder to prevent him from exploding like a firecracker.

"Mr. Poindexter, as it happens, is away," he said smoothly, "and Tom will be staying with us until his return."

Mrs. Fletcher shuffled through her papers. "I'll need your address," she said. "We need to know where adopted orphans are staying."

"Certainly," said Mr. Bromley. "You can find us at 20 Grosvenor Square."

Her pencil faltered. "*Grosvenor* Square?"

He might've said "Buckingham Palace," for the look of reverence that now came over her. Grosvenor Square, where London's richest and most fashionable families hung their hats at night! Grown-ups are such snobs.

Mr. Bromley took no notice of her new tone. "Number twenty," he supplied once again.

"I'll be sure to come by," she burbled.

"Please do." He bowed courteously. "Now, if you'll excuse me, madam—"

"I must be going," she said hastily. "I'll look forward to the pleasure of a visit to your home. To check on *dear* young Thomas."

"By all means," replied Mr. Bromley. "Good morning, madam."

The bell on the door tinkled as it closed behind her.

"*Dear* young Thomas!" I sputtered.

Alice watched thoughtfully as Mrs. Pearl Fletcher's high-heeled boots hurried past the high shop window of the garden-level store and down the street. "I don't think she was very sincere," she said slowly. Strong words from Alice, who can't bear to say anything unkind about anyone.

"I'm sure she feels she's doing an important work," Mr. Bromley said, "as, indeed, she is. Thank goodness someone looks after the welfare of adopted children."

"I'd thank goodness *more*," I muttered, "if that someone wasn't her."

Mr. Bromley looked away to hide a smile. But Tom was in no laughing mood.

"What'll I do?" he said. "She won't stop coming around, and when she discovers Dad's gone…"

"Which is why," I said firmly, "we're going to find him and bring him back."

"Well said, Maeve," Mr. Bromley said. "Now, Thomas, where is your father's office? I'd like to begin there and have a look at his papers."

Tommy hesitated, then pointed toward a door. "It's over there, sir, but I doubt there'll be anything to find there."

"You never know," the older gentleman replied. "Papers and ledgers and such things can tell a lot. What looks dull and meaningless to a young person might communicate a great deal to a grown man." He pulled open the door to Mr. Poindexter's dim office and disappeared inside.

Tommy sighed and shook his head. "I don't think he'll find anything there," he said. "Dad hasn't been in there in weeks. He always says it's too cluttered to find anything. He threatens to clean it up, but never does."

"Then where would his personal papers be?" I asked. "Recent mail and so on?"

"Follow me."

Tommy led us up the stairs, above the shop, to their living quarters. We passed along a corridor, then followed him through a door. "Here's his bedroom," he explained, "and this is the writing desk he uses most of the time."

As usual, I blurted out something foolish. "What a mess!"

Tom shrugged. "It wasn't so bad before the thief rifled through it."

"Oh."

Thief or no thief, the room was rather a disgrace. The bedclothes were rumpled, and the small bedside table was piled high with books and gadgets. A magnifying glass. A kaleidoscope. An ashtray. Another framed photograph of him with Tom. A small mirror hung over the washbasin, and on a shelf sat a hairbrush—for what hair Mr. Poindexter had left, around the edges, so to speak—and a toothbrush.

On the opposite wall stood an old wooden armoire, open and revealing an assortment of shirts, waistcoats, trousers, and belts. In one corner stood a folded-up tripod and a telescope for studying the stars. A rugged trunk and a shabby pair of traveling bags crowded into the space behind the door. A footlocker lay open at the foot of the bed, displaying a wooden camera, a pair of binoculars, and other curious implements. Any other day I'd stop to examine, with no small envy, all these wondrous tools for exploration. Mr. Poindexter, as his shop sign proudly declared, was a world traveler. I longed to be one, too.

"Tom," Alice said, "what's missing here?"

Tom glanced at her. "Sorry?"

"What isn't here?" Alice asked. "If we look for what's not here, we might learn something about where he thought he was going."

Clever Alice. She has a great deal more brain than many grown-ups supposed such an angelic, pink-cheeked, golden-haired girl could have.

Tom poked around the room. "His spectacles are gone," he began, "and his wallet."

"Good, good," Alice said encouragingly, though I couldn't see how that told us much.

I drifted over to the writing desk while they continued their study. What I really wanted to know was, had Mr. Poindexter taken the djinni with him? He must have. That would explain how he could've vanished so suddenly, late at night. If I *did* find the sardine tin where rascally old Mermeros kept house, so to speak, then I would know Mr. Poindexter hadn't taken the djinni, and he must be somewhere reachable by train. That would be so, so much better—though why he would've gone off without a word on a late-night train, I couldn't imagine.

But how could I ever know for sure if he'd taken the djinni? His hiding place for the sardine tin was bound to be as well locked and hidden as prisoners in the Tower. If the thief couldn't find it, how could I? Mr. Poindexter would never want Tommy to know he had Mermeros. Neither did I.

I searched through the writing desk. Various papers were strewn inches deep across its surface. Opened letters, bills, telegrams. Nothing that seemed important.

A curious device with two holes for eyes sat in one corner, atop the papers.

A stereoscope, I realized, much like the one we'd seen at the Crystal Palace. Had he bought one there? I held it up and looked through the holes, but saw nothing. Where I expected to see the Swiss Alps, or Niagara Falls, I saw nothing at all.

"Dad got that in Monday morning's post," Tommy said absently, seeing me studying the stereoscope. "From someone who wanted to sell him something for his shop."

"Mr. Poindexter wants to sell stereoscopes?" inquired Alice.

"No," said Tommy. "He wasn't interested."

Poor Tom. A night's sleep and a hot breakfast hadn't rid him of that distant, distracted air he'd had last night. He just wasn't himself for worry. Neither would I be, I thought, if I were in his shoes.

Shoes.

I knelt and looked under the bed and saw some sort of box. I slid it out and opened it.

"Well, he hasn't gone hunting." I hoped to lighten the mood by saying this. There in the case sat a gleaming rifle.

Tommy's face went pale. "No," he said. "But his pistol is gone."

Alice and I looked at each other. She gulped.

"Mightn't he have taken his pistol for, er, shooting birds?" she asked timidly.

Tommy shook his head. "I don't think so."

"This means," I said, for there was no point beating around the bush, "that wherever he was going, he expected to find danger waiting for him."

Tommy sat down upon the bed, as if standing had become too much. "And since he hasn't come back," he said, "evidently, he was right."

CHAPTER
10

"W e have to tell Grandpapa," Alice said. "He'll know what to do."

"Wait a minute," I said. "We will, but let's keep looking. A few more minutes won't make any difference one way or another."

I searched through all the small cubicles and drawers in Mr. Poindexter's writing desk.

"He didn't take his toothbrush nor his hairbrush," Alice said to herself. "Is that all of his luggage, Tom?"

Tom nodded mutely.

"Then, if he took no bags with him, he doesn't seem to have intended to be gone overnight." Alice frowned.

She was right. Things were looking worse and worse. I was certain my theory was correct. Mr. Poindexter had gotten into some kind of trouble involving Mermeros, the djinni.

"Tom," I said, "does your dad have a place to keep his most valuable things? Money, or especially important papers? Things like that?"

Tommy shook his head. "I suppose he must have something like that," he said slowly, "but he hasn't ever told me about it." His eyes narrowed. "Why do you ask?"

I looked away. "No reason." I tried to sound careless.

I kept on searching. I looked through the footlocker, the trunk, and the other pieces of luggage.

"You seem like you're looking for something particular, Maeve," Tom said.

Alice's eyes met mine in alarm.

I tried to sound casual. "What do you mean?"

Tom watched me closely. "You wouldn't be looking for a sardine tin, would you?"

For a moment, there was silence in Mr. Poindexter's chamber.

"You're worn out, Tom," Alice said soothingly. "Let's get you back home for some dinner."

"This *is* my home," Tom said stiffly, and Alice shrank back.

"No, Alice," I said. "Tom asked a fair question." I didn't like what I was about to do, but it was time for the charade to end.

"Yes, Tom," I told him. "I'm looking for Mermeros."

I could almost hear the cogs in his head whirring as he grappled with this new information. His mouth hardened into a straight line. "And why would my dad have your djinni?"

I squeezed my fists tightly, perhaps to keep from giving myself the poke in the chin I deserved just then.

"I made a bargain with him," I told him.

"You'd made a bargain with *me*," Tom protested.

That wasn't actually, technically, one hundred percent true, but Tom had believed it to be the case, and I'd never corrected his thinking. Which, come to think of it, turns out to be another type of almost-but-not-quite lie.

How was I ever going to explain my way out of this? *Try the truth on for size*, I told myself, since I'd run out of other options.

"Mr. Poindexter believed you weren't fully well, in your mind," I said, as gently as I could. "Remember? Because you told him all about how Mermeros took us on a magical journey to Persia, and we battled ancient demon beasts."

Tommy nodded. "I know. He couldn't believe it, no matter how much I told him."

"I wanted to prove it to him," I said, "by showing him the relics we brought back with us from Persia."

"I remember," Tom said impatiently. "Mermeros's sorcerer father came and snatched them back from you." He frowned. "I don't see what this has to do with you breaking your deal with me."

"It meant I couldn't prove you were telling the truth," I told him. "I happened to run into Mr. Poindexter on the street one day, just coming out of the orphanage. He told me he'd been planning to take you on as an apprentice, but had changed his mind because of how you clung to unbelievable statements about a magical djinni."

Tommy's brow furrowed. He didn't like where this was going, just as I knew he wouldn't.

"So when we finally managed to get the djinni back from nasty Mr. Treazleton's nasty servant, the ginger-whiskered man, thanks to Alice," I said, and Alice looked down at her boots, "I came here to the shop. I made Mr. Poindexter promise that, if I could prove to him the djinni was real, he would have to admit you were in your right mind. He agreed."

"So you showed him Mermeros?" asked Tom.

I nodded.

"You still could've kept your promise," Tom insisted, "and given him to me. Mr. Poindexter would've taken me on as an apprentice."

I sighed. "But what if he didn't, Tom?"

He said nothing.

"At your next birthday, you would've gone off to work at the cotton mills. Like your friend, Jack."

Tom rose to his feet. "So you traded your djinni for him to adopt me," he said. "You *sacrificed* your djinni and *bought* a father for the poor, wretched orphan."

Ordinarily, boys who use that sneering, sarcastic tone with me walk away with bloody noses, but I knew what was going on inside Tom's heart, and for once I kept my fists to myself.

"No, I didn't," I said quietly. "I made a deal with him that I would give him Mermeros if he made you his *apprentice*. I never mentioned adoption."

"That was all his idea, Tom," Alice said gently. "Maeve had nothing to do with that."

"Were you there?" Tom asked curtly.

"Why, no." Alice seemed stung. "But Maeve told me all about it at the time."

"That doesn't mean much, then," said Tom. "What Maeve says, and what she means, are often two very different things."

I took a deep breath, and counted to ten. I knew Tommy was angry because he was scared, with Mr. Poindexter missing, and now he had the added horrible thought that his new life was built upon a lie—that his dad hadn't adopted him out of love, but because it was part of a business deal. *You want the djinni? Fine, you've got to take the kid.*

"It's true, Tom," I said, as calmly as I could. "Mr. Poindexter already had the adoption papers drawn up. He only hesitated because he worried you weren't well."

"But once you'd proven to him that I *was* well," Tom said bitterly, "that should've been enough. He shouldn't have needed extra persuading. Unless, that is, he never really wanted me in the first place."

I took hold of his arm. "That's not true, Tom," I said, "and it's not fair to your dad." I pointed to the framed photograph of the two of them. "Your dad loves you. I know he does. He adopted you because he wanted you to be his son. You know how he feels. Just look at him."

Tom glanced at the photograph, then looked away.

"I think you're right," I told him. "I probably didn't need to offer the djinni."

"So you threw it away for nothing?"

One more deep breath. "I didn't know what Mr. Poindexter had planned," I said. "I wanted to be sure you never ended up in those cotton mills."

"A djinni of my own would've made sure of that," said Tom.

"Would it?" I said. "Seems to me, a djinni turns out to be nothing but trouble. Look at us now. We're fighting over Mermeros, when we should be looking for clues as to where your dad has gone. Nothing works out right once magic enters the picture."

"I disagree."

We both turned and stared at Alice. I would've bet good money that such words had never come out of Alice's mouth before in her life. If Alice has a fault, it's that she's one of those obliging people who can't bear to disappoint anyone. That's never been my problem. Just ask my mother.

"I disagree," Alice repeated, shattering her previous record. "Magic is what brought us all together. With Tom, I mean, as a friend. And magic gave us spectacular adventures we'll never forget. Without those adventures, we might never have met Mr. Poindexter, which means Tom wouldn't have met him. Morris wouldn't have found a proper home, and Tom wouldn't have, either. For all the trouble it's caused, magic has done us a great deal of good."

From downstairs, we heard Mr. Bromley's voice, calling to Alice.

"Coming, Grandpapa," she called back to him. "Just a moment." She turned back toward Tom. "You can disagree with her, Tom, but Maeve was trying to do the right thing. Let's not have quarrels now. It helps nobody, and certainly doesn't help us find your dad."

Tom swallowed and looked away. Finally he held out his hand to me. I shook it. Friends once more. At least for now.

"Good. I'd better go see Grandpapa." Alice took one of the shabby carpetbags and handed it to Tom. "Why don't you pack up some clothes and meet us downstairs in the shop?" They both went out the door, leaving me alone in the room with my thoughts.

Well. Now what? Time was running out. I'd come no closer to finding Mermeros's sardine tin, nor had I expected to find it. I was pretty sure Mr. Poindexter had taken it with him. I needed to look at our larger problem: finding him. Where could he have gone? This talk of toothbrushes was all very well, but I couldn't see where it had gotten us.

I sat down on the bed and tried to think. If I were Mr. Poindexter, owner of a London shop, and new father to Tom, what would persuade me to take off on a late-night journey without telling anyone? Why would I leave my son home alone?

And why would I use magical wishes in order to do it? Once those wishes were spent, as I well knew—and so did Mr. Poindexter—one never got them back.

I would do it, I decided, if I felt that I had no choice. It would have to be something urgent. An emergency. Something worth giving up wishes for. And I wouldn't go, I thought, unless I felt quite certain that I could return as quickly as I'd gone—which would require a djinni's help.

But what kind of emergency could have arisen on Monday evening? And why wouldn't Tom have known anything about it?

His dad must have received some kind of information. A letter, or telegram, or message of some kind, delivering the urgent news.

"Maeve!" Alice's voice called to me from down the stairs. "It's time to go."

I glanced back at Mr. Poindexter's untidy writing desk and made my decision. I seized the other carpetbag on the floor and swept the contents of his writing desk into it. I brought Mr. Poindexter's camera, binoculars, and magnifying glass. They could well be useful tools for a detective, if Mr. Sherlock Holmes was right about anything, and I had a feeling we had some detecting ahead of us. On an impulse, I took the stereoscope, too, even though it lacked a photograph. I buckled my clumsy bag shut and hurried downstairs.

## CHAPTER
## 11

Back at Grosvenor Square, Alice, Tommy, and I sat at lunch in the kitchen, while Mr. and Mrs. Bromley took over the dining room, entertaining their guest, one chief inspector Mr. Andrew Wallace from Scotland Yard. Evidently Mr. Wallace's father and Mr. Bromley had been friends, once upon a time, in their old school days.

We knew they were involving the police bureau because they were truly afraid for Mr. Poindexter, and they wanted the police detective bureau's help. We knew it, and it made our cold chicken salad stick in our throats.

The Bromleys' cook, Mrs. Tupp, took pity on us and set out a plate of her famous coconut cakes. This gave me an idea.

"Let's take these upstairs," I whispered, "and figure things out."

Alice nodded and brought the coconut cakes. We thanked Mrs. Tupp on our way out and headed upstairs to Tommy's room. A cozy fire was burning on the hearth, and we sat around it on the floor.

Tommy was the first to speak. "Do you really think my dad went somewhere with Mermeros?"

I nodded. "It's the only theory that makes any sense."

I hated to hear the sorrow in Tom's voice. "Then why isn't he back?"

Alice's face was drawn with worry. She looked to me to say something.

"I imagine," I said, "someone has stolen the djinni from him. Which would leave him stranded."

"But that means," Tommy said, "he could be anywhere in the whole wide world. We'll never find him."

"That's what the police are for," Alice said soothingly.

Tommy wouldn't be comforted. "If he's...in some faraway place, like Morocco, or Saint Petersburg, or... Panama, Scotland Yard will never, ever find him."

"You're right," I said. "We're going to have to find him ourselves."

Alice's eyes goggled. "But, Maeve," she protested, "how on earth could *we* get to him?"

Tom's face, however, lit up. "Maybe he's on his way back now, on a long ocean voyage!"

"That's right." Alice seemed relieved at the thought. "That could explain what's taking him so long."

I hated to rain on Tom's hopes, but I had my doubts. "I don't think Mr. Poindexter has gone that far away," I said. "I think he's bound to be somewhere in the British Isles."

Alice looked perplexed. "Why do you say that?"

I took a bite of cake. "It's mostly a hunch," I said, "but look at it this way. If Mr. Poindexter was planning to go to, let's say, Hong Kong, he would've made arrangements for you, Tom, in case of a delay. Or at least left a note."

"Like we did, when we traveled to Persia?" Alice gave me an arch look.

"Fine," I said. "Point taken. We didn't leave a note. But Mr. Poindexter's a grown-up. A father. He's supposed to think ahead."

Tom took a bite of cake, too. I was glad to see him eat. "So you think he didn't leave a note because he didn't feel he was going very far?"

I nodded. "That's my theory. Unless..."

Tommy's eyes bulged. "Unless *what?*"

I told him about Mrs. Gruboil's visit, weeks before, even before our outing to the Crystal Palace.

"You think your old *cook* has kidnapped my dad?" asked Tom incredulously. "That phony baroness who stole Mermeros back at your school?"

I shook my head. "I couldn't believe it of her."

"You underestimate her, I think, Maeve," Alice said. "Surely you don't think she couldn't pull off the crime simply because she's a *woman?*"

"Not on your life!" I cried. "Women can do anything. I only say it because she's Mrs. Gruboil." I shook my head. "I'm certain that's all a coincidence. Mr. Poindexter left home freely. He must have received some kind of message." I snapped my fingers. "I'll run up to our bedroom and get the bag I brought of papers and things from your dad's desk, Tom. I'll bet there's something there. Some letter or telegram that will give us a clue." I paused to think. "You said he was acting perfectly normal on Monday. Then, after you'd gone to bed, he took this wild journey. It must be that on Monday evening, he received some information that made him feel he must drop every-thing and leave immediately."

I hurried up the stairs to the third floor, where Alice and I shared a room, fetched my bag of loot, and brought it back down to Tom's room on the second level. I took out the larger objects, then dumped out the papers, and we began prowling through them.

Tom was able to dismiss many of them immediately. "That's Dad's aunt in Liverpool," or "that's one of his antiquities dealers," or "I think that's a friend from his school days." We read the letters all the same, looking to see if anyone from Mr. Poindexter's past life had sent him a plea for help, but no letters seemed out of the ordinary. Frightfully dull, in fact. I resolved that when I grew up, if I had nothing interesting to say in a letter, I wouldn't bother to send one.

When all was done, we were left with just a few pieces we couldn't explain. First, a short letter in an odd, shallow, cramped hand. Alice read it aloud.

Gretigwode Manor, Dunstable, Bedfordshire
To Mr. Siegfried Poindexter, Proprietor, the
Oddity Shop, Mantlebury Way, London

Dear Sir,

Though I rarely travel to the metropolis,
I have become aware of your shop by
reputation. I am informed that you are a
discriminating collector and purveyor of
curios, artifacts, and, as you so quaintly put
it, "oddities." I take the liberty of writing
to make you aware that I am in possession
of a most extraordinary object which,
though modern in its outward appearance,
is inwardly as mysterious as a crystal ball
or any other ancient tool of divination. I
refer, sir, to a camera that can photograph
the future. If you would pay me a visit at
my home, the journey will prove worthwhile.

*I can promise that in all your days you will not have laid eyes upon a more wondrous device. Someone in your line of business will not want to miss such a marvel as this.*

*Sincerely yours,*
*Professor M. Fustian*

"A professor?" Alice looked at us wonderingly. "With a camera that can photograph the future?"

Tommy shook his head. "Dad got the letter a few days ago. He thought it was a joke. He said he gets letters like this from time to time, with people assuming, because of 'Oddity' in the name of his shop, that he'd want buy all sorts of crackpot things."

"Like djinnis," I muttered. "Do you think he answered the letter?"

"I doubt it," said Tom.

"There's no envelope," I noted. "Tom, do you remember when he received the letter?"

Tom tried to think. "Perhaps a week ago?"

"Dunstable's not far from my home," I told them. "It's pretty much the next big town over from Luton, in Bedfordshire."

"Maybe your parents know of this Mr. Fustian, then," offered Alice.

Something seemed to move out of the corner of my eye, but it must've been coals shifting in the grate. I shuffled through the remaining papers. I found no other letters from Professor M. Fustian, but I did find a short slip of paper with handwriting that seemed similar. It read: "Proof of the astonishing abilities of my prognosticating camera." I looked at Alice. "What's 'prognosticating?'"

"Telling the future," she explained.

"Ah." I waved the slip of paper in the air. "*What* was the proof? What does this slip refer to?"

Alice pointed at the camera I'd already removed from the bag. "Is that the magical camera?"

"No," I said. "That's Mr. Poindexter's own camera. The one he used at the wedding and brought to the Crystal Palace."

I reached for the stereoscope, and fitted my eyes to the lenses, and looked inside it once more. Where fanciful pictures ought to appear, there was nothing. Just solid blackness. "Didn't you say, Tom, that this had arrived recently?"

"I believe so," Tom said. "I brought him a package of about that size, when it came by post. That night, I saw the stereoscope in his room. I'd never seen it before. So I thought it must've been what came in the box."

I tried holding the stereoscope up toward the light of the window, but it made no difference. All was dark.

An idea was beginning to take shape. "A stereoscope holds a photograph," I said, "and a camera that predicts the future, real or fake, would produce *photographs*, right?"

"Correct," Alice said slowly. "Is this a trick question, Maeve?"

"She's right," Tom said. "Someone sent a letter and an object. The object is supposed to prove the existence of the magical camera. What if this stereoscope is the object? It's new enough. And it's supposed to have a photograph in it."

"Of the future." Alice sighed.

"If this contraption is supposed to prove something magical, it's doing a lousy job of it." Something out of the corner of my eye seemed to move once more, but when I looked, it was nothing more than a glimmer. Firelight bouncing off the fireplace tiles. I set the stereoscope down and shuffled through the papers. "Here's a post office telegram envelope. Dated Monday. Now we're getting somewhere." I handed it to Tom. "Do you remember a telegram arriving Monday?"

Tom frowned. "I don't." He pointed to the date on envelope. "But obviously, it must have come. I was reading for a while in my room, so maybe I never heard the bell."

Tom, reading? That caught my attention. I didn't think he was the bookish sort.

"What were you reading, Tom?" I inquired.

"*The Adventures of Tom Sawyer,*" he said. "By an American. Mr. Mark Twain."

"Another Tom," I said. "Is it any good?"

He managed a smile. "You'd like it, Maeve."

Alice made a little cough to let us know we were wandering off the point. She took a thoughtful bite of coconut cake, and chewed and swallowed it carefully before speaking, unlike certain nameless other girls who shared a room with her.

"Have we learned anything?" she inquired.

"We've learned it wasn't Mrs. Gruboil," I said firmly. "Perhaps she could find some criminal to work with her, but not a professor, nor someone who knew how to sound like one."

"These letters and envelopes and things might have nothing whatsoever to do with Mr. Poindexter's plans," Alice pointed out.

"The telegram must be connected to it," I pointed out.

"But since we only have the envelope," she said, "and not the message inside it, it doesn't do us much good."

Tom sat up taller. "Would the post office have a record of what the telegram said?"

"Or at least," added Alice, "where it came from?"

"If they did," I said, "I doubt they'd tell it to us."

"But they might tell it to a police detective," Alice suggested. "Should we go downstairs and show it to the detective from Scotland Yard?"

"We can do that," I said, "but I wish we could figure out what it all means first." I looked around. "Where's the bag? Maybe the telegram fell out."

Alice pointed across the room. "It's over there. Next to the other one."

I looked where Alice had pointed. Tom's room, like all the bedrooms at the Bromley's Grosvenor Square town house, was spacious and elegant. The two shabby carpetbags seemed horribly out of place here. But there they sat, end to end on the carpet, like a pair of kittens, nose to nose.

An odd feeling came over me. "Who put the bag there? Did you, Tom?"

He looked up, puzzled. He hadn't been paying attention. "What do you mean? I didn't do anything with yours. I put *my* bag, the one with my clothes in it, behind the wardrobe after Mrs. Harding put away my things."

I pointed to the two carpetbags, side by side in the middle of the carpet. "*That's* not behind your wardrobe. And I never went anywhere near that spot."

We looked at each other.

"Do you know something," Alice whispered. "More than once, as we sat here talking, I had the odd feeling something was moving behind my back."

"Me too!" I cried.

"But when I turned to look," continued Alice, "I couldn't see anything unusual."

"Look at those bags," I said. "Were they placed like that before?"

She bit her lip. "I don't think so."

Tom glanced at the bags, then back at the pile of mail and papers. "I don't know what you're on about," he said. "They're just dad's old carpetbags. He's had them forever. One of you must've accidentally slid them that way. Or, maybe, Maeve, you forgot where you put it."

"I *didn't*." Any other day, I would've gone to war over this, because I knew I was right. Tom wanted to focus on finding his father. This matter of the bags must've seemed to him like a needless distraction.

But I couldn't stop thinking about it. As Alice and Tom pored over the papers once more, I crept over to the bags and examined them.

They were a matched pair, both cut, it seemed, from the same rug. Faded browns and reds and dark greens swirled in the dusty pattern. Well-worn leather handles were riveted to strips of leather sewn to both top edges of the bags. They looked like they'd traveled the world and logged countless miles. Is it possible for a girl to envy a pair of bags? I did. I longed to have seen the sights these bags had seen, and tromped in the faraway dust that filled their crevices and corners.

Someday.

Right now I needed to determine whether these bags had traveled a few feet across the bedroom floor while our backs were turned.

I separated the bags by a few inches, then went back to see what Tom and Alice were up to. The tiny hairs on the back of my neck prickled. I was desperate to turn around and spy on the bags, but I told myself to wait. I bided my time and ate another coconut cake. Finally, I turned back.

The bags were touching each other again.

I tiptoed to the door and closed it gently.

"Alice," I whispered. "Tom. I did an experiment. I moved the carpetbags apart, then walked away and didn't look. They moved back together again! We have a pair of magic carpetbags!"

Alice's jaw dropped. Tom looked at me as though I had trees growing out of my ears.

"Dad's had those bags for years," he insisted. "If they were magical, he'd know it."

"Are you sure, Maeve?" asked Alice.

"Of course I'm sure." I folded my arms across my chest. "Why don't you believe me anymore, Tom? What's gotten into you?"

He kept on shuffling through papers. "This is a rotten time to pull a prank, is all. How do we know you didn't move the bags yourself?"

Once more, I tried counting to ten. "Because I *didn't*." I marched back over to the bags and separated them by six inches. "Do you both agree that they've been separated? Now, I'll sit over here by the fire, and we'll see what happens in a few minutes."

Alice sat up tall. "I believe you, Maeve."

"Thanks, Alice."

"Do you know," Alice said, "I think Maeve has a knack for finding magical objects. Or perhaps it's that they find her. Something about her draws them."

"Maybe she's an evil sorceress."

Being a sorceress wouldn't bother me. Miss Salamanca, headmistress of my old school, would certainly have called me evil.

I wanted to look back at the bags, but I was pretty sure they needed more time. So I picked up the useless stereoscope once more and examined it thoroughly.

Why didn't it work? Here at the back was the pane of glass, letting in the light. Here in the slot was a cartridge which would ordinarily hold a photograph. I tugged at it, but it wouldn't come free. Here at the top was a hinged door that gave a glimpse at the inner workings. I tried to pry it open, but it didn't want to budge. I bashed it with the side of my fist, which loosened it slightly.

Finally, it opened. Inside the chamber, which ought to have been empty, were tightly stuffed cloths. Socks, of all things! No wonder neither light nor pictures came through the viewer. I tugged them out, and a pair of tiny pictures appeared, though what they depicted, I couldn't tell.

"Those are my dad's socks," Tom told us.

I held the scope before my eyes, pointing the glass pane toward one of Tommy's windows, and gazed inside.

"Look, Maeve!" Alice cried. "The bags *are* back together again!"

I didn't care. I cried out in terror as the stereoscope fell into my lap. What I'd seen, I couldn't unsee.

A view, at twilight, from the top of a tower, looking down the tower's stony height. In the foreground, a figure, having just fallen, or been pushed, from between the battlements, its limbs flailing as it fell.

The terrified face of the figure was Tom's.

# CHAPTER 12

Tom reached for the stereoscope. Instinctively, I pulled it back. He must *not* see this. It would be more than any one person could bear to see. Imagine if it had been my face in the photograph.

*A camera that can photograph the future.*

No wonder Mr. Poindexter had stuffed his socks in here before leaving. It was a wonder he hadn't thrown the whole thing into the fire. Tom *mustn't* see it.

"What's the idea, Maeve?" demanded Tom. "Let me see."

"What is it, Maeve?" Alice's voice was concerned. "What happened?"

I held on tightly to the stereoscope. "You mustn't look at this, Tom," I told him. "I'm serious."

Tom's face reddened. "But Alice can?"

"No one should." I wrapped my arms tightly around the hateful thing.

Alice looked at me thoughtfully. "Maeve," she said gently, "I don't think you can shield Tom from whatever you saw. This is *his* problem. *His* father. You can't protect him from it."

She was right, and I knew it, but that didn't mean I had to like it. I handed her the stereoscope.

"You look first," I told her, "and if you still think Tom should see it, show it to him."

Alice hesitated, then peered through the lenses of the stereoscope. It took her a moment to register what she was seeing. A little cry escaped her lips.

Tom didn't wait for Alice to decide to give him the stereoscope. He took it from her and stared into its depths.

He gazed into it for a long time.

When he set it back down upon the carpet, his face was pale.

"This camera," Tom said slowly, "which can see the future, sees *me* being pushed off a tower?"

"Maeve," Alice said, "I think we need to tell Scotland Yard about this. And my grandparents. Let's go see if that detective gentleman is still here."

"They'll never believe us," I warned her.

"They must," Alice said. "This has gotten too big to keep to ourselves."

I looked at our friend, who sat on the floor with his arms wrapped around his knees. "Are you all right, Tom?"

He startled awake, as if he'd been far away. "Hmm? Fine. I'm fine."

But he wasn't fine. Not after his dad went missing, and certainly not after that horrid picture. Anybody could see that.

"Come on," I told them both. "Let's go downstairs and tell them everything."

★ ✸ ★

"A djinni."

Detective Wallace peered over the tops of his half-moon spectacles.

Alice nodded. "That's right."

We'd made Alice our spokeswoman, in the hope that the adults might believe her. She dreaded it, but she looked them all straight in the eye and told her story without flinching.

"My dear young lady," Detective Wallace said patiently, "Mr. Poindexter's shop, as you know, was burgled recently. He reported it to the bureau. It's far more likely that Mr. Poindexter's disappearance is somehow connected to that *actual* crime than that it has anything to do with a fanciful tale about magic and djinnis."

Alice's grandmother clutched her husband's arm and whispered urgently in his ear. I could see their worried glances darting back and forth between me and Alice. I knew what they were thinking.

*Perhaps Miss Maeve Merritt puts ideas into dear Alice's head. Perhaps she isn't quite the ideal companion for our precious girl.*

"I know this is hard to believe," I said, "especially coming from us. Mr. Poindexter saw Mermeros, but of course, you can't ask him. There is one other adult who has seen him. My father. You could ask him."

*Sorry, Dad,* I thought, *for dragging you into this. But Mr. Poindexter's disappearance leaves me no choice.*

"And your father is...?" inquired Detective Wallace.

"Mr. John Merritt, senior investment manager, St. Michael's Bank and Trust." He'd had a promotion, and jolly well high time for it, too.

The detective glanced at Mr. Bromley, who coughed.

"A fine, upstanding man, I would say," Mr. Bromley said, though he didn't seem too eager to say it just then. "Someone of sound judgment."

"I really think we need not bother with such distrac—"

"Can you get in touch with Mr. Merritt, dear?" Mrs. Bromley interrupted the detective, addressing her husband. "I feel I *must* know."

Mr. Bromley nodded and left the room, presumably to place a telephone call to St. Michael's Bank. *Oh, Daddy. Please don't be vexed with me.*

In his absence, the detective fiddled with the stereoscope and looked over the letters and envelopes we'd provided him. We'd decided not to tell him about the carpetbags. What would be the point? Our story sounded ludicrous enough already.

In no time, Mr. Bromley returned to the table. "Mr. Merritt is on his way," he said.

The detective peered once more into the stereoscope, then back at Tom as if memorizing his face, then back into the stereoscope. Finally he handed it to Mr. Bromley, who had already seen it once. "What do you make of this?"

Mr. and Mrs. Bromley studied the image once more.

"It's astonishing," Mrs. Bromley murmured.

"Most disturbing," added her husband.

The detective turned toward them and asked, in a low voice, "Could the boy's father have perpetrated this as a hoax?"

Did he think we wouldn't hear him? Tom's jaw clenched.

"Mr. Poindexter would never," I said stoutly.

The detective's gaze in my direction was unamused.

Mr. and Mrs. Bromley exchanged worried glances.

"I feel quite certain that Master Thomas is speaking the truth," Mr. Bromley said quietly. "His father is gone. When he arrived last night, he was terrified."

Detective Wallace turned to Tom. "Can you give me the names of some of the hospitals and mortuaries you visited last night?"

To check up on his story. If Tommy was angry at being doubted, he hid it well, and answered the detective's questions calmly. Mr. Wallace asked permission to use the Bromleys' telephone and stepped out of the room for a while. Presently, he returned.

"I have someone checking up on the young man's statement that he searched those hospitals and mortuaries," the detective said. "You must understand, however, that I can't very well open an investigation into someone who's gone missing because he's taken a journey with a djinni. The best I can say is that Mr. Poindexter appears to have gone somewhere by his own free choice, abandoning his orphaned son, who will need to be returned to the orphanage or home that housed him previously."

A small cry escaped from Mrs. Bromley. "Surely he can stay with us until this matter is resolved?"

The detective shrugged. "For the time being, certainly, but if Mr. Poindexter can't be located, there are rules that must be followed. Unless you are proposing to adopt the young man yourselves?"

The Bromleys were quiet for a moment.

"Excuse me." Tom spoke politely, but I could feel the fire burning inside him. "My father is missing. Shouldn't finding him be what's important now?" He nodded toward the Bromleys. "I'm very grateful to you both for letting me stay here, for now."

The detective watched Tom thoughtfully. Mrs. Bromley's face melted into sympathy.

The doorbell rang. We heard Mr. Linzey, the butler, cross the foyer and open it, and I recognized the distinctive tone of my father's voice. Moments later, Mr. Linzey showed him in.

My stomach squirmed. What would Dad say? Would he worry about his reputation as a man of business, a man of sense? Had he persuaded himself that he imagined seeing a djinni?

I should've known I could count on my dad.

He crossed the room resolutely and addressed the adults there. "Mrs. Bromley," he said with a bow. "Mr. Bromley. Inspector. Everything my daughter has told you about a supernatural djinni is true. I would never have believed it if I hadn't seen it with my own eyes, but see it, I did, and I'm prepared to swear to it."

CHAPTER

13

We returned to Tommy's room while the adults held an urgent council of war. Mr. Wallace, it was plain, was not convinced. The Bromleys were too polite, and too kind, to disagree with my father to his face, but I could tell they were alarmed and upset by what he said. Father wasn't someone you could easily dismiss. But djinnis? Here, in modern London?

Of course they couldn't believe it. I wouldn't have believed it either, if I hadn't met Mermeros myself.

Mr. Wallace kept the letter, the envelope, and the papers, and it seemed, from what he said, that he planned on tracking down the telegrams. He even said something about telephoning the local police in Dunstable to have them stop by this Gretigwode Manor to see what they could learn, and what they knew about "M. Fustian." He took his hat and coat and left.

We slipped upstairs while the Bromleys and my father made awkward conversation.

When we opened Tom's door, the first thing I saw was what I *didn't* see.

The carpetbags were missing.

Morris the owl was still there, perched on a curtain rod, looking as ruffled and terrified as a farmyard hen who'd just seen a fox.

We searched all around the floor for the bags and in the wardrobe. They were gone.

"Maybe the housekeeper thought they looked dirty and took them somewhere else?" suggested Tom.

I heard a faint scuffling.

"Alice. Tom," I whispered. "Look."

They looked up. There, atop the tall armoire, partially obscured by a decorative woodwork facade, huddled the two bags. For all the world like two naughty children caught in a corner with the jam pot.

"They're laughing at us," whispered Alice.

They made no sound, but they did have a sort of wriggly-puppy look about them. Highly amused with themselves.

"They went up there on purpose," I told the others. "I'm certain of it."

"You mean, they can *fly*?" demanded Alice.

"Jump, at any rate," I said.

Tommy, the tallest of us three, reached up and pulled the bags down.

"I swear to you," he said, "these bags have never done anything like this before. Dad brought them when we took that weekend trip to Brighton. I think he's had them for years."

"It's Maeve," insisted Alice. "There's just something about her."

"Hogwash," I told her.

"If Dad had magic bags," said Tom, "he would've told me." He paused. "Then again, he did say they were his lucky bags. He said he's lost them more than once in his travels, yet they always turn up."

"Let's have a look at them, then." Alice knelt down on the floor to examine the bags.

I sat beside her and poked at the other one. "If a bag could talk..." I muttered.

"Who cares about talking?" asked Tommy. "If these carpetbags can fly—"

He and I stared at each other. For a moment, I saw, with relief, a glimpse of the old, adventure-loving Tommy.

Alice continued her exploration. "They must come from the same original carpet."

"*Magic* carpet," I corrected.

"But why would anyone ever cut up a magic carpet?" Alice said. "It seems criminal!"

"Maybe," suggested Tom, "they didn't know."

"Or maybe," I mused, "that magic carpet had gotten somebody

into heaps of trouble, and someone thought it needed to be stopped."
I leaned back against the side of Tom's bed. "Oh, what wouldn't I give to have a magic carpet of my very own!"

Alice's face grew truly alarmed. "I'm not sure that's wise," she said. "Remember all the trouble we got into, the last time we took a magical journey?"

"Ah, but think," I said. "Mermeros himself was the source of our trouble, the stinky old fish. Don't you see? *He* dragged us right into the midst of his horrid, ghostly family—"

"Because you wished him to," added Tom.

I ignored this. "And *he* nearly made me spend another wish, just to make it back home!"

"But he didn't, because *you'd* put him into mortal danger," pointed out the ever-helpful Tom.

I'd had enough of this. "You're missing the point," I said. "Mermeros, as a means of magical transportation, was disappointing. He insulted us six ways from Sunday. You only get three wishes, tops. Worst of all, it cost us a wish to go anywhere, and a wish to come back."

Tom's voice, when he spoke, was small. "Maybe that's my dad's problem now."

"Whereas," I said, feeling we needed to stick to cheerier subjects, "a magic carpet is an unlimited source of fun, with none of the rudeness. It's perfect!"

I looked about me, but my audience wasn't getting into the spirit of things. Alice worried, as is her way, and Tom was nothing but a slump of sadness.

I jostled them both with my elbows. "Well, what do you say?" I tried to sound jolly. "Where can we go to test these out?"

Alice laid a hand on my arm. "Maeve," she said, "hadn't we first ought to focus on trying to help find Mr. Poindexter?"

I wish I could say I'd thought of it sooner. I wish I could say it had been my idea all along, for that would make me sound a good deal cleverer than I was. But Alice's words burst upon my mind in a fireworks display of the most fantastic idea since girls' cricket.

"We've done our part and told the police," I told her. "They'll do their best, I'm sure. But now it's up to us."

Tom's mouth hung open. He and Alice exchanged a look that said *Maeve's off her chump again.*

"What faster, better way is there to reach Gretigwode Manor, Dunstable, Bedfordshire," I said, "than flying by magic carpet?"

CHAPTER
14

B ag," Alice corrected. "Magic carpet*bag*."

"It's a bonus," I told her. "All the comforts and conveniences of your classic magic carpet, plus storage space and easy carrying handles."

"You could sell them for a living." I was glad to see Tom crack a joke.

"Well, come on, then," I told them. "Let's grab our hats and coats, and go test these out."

Alice gulped. Tom rolled his eyes.

"What?" I demanded. "Don't tell me you're too afraid."

"It's not fear, Maeve," Alice scolded. "And you shouldn't try to goad people like that."

"Just friendly persuasion," I said. "What is it, then, if it isn't fear?"

Alice went to Tom's bedroom window and pulled back the drapes. "Practicality," she said. "Have a look, Maeve. Where in the park do you suppose it's safe for us to test out our 'flying carpetbags' where no one can see?"

I didn't like to admit it, but she had a point. As I drew near the window, I saw that the park across the street buzzed with people enjoying a clear and sunny day (by London standards, I mean) in spring. Little children flew kites. A group of private-school lads in uniform did a series of dismal-looking exercises, though the moves they invented when their gymnastics instructor wasn't watching were highly entertaining. Nurses and nannies kept watch over toddlers, and older sisters pushed their infant siblings in prams.

Alice was right. There was absolutely no piece of sky where we could soar in the air unseen. Neither was there any space to the rear of the house to put to use.

"Fine," I said. "We'll use the ballroom."

We tiptoed down the stairs and crept along the main entry foyer toward the rear of the house. Alice opened the door and poked her head inside, then beckoned for us to follow her in.

Our footsteps on the patterned mahogany floors echoed across to the tall windows, bouncing off the painted ceiling on their way back to an awestruck Tommy. He'd been a frequent guest in the Bromleys' grand home, yet he had never been in a room this resplendent before.

I could read his mind exactly as he gazed in wonder at Alice. *I knew you were rich, but not* this *rich.*

Poor Alice. She could read the look, too, and she hated that sort of thing.

To be frank, this room had never been my favorite one in the Bromley's town house up till now. It was absolutely encrusted with marble statues, and its walls were nothing but ornate, gilded plaster carvings all the way up to the ceiling. Worst of all, its entire function was *dancing.*

But it was huge. Two full stories tall, and long enough to—well, if not to play cricket, at least long enough to get a running start to avoid someone asking you to dance. Late afternoon sun poured through the French doors, spreading checkerboards of light far across the floor.

We set the carpetbags on the very middle of the grand floor, right underneath the crystal chandelier, and stepped back a bit.

"Well?" said Alice. "Now what, Maeve?"

As if I should know!

"Fly, carpetbags," I told them, rather majestically, if I do say so. My voice rushed back at me. The carpetbags, however, did not.

"Fly, magic carpet?" I tried.

"Please?" ventured Alice.

The bags inched toward each other until their corners touched. They leaned in together.

"I do believe they're gossiping about us," declared Alice. "That's not polite, you know."

"You're talking to carpetbags," I whispered.

Alice was undeterred. "Gossiping isn't polite for carpetbags, either."

Tommy knelt down and examined the one closest to him. The bag didn't seem to mind.

He turned to me. "What do you think, Maeve?" he said. "Suppose they can't fly by themselves? Perhaps a magic carpet needs passengers."

"How does one ride a carpetbag?" asked Alice.

I had an idea.

"Normally," I said, "when one travels, they carry their carpetbag. They drag *it* around. What if the opposite were true?"

I seized the handles of one of the bags. "Magic Carpetbag," I said, in the sweetest voice of which I'm capable, which isn't very sweet, "oh, Magic Carpetbag, I don't suppose you'd want to carry me for a spin around the room, would you?"

*Well.*

What happened next is hard to describe. It was as if the Topsy-Turvy Railway at the Crystal Palace had suddenly appeared at Grosvenor Square. Up, up, up the roller coaster swept your body, while your stomach stayed somewhere on the ground, until, *whoosh*, you were at the top, stomach and all, then you were falling, absolutely shooting downward, it seemed, while your stomach flapped behind you like underdrawers on a clothesline.

*That's* what this felt like.

That carpetbag shot forward and up into the air, swooping me along with it, with a jerk and a rush that left my insides out and my legs flailing.

"Maeve!" squealed Alice.

The carpetbag catapulted me up to the ceiling and led me on a tour of it. Ceiling cherubs and chandelier cobwebs and rushed by as Alice and Tom gaped at us from below.

I glanced back down and realized how high, how desperately high I was, and for a moment I felt wobbly. My grip loosed on the carpetbag just as it had made up its mind—its *mind?*—to explore the far corner of the ceiling. I hung suspended for a moment, just as I had atop the loop-de-loop, then tumbled through the air.

It must've been the work of only a split second. But it felt like forever.

*Thump.*

My jaw clamped down on the tip of my tongue as something caught me from beneath. As if I'd landed on a horse.

I once saw a picture of the riders in an American rodeo. There I sat, bucking around in the air on the back of a steed with no reins, no mane—no head, even.

The carpetbag had caught me.

And the whole while, that carpetbag was laughing. *Isn't this fun?*

I know it doesn't make sense. I couldn't hear it, but I felt it, just as I'd felt its whoop of glee when it first yanked me off the floor.

I rode the carpetbag around the grand hall, up, down, and sideways. The bag was definitely in charge. Now, in the distance, I heard Tom's laughter, and the next thing I knew, there he was, dangling from the other bag's handles, being yanked around the room like a rag doll a child dangles by its cloth-mitten hand.

"Come on," I told the bag. "Let's go get Alice."

The bag zoomed straight toward her, skimming not far above the floor. Alice reached for me—I think she meant to save me by snatching me off—but instead I seized her by the wrist and hoisted her up in the air with us.

"*Ohhhhhhh!*" she cried, her voice climbing up the musical scale as her body mounted into the ballroom's lofty upper atmosphere. "Maeve, let go!"

"Look down," I told her.

She did so. "Maeve," she panted. "*Don't* let go!"

"Put Alice down," I told the bag. Instead, it whizzed faster, round and round the room, nearly crashing us into a wild-eyed Tom. I like to think I'm strong, but my grip on Alice's hand was slipping.

"I think we should set Alice back down on the floor, Carpetbag," I told it in the friendliest way I knew how. "Don't you think so?"

The bag's pace slowed. It spiraled downward in leisurely loops.

Alice's feet hit the floor. She gasped with relief. "Oh, thank goodness."

Tom, however, was having a time of it. His carpetbag seemed to have gotten ideas from mine. It flew Tom up to the ceiling, wiggled itself free of his clutches, then swooped downward to catch him right before he fell.

"Stop it!" Tom laughed. "No more! Hey! You cut that out! No, no! I mean it!" All to no effect. As if he were barking orders to a naughty, rambunctious dog, one having far too much fun to obey.

From outside the room, a high voice called. "Alice! Alice, dear, where are you?"

Alice looked at me in horror.

"Carpetbag, please," Alice cried softly, "put Tom down!"

Still nothing.

"Now, carpetbags," I told them both. "Let's save the fun for later on, shall we? Maybe we can find a time to go *outside*."

The carpetbags stopped—actually stopped—with Tom dangling from both handles, and reluctantly, I swear, set us both down on the floor.

The ballroom door opened, and Alice's grandmother, Mrs. Bromley, came in. She gazed at each of us in wonder, and then at our dingy carpetbags on the floor. Her eyebrows rose quizzically, but she said nothing.

Alice swallowed. "Yes, Grandmama?"

Mrs. Bromley roused herself slightly. "Thomas, Maeve, Alice dear. It's time for tea."

"Thank you, Grandmama," Alice said sweetly. "We'll be right there."

Tom scurried the carpetbags back up to his room, and then he, Alice, and I entered the drawing room, still flushed with excitement at our new carpetbags. My father, I was pleased to see, had stayed. Mrs. Harding had arranged an inviting spread of sandwiches, cheeses, and fruit, and Mrs. Bromley was pouring Dad's cup of tea. Mr. Abernathy, the tutor, who joined the family at teatime, was just becoming acquainted with my father. It seemed, from the way they were talking in low voices, that the tutor only just been brought up to date on the latest developments in Tom's troubles. I was glad. He'd been downright peevish about us postponing today's schooling, though he couldn't say it aloud when he saw Tom's anxious face.

Tom spoke up before even looking at the food. "Is there any word about my father?"

Mr. Bromley gave him a sympathetic look. "Not yet, my lad. It's early still."

"Inspector Wallace said he would ask the county police to send someone over to Gretigwode Manor to investigate," my father said.

I helped myself to a salmon-cucumber sandwich. "Good," I said. "When they've arrested the owner, we'll learn the truth."

"They won't arrest him without evidence, Maeve," Dad said gravely. "A few letters and a stereoscope aren't enough to charge a man with kidnapping."

"But when they search the manor, they're sure to find evidence," I pointed out.

Mr. Bromley shook his head. "A search requires a warrant, Maeve," he said. "No magistrate would grant a warrant based on what little we know so far."

My heart sank. Tom's face paled.

Mr. Abernathy took a sip of tea. "What did you say the name of the house was?"

"Gretigwode Manor," I told him, "in Dunstable."

"I thought that's what you'd said. Gretigwode Manor," he mused. "I took a Saturday tour there, on my day off, last summer, I believe it was. The owner seems to go in for the eccentric, shall we say, and the mystical. A wonderful old Gothic tower."

Those of us who'd seen the photograph of Tom falling off the tower didn't find this image very wonderful.

"*Gretig* is Dutch, I believe, for eagerness—or greed," Mr. Abernathy mused aloud to nobody in particular.

"Don't tell me you also speak Dutch," I cried. The man's knowledge of languages boggled the mind.

Mr. Abernathy chuckled. "No, Maeve," he said. "After visiting the manor, I became curious. I looked it up." He took a sip of tea. "Whom did you say the owner was?"

My father answered. "Professor M. Fustian."

Mr. Abernathy sat upright. "You don't say. Fustian?" His eyes lit up. "How many Fustians can there be?"

*Six*, I wanted to say, because an absurd question deserves an absurd answer.

"Fustian," Mr. Abernathy repeated. "I knew a Mortimer Fustian, back at Oxford. I wonder…"

"What was he like?" I asked. "Did he seem like the sort that might kidnap a man?"

(As an aside, one thing I appreciated about teatime, and all meals at the Bromleys' home, was that young people were welcome to engage in conversation with adults and ask questions. There was none of this "Children should be seen and not heard" rot you often find.)

"Good heavens, no, not a kidnapper," said Mr. Abernathy. "Professors don't kidnap people, my dear. They lack the resolve. They can scarcely decide what to eat for dinner. When I knew Morty—if we're even talking about the same person—he was reading for a master's degree in history."

"Scarcely sounds like the violent type," my father said.

Mr. Abernathy's expression took on the slightly guilty look of one about to gossip. "He was rather a strange bird," he said. "The boys in the dormitory used to heckle him awfully. I'm surprised he's become a professor. Can't imagine any college that would graduate him, much less hire him. He's... Well, it's awful to say it, but he's become a laughingstock in most academic circles."

This caught my attention. "Why?"

"Well," Mr. Abernathy said, "though he studied history, his real fascination was with, how shall we say, myths and legends of magical objects. Magic talismans, cursed artifacts. The occult, some would say. I would call it, the bizarre and improbable."

"What's wrong with studying mythology?" inquired Alice. "Isn't that what we're doing when we read the *Iliad* and the *Aeneid*?"

Mr. Abernathy nodded. "An excellent question, Miss Alice, and of course, you are correct. We give myths a great deal of our attention in classical studies. But Mortimer..." He coughed. "Morty seemed to *believe* in it all. He seriously expected the faculty to grant him a degree for a thesis arguing that many of these mythical, magical, and legendary artifacts were real, and that Britain should harness their power to advance the empire." He smiled. "Imagine, Her Majesty's government employing *magic wands* and whatnot to enforce its laws. The army, fighting its wars with King Arthur's sword, Excalibur." He winked at me. "Employing djinnis to help insure a favorable year for the crops."

He looked around the room to see if others shared his amusement. No one did. Mr. and Mrs. Bromley's eyes were wide as soup plates.

"Well?" I asked Mr. Abernathy. "Did they?"

He blinked. "Did they what, Miss Maeve?" he asked. "I mean to say, did *who* do *what*?"

"Did the Oxford, er, faculty, grant this Mortimer person his degree?"

Our tutor looked shocked. "Certainly not," he said. "He wasn't even invited to revise his paper. He was politely invited to pursue his studies elsewhere. Thrown out on his ear, in other words. I recall he was very bitter about it."

A rich, eccentric would-be professor who believed in djinnis. Could there be any doubt?

"Imagine old Morty owning Gretigwode Manor," Mr. Abernathy said. "You just never know."

"Dad," I said, "can we go take the Saturday tour at Gretigwode Manor tomorrow?"

Tom's eyes grew wide. He sat up straight in his chair, tense and waiting.

My father cast a helpless look at the Bromleys, who both found their sandwiches to occupy their full attention just then.

He turned back to Tom and watched him thoughtfully.

"All right," Dad said. "I'll take you on the tour tomorrow, Maeve. You can come home with me tonight."

I bounced on the sofa, toppling a sandwich onto the rug.

"Your mother will be, er, delighted," Dad said, "to have you join us for Sunday dinner."

*Aha.* The proposal dinner, where Matthew Hopewood would take Dad aside and ask him for permission to marry Polly! Now I wouldn't need to hear about it secondhand from Evangeline.

"Can Mr. Poindexter join us for Sunday dinner, too, Dad?" I cried. "He and Tom? After we've found him in Dunstable, I mean."

My father wiped his mustache carefully with his napkin. "Certainly," he said quietly. "Let us hope for that." He smiled at Tom. "Mrs. Bromley, might I borrow young Thomas for the weekend as well?"

"Certainly." Mrs. Bromley's face contorted with worry. "In this instance," she said apologetically, "I'd much rather Alice stay far away from any...unpleasantness. Given that there could be danger, I mean. Though of course, going on a public tour, I'm quite sure—"

Her voice faltered.

"Perfectly understandable, madam," my father said. "If I were Miss Alice's father, I should wish to keep her away from trouble as well." He gave me a rueful look. "But as I'm Maeve's father, I think I'm better off escorting her *into* trouble, where I can at least keep an eye on her. Heaven knows she'll find her way into the thick of trouble, with or without my help."

Mr. Abernathy shook his head with an injured air. "My pupils have been preparing all week for an examination..." His face softened slightly when he looked at Tom. "But, I suppose, examinations will keep. Miss Alice, since Miss Maeve is abandoning us, you may have tomorrow morning off."

"Thank you, sir."

"And, Miss Maeve, I trust you will employ your time off this weekend in extra study."

I sealed my lips shut. Better that than to tell a lie.

Alice, I could tell, was disappointed not to go, but she put a brave face on it. "Come on, you two," she told Tom and me. "Let's go upstairs. I'll help you get your *bags* packed for the trip."

CHAPTER
16

T here it is."

I pointed to the tall tower beginning to emerge into view from the woodland surrounding Gretigwode Manor. Tom's face was grim as he took in the sight.

Our feet crunched on the gravel as we climbed the winding drive leading to the old manor home. Other tourists straggled behind us, but we pressed on with a purpose. The humid air buzzed with insects in the shrubbery, while grim clouds brooded overhead. The gray stone of the tower felt like a darker slice of sky.

"My dad's somewhere in there," Tom said softly.

"We'll find him," I said.

My father cast a worried look our way. Part of him, I felt sure, wanted to warn us against leaping to conclusions. The other part of him wanted to keep hope alive. Mr. Poindexter, trapped somewhere in Gretigwode Manor, was a much better thought than him *not* being here.

"Get your licorices, your peanuts, your marshmallows and toffees! Get 'em here, ladies and gents!"

A boy around my age emerged from a shady waiting place amid the shrubberies lining the path. He wore a blue serge jacket and a matching cap, and a pair of short gray trousers. When I first saw him I blinked, thinking somehow Tom had moved from my left side to my right. This boy wore a shallow box at his waist, slung from a strap around his neck and packed with shiny packages of sweets and snacks. In London you often see lads like this at street corners, but here, in the serene, leafy wilderness surrounding a stately old English manor home, he seemed as out of place as a clown.

"Two pence a package," he declared. "What'll it be, miss? You never had such marshmallows as these."

*Miss?* From a cheeky boy my own age? If my dad hadn't been there, I'd have told him off.

"I'm sure I haven't," I told him, "but we're in a hurry to catch the one o'clock tour, and we haven't time for marshmallows."

"Ah," the junior salesman replied. He fished through his box and pulled out a grimy printed leaflet. "Then you'll be wanting this. All the secrets of Gretigwode Manor. Price, one penny."

"What secrets?" I demanded.

"That's stealing," he said, with a severe look—the scalawag! "Secrets cost a penny."

My father produced a sixpence from his pocket. "Three bags of peanuts," he told the boy.

"Appreciate your business, sir," he said, tipping his cap to my dad and handing over three pouches of peanuts in brown paper. "And for you, miss? Tell you what—special price for you. Secrets of Gretigwode Manor, yours for a halfpenny."

*Fine.* Producing a halfpenny to get rid of this impudent person began to seem like a bargain, which was no doubt his strategy. I pulled one from my small coin purse. This boy had a faintly horsey smell about him, which made my nose twitch.

"Do they know you're out here?" I asked him. "The people up at the manor. Do they know you're selling to the folks who come for the tour?"

He pocketed my coin with lightning fingers. "Strictly speaking, no," he said, "but more or less, yes." He handed me my leaflet.

I took the paper and kept on trudging up the walk, hoping this pest would take a hint. We'd bought his silly stuff. He should move along now.

Instead he fell into step alongside us, as if he planned to join our tour.

"Name's Charlie," he announced.

"There are more visitors on the path behind us," I told him. "I'm sure *they'd* like to try your marshmallows."

He ignored the bait. "I do a brisk trade here every Saturday." As if we'd asked.

"And how, Charlie, do you come to know all the secrets of the manor?" my dad inquired.

"My big sister works there," he said proudly. "Chambermaid."

"I see," Dad said. "You have inside connections."

"'Sright. I'm here all the time. Sometimes I do a bit of a job for them, here and there, when they need help."

"What are the people like?" Tom showed the first bit of sense any of us had thus far. "The ones who live in the house?"

"It's just the one," said the unflappable Charlie. "Bachelor gentleman. Old. Older than you, even, sir."

"Indeed?" Dad coughed to hide a laugh. "He must have one foot in the grave."

"Oh, he gets around all right," said the expert on Gretigwode Manor. "Has his hobbies and whatnot. Collects things." He leaned in close. "Does a bit of *science*, don't you know." As if this were practically witchcraft. "That's a bonus secret. You won't find it on the leaflet."

A sign just ahead pointed to our right toward an opening in the hedge, indicating we had reached the house itself.

"Do me a favor," Charlie said. "If anyone asks, say you bought the peanuts in town, will you? Oh, and don't let anybody see the sheet of secrets. Then they wouldn't be secret, see."

And he was gone, though I heard his voice from around the bend. *"Get your licorices, your peanuts, your marshmallows..."*

The path turned, and we beheld Gretigwode Manor. Rows of prickly yew trees lined the long drive leading toward the grand house. It wasn't a castle, but it might as well be. Its massive, dark stone face glared down at us, with deep-set windows like glaring eyes. Its two towers were spiked weapons. It called to mind a guarded keep where prisoners were tormented until their spirits broke. A wide double-door of oak beams practically bellowed, "Abandon hope, all ye who enter here." I'd been a fool to think I could somehow break in and save Mr. Poindexter. It would take a battering ram.

Or, with luck, a tour pass.

We lined up behind a few other people at a door that advertised the starting point for the tour, and Dad paid our entrance fee. To pass the time, I silently perused the "Secrets of Gretigwode Manor" Charlie had sold me, and learned the following doubtful facts:

1. The high tower was haunted by the ghost of some lady of the manor from centuries past, who died on her wedding day. You can still hear her shriek.

2. During the English Civil Wars, Roundhead soldiers were often quartered at the manor, and at one point,

Royalist prisoners were locked in the dungeons, while noble captives were sequestered in the tower.

3.  His Majesty, King George III, once spent the night here, in 1781, raving in the Purple Room about the loss of the American Colonies.

4.  The weapons room contains the sword of one Sir Edmond de Beaumont, who fought alongside William the Conqueror in 1066.

5.  One of the house's past owners was a captain of a merchant fleet and, quite possibly, a pirate.

I folded the paper and stuffed it into my little coin purse. There were more "secrets," but the tour was starting. Historical trivia clearly wouldn't help us find Tom's dad today.

The tour guide, when he greeted us, had a pink, runny nose and a stuffed-up sounding voice to match. A few of the parties coming along after us on the walk to the manor had arrived in line behind us, so we made a group of about fifteen people, mostly elderly ladies.

"Good morning, ladies and gentlemen," our guide sniffled. "Welcome to the tour of the historic Gretigwode Manor. You will be shown through many of its magnificent chambers. Would you be so good as to remember that the manor is an occupied, private home?

Therefore we ask you kindly to stay with the tour group, within the roped-off areas only, and especially, we ask that you not touch anything. We will begin in a hallway where you may hang your coats and hats, and store your umbrellas. Thank you, and we hope you enjoy your tour."

He recited the speech as though he'd given it hundreds of times before, which, probably, he had. He pointed out some outdoor items of interest—a statue, some old trees. I itched to get inside.

Tom leaned over to whisper in my ear. "How will we break away from the group to go searching for Dad?"

"I'm not sure," I whispered back. "We'll have to look for our chance."

"Is the master of the house in residence now?" my father asked casually. "Or does he spend most of his time elsewhere?"

"Professor Fustian makes Gretigwode Manor his year-round home," the tour guide said, "though he is very fond of boating and spends part of each year sailing the Mediterranean aboard his yacht. This way, please."

He led us through a side door which brought us into a stone-paved corridor lined with pegs for coats and hats. I waited for my turn to hang my coat and found myself standing beside the umbrella stand. It was a giant vase of white ceramic, decorated all over with a blue china pattern. Imagine, even a humble umbrella stand being a work of art! But it wasn't the outside of it that caught my eye. It was a crumpled thing inside.

While everyone else fussed with buckles and buttons, I bent down swiftly and snatched the thing up. Tom and Dad both saw me looking at it, and they came closer to see what it was.

Just a small square of cloth. A man's everyday handkerchief. Pale gray, with initials embroidered in white thread. "S.E.P.," for Siegfried Ernest Poindexter.

Tommy's face went pale as chalk (if chalk had freckles). Dad took the handkerchief, folded it, and stuffed it into his breast pocket. He held a finger over his lips. I nodded. I wouldn't say a word.

My heart pounded so hard in my ears that I couldn't even hear the droning voice of the tour guide. He led the group along the corridor and out into a grand entrance hall, and from there into a weapons room. Suits of armor stood at attention along the full length of the room, while the walls were littered with spears, clubs, maces, and swords and daggers of every description. A cheerful room, in other words, perfect for a ladies' tea party. The sword of Sir Edmond de Beaumont looked just as dull and battered as the others. I shuddered and moved on.

Next we came to a portrait gallery proudly displaying a long row of furious-looking dead people. After that, the dining hall. It felt more like the scene for a feast of Viking raiders than a room for a modern gentleman to take his evening soup and cutlet.

As we entered the room, a white-clad cook or other kitchen staff rose suddenly from a hutch she'd been looking through. She turned, and I clutched Tom's wrist.

"That's Mrs. Gruboil," I whispered.

It was. It was her shape, dressed in the uniform I first knew her in, with that piggish face and those beady, suspicious eyes. She'd rose from the cupboard with the air of someone caught red-handed. I slipped quickly behind Dad. No good could come of her seeing me.

But what could she be doing *here*, at Gretigwode Manor, all the way up north from London in Dunstable? How had the "baroness" become a cook once more? Had she really lost everything? For a moment, I actually pitied her. Then I came to my senses. If Mrs. Gruboil was working as a servant at Gretigwode Manor, she had to be up to something, and that something had to involve Mermeros. This was no ordinary job for her.

She turned and disappeared through the room we'd entered through, keeping her eyes rooted to the floor the whole time. She hadn't seen us, I was sure.

Tom's gaze met mine. I knew we were both thinking the same thing. If Mrs. Gruboil was here, that was even worse news for his missing dad.

We trudged along on the tour, hearing none of what the stuffy-nosed tour guide said. With every room, the manor house felt more and more like a castle of evil. Where in this old Gothic pile could Mr. Poindexter be hidden? And what was "Baroness" Gruboil's hand in the game?

I pulled that Charlie boy's grimy pamphlet from my coin purse. "Secrets of Gretigwode Manor." I skimmed the lines.

*During the English Civil Wars, Roundhead soldiers were often quartered at the manor, and at one point, Royalist prisoners were locked in the dungeons…*

*Prisoners. Dungeons.* Of course a dismal old house like this would have dungeons!

The tour guide was showing us some ancient ladies' sitting room, lined with dull tapestries, when I seized my chance.

"Does the manor have dungeons?" I asked.

He gave me an indulgent smile. "Youngsters always want to know that," he said. "There is a cellar, but it's been modernized with several comfortable rooms. The present lord of the manor is a scholar, and he keeps books and equipment downstairs. It isn't part of our tour."

The rest of the party moved slowly into the next room, but I hung back, tugging Tom's sleeve.

"We've got to get downstairs," I told him. "I'll bet anything one of those rooms is a prison cell for your dad."

"What if we run into Mrs. Gruboil again?" he whispered.

I tried to think. "Pray we don't."

We crept back, retracing the former route of our tour. A doorway in the middle of a corridor opened, and an enormous man stepped out. If the strongman swinging the hammer at the Crystal Palace had dressed for a funeral, he'd look like this man.

Tom and I ducked out of sight and watched him leave. He turned away from our direction and strode down the hall and out of sight.

But I'd seen enough. The doorway he'd come through led to a *down* staircase.

"Come on," I told Tom. We slipped through the door and crept downstairs.

If I'd expected cobwebs and dust, I was mistaken. The downstairs was indeed modernized, clean and bright, with wallpaper and carpets and electric lamps.

We saw no one. The room we arrived in first looked like a museum. Glass cases filled with odd bits of stone and crystal, and ancient-looking artifacts, lined the walls. Beyond the room stretched a passageway with doors on either side.

"This is the dungeon?" Tom whispered. "Do you think my dad's in one of those rooms?"

"He's got to be," I said. "Let's go find him."

But we were disappointed. One room held roll upon roll of maps and nautical charts. Another room held a writing desk cluttered with papers. One room appeared to be some sort of workshop, with low lamps and a wide countertop littered with paintbrushes, tiny knives, and pots of glue. The fourth room was dim- I couldn't tell what it contained, but when we heard footsteps coming down the stairs, we hurried inside it and flattened ourselves against a wall.

We held our breath and waited as the footsteps drew near. Tom pointed toward a corner, behind a tall cabinet of drawers, and we tucked ourselves in there. I realized that at least one of the strange objects in the room which I couldn't at first recognize was a camera, on a tripod, covered with a velvet cloth.

Tommy and I looked at each other. "The camera that sees the future?" he whispered.

That's when I took a closer look at the papers on a nearby counter. They weren't, in fact, papers. I picked one up and we both stared. It was another copy of the photograph of Tom, falling off the tower. The tower here, at Gretigwode Manor. Underneath it in the pile was the crumpled calling card of Siegfried E. Poindexter, Proprietor, World Traveler, Chief Buyer, and Proprietor, The Oddity Shop.

"That's all the proof we need," Tom whispered. "We're in the right place. He lured my dad here. It's definitely him."

The door opened quietly. We hadn't heard footsteps. We pressed back against the shadows.

"Maeve?" a voice whispered. "Are you in here?"

I sighed with relief. "Yes, Dad."

My father groaned with exasperation. "What on earth were you thinking? You can't just wander off from a tour like that! Any minute now, they'll discover us missing."

"But, Dad," I cried. "Mrs. Gruboil is here!"

He frowned. "Who?"

"The cook from Miss Salamanca's School. The one who stole Mermeros from me, and made herself a phony baroness until we stole it back, and then showed up at the Bromleys' home the other day, making threats—"

"You can explain your cook's life to me later." Dad pressed his temples as if a headache were coming on.

"But, Dad!" I cried. "She's a clue! She's got to be."

"Shh. Never mind that now," he said. "Come along, both of you. We've got to get back upstairs before they find us down here."

I couldn't leave. I couldn't let go. My hands gripped the countertop.

My dad's not one to get overly heated with anger. He keeps himself under control. Today, however, he simmered to a boil.

"I know you want to find Tom's father," he said, "and believe me, I want to find him, too. That's why we're here. But you can't just go running off without telling me, and taking matters into your own hands. You'll ruin everything, and we won't come any closer to finding Mr. Poindexter."

Tom took the picture from me and thrust it at my dad. "Mr. Merritt," he said, "I think you should take a look."

Dad hesitated, just one second, before overruling Tommy. That second was enough. He saw the photograph. He stared at it.

"Good Lord," he whispered. "We have to call the police."

"My feelings exactly."

We whirled around to see two people standing in the doorway— the tour guide, and a servant in a black dress and a white apron and cap. It was she who'd just spoken, in acid tones.

My father pivoted on his heel and addressed the pair. "I do apologize, ma'am, sir," he said. "My daughter wandered off, and got lost, and—"

"A likely story," the woman snapped. "You're nothing but a pack of thieves, come to plunder Mr. Fustian's treasures. I'm calling the constables."

"We *asked* you kindly to stay with the tour group," our sniffly guide said, then shut the door behind him. A second later we heard a bolt click into the lock.

My father stood, blinking, a stunned expression on his face. "We're prisoners," he whispered. "They've locked us in, by thunder!"

"Just like they've locked up my dad," Tommy said. "They're monsters."

"What'll we do, Dad?" I asked.

"*Do?*" he echoed. "I don't want you *doing* anything. Your insistence on doing things yourself is why we're in this mess." He shook his head and sighed. "We'll wait for the police to come," he said, "and I'll do my best to talk our way out of this. With luck, we can chalk it up to a silly misunderstanding."

"You could give them a false name," I told him. "Don't tell the constables who you really are."

"Maeve," my father said sternly. "I'm disappointed in you. We don't *lie*."

"Yes, well," I said, "we don't get arrested, either."

"When they come," he said, "you'll let me do the talking, if you please, young lady."

"Don't you see, Dad?" I asked, pointing to the velvet-draped camera. "This must be it. This must be the camera that photographs the future!"

My father sighed. "Maeve," he said, "*think*. There's no such thing. There can't be. There absolutely couldn't be."

"Who's to say?" I demanded. "If a djinni can come from a sardine tin, why couldn't a camera photograph the future?"

Dad shook his head wearily. "What's that Oxford chap teaching you?"

"Maybe," I said, "maybe the camera lens is a piece of glass from a crystal ball."

"Begging your pardon," Tom said, "but I don't think it's the camera that matters." My father turned to look at him. Tom went on. "My father's here, in this house," he said. "Can't you feel it? He's here, somewhere. We can't leave till we find him."

"We're locked in, Tom," I pointed out. "The constables will certainly escort us out the door when they come. And we won't be welcomed back."

"But we're so close!" Tommy cried. "He's here, somewhere. We found his handkerchief. We found his business card. We have proof."

"And Mrs. Gruboil!" I reminded them.

"What will I tell your mother?" my father moaned. He began pacing the floor. "What if someone from the bank hears of this?"

"False name, Daddy," I repeated. "False name."

(I've been known to have a corrupting influence on other people's morals, but my father, I thought, could weather the onslaught.)

We waited. We tried the door, but the bolt held true. Dad fingered the business card and the photograph of Tom, all the while shaking his head and muttering. The horror of our plight began to settle more heavily upon me. Here my father sat, locked in a room, about to be arrested by the police, perhaps, and it was all my fault. And what if the bank did hear about it?

Had I done it again? Had my bumbling actually threatened my father's career and my family's livelihood?

But we *had* to find Mr. Poindexter! What if he was in mortal danger, even now?

Time slithered along torturously. I wondered if this was how Marie Antoinette, the deposed French queen, had felt, waiting in prison for her execution.

We heard a key in the lock. Dad thrust the picture at me. "Put this back!" Quickly, I returned it to its place on the counter.

The door opened. The enormous man in the funeral clothes appeared in the doorway, with murder in his eyes, and beside him, the indignant housekeeper.

"The police for you, if you please," she said tartly. She stood aside to usher them in.

A middle-aged officer appeared at the doorway with a "Now, what's all this?"

A second officer followed on his heels, and stopped us cold. There, in a blue uniform, with bright brass buttons, a wooden baton, and a horrified expression, stood Polly's own Constable Matthew Hopewood, of the Bedfordshire Police.

M r. Merritt!" Constable Hopewood cried. "Sir!"

His face flushed violet. So much for Daddy using a false name.

The indignant housekeeper turned to Matthew in disbelief. "You know this...this *person*?" As if her good breeding prevented her from using the word she would've liked to use.

Constable Hopewood hesitated. In that moment's delay, I saw a glint of steel flash in my father's eye. Matthew Hopewood may have just failed an unwritten test. Polly's hopes might've gone up in smoke.

"I am acquainted with this gentleman," Matthew Hopewood said, *very* carefully, "and his family. Including his daughter here, Miss Maeve, and her friend, young Thomas."

"He's a thief!" cried the housekeeper. "He snuck off from the tour, and—"

"I beg your pardon," my father said smoothly. "I believe there's been some misunderstanding. I apologize for leaving the tour. My daughter wandered off from the tour group, no doubt due to her *great* curiosity." He cast a sideways glance at me. "When I discovered her missing, I searched and found her here."

"By mistake," sneered the housekeeper.

"You are welcome to search my person," Dad said. "I have taken nothing whatsoever."

The other officer conferred quietly with Matthew Hopewood. "It does seem as though this has been a bit of a misunderstanding," the older officer said soothingly. "Of course, a father would be anxious about a daughter going missing, and young people will be curious and lose track of things."

My father took a deep breath. Yes. This was looking promising.

Then we heard a voice from outside the room, in the corridor. An older man, from the sound of things. The senior officer left the room to greet the speaker, and the large man and the housekeeper followed, leaving us alone with Matthew, who couldn't seem to look my father in the eye.

"You again?" the speaker's voice said.

"It's fortunate that we were so close by," the constable said. "We'd only just left."

Left Gretigwode Manor? *Why?* I wondered.

"You've caught my thief?" asked the unseen voice.

"Now, I don't believe there's cause to assume anyone is a thief," the older officer said. "A man and his daughter, and the daughter's friend. Seems the young people became separated from the rest of the party."

"Rubbish," the voice declared. "I'm telling you, I've had two attempted burglaries in my home this week alone. This group is bound to be connected to it."

Dad, Tom, and I stared at each other.

"Now, sir," the constable said, "those may be unrelated. I do believe this may just be an innocent mistake."

"Of course they're related," the voice said. "Snooping around in my private chambers? This level of the house isn't even part of the tour."

The long-suffering officer tried once more. "Begging your pardon, sir, but you told us this morning at the bureau that nothing had actually been taken."

This *morning*?

"The fact that a burglar fails to burgle does not mean he's invited to prowl around my property," cried the voice. "Arrest them. I've had enough of people poking and prying around my home. I've half a mind to put an end to these tours altogether. If people haven't the decency to respect a man's property, they shouldn't be welcomed here."

"But, sir..." the officer said, placatingly.

"Arrest him on charges of trespassing," the voice insisted. "If you find stolen property, charge him with theft as well. My friend, the magistrate, will hear of this."

While this was happening, Matthew Hopewood didn't dare meet Dad's gaze. "He's a bit upset today," he whispered miserably. "There've been some...incidents lately. And then we received a request from a London investigator to come here and ask questions about some shopkeeper's disappearance. It put him in a very bad temper."

I took a deep breath to tell Constable Hopewood exactly who that shopkeeper was, but my father silenced me with a look.

The senior constable and the curious household staff filed back inside. Mr. Fustian didn't follow them.

"You heard Mr. Fustian," the older police officer said. "Arrest this man, Hopewood."

Matthew Hopewood's blond-whiskered face took on a greenish hue.

"John Merritt," he said faintly, "you are under arrest, on suspicion of trespassing and attempted theft."

"Aren't you going to cuff him, copper?" growled the massive man in black. He had a thick American accent, and an unpleasant one at that.

Matthew Hopewood looked like he wished to fall through a hole in the floor and disappear.

My father held out his wrists and watched as his daughter's beau snapped handcuffs around them. He waited until Matthew Hopewood found the courage to look him in the eye.

"You must do your duty as an officer," he said, "and I, as a father, must do mine."

I wondered, just then, which daughter my father was thinking of. From the look on Constable Hopewood's face, he was wondering the same.

"Maeve," my father said, looking significantly at me, "don't cry, my dear."

My mouth hung open. I'm not a crier, and I certainly wasn't tearing up just then.

"Why don't you take my handkerchief from my breast pocket," he told me, arching his eyebrows. "You may need it."

O-ho! Now I understood. Good old Daddy! I pulled back his jacket and reached inside the inner pocket, drawing out Mr. Poindexter's gray embroidered handkerchief. One of our vital clues.

"Gather up anything you may have *left*," Dad said, "and we'll follow these good officers to the station."

While the suspicious adults steered my dangerous criminal of a father out of the room, I casually slid my hand over the counter, palming the photograph of Tom and Mr. Poindexter's calling card. I slid both into my pocket and followed the grown-ups out of the room.

We made our way upstairs and were marched out the front door by the officers. Strangely—or not so strangely, when you consider how gossip spreads among domestics—a whole queue of household staff flanked us in the entryway, watching with wide eyes as we were led outdoors. Like a receiving line of humiliation. And there, near the door, in her white starched apron and cap, stood Mrs. Gruboil, with a gloating look of triumph in her eyes.

## CHAPTER 19

They drove us in the back of a police wagon to the police bureau in Dunstable. He said nothing, but I could tell Tom was desperate not to leave Gretigwode Manor. Every turn of the wagon wheels carried us farther away from finding his father. How would we ever come back now?

I sat there seething at the image of Mrs. Gruboil seared into my brain. Professor Mortimer Fustian was all but forgotten in my wrath at that wretched, ruthless cook. Were they working together? They must be. But how? Why? Why would she don a cook's uniform once more? How would it help her get Mermeros back?

The heavy clouds which had been massing overhead all day finally broke into rain, drumming on the roof of the close-topped wagon as we rode along in silence. We could hear the driver grumbling about it even over the noise.

We reached the bureau, and the senior officer clambered out and beckoned my father to follow. They intended to question him, it seemed. As Dad climbed awkwardly out of the wagon, he leaned in close to me and hissed two words of warning.

"*Say nothing.*"

I nodded.

Satisfied, he turned to the senior officer. "Constable," he said, "as Officer Hopewood is acquainted with my daughter and her friend, could he be permitted to escort the children home and leave them in the care of my wife and daughters?"

The officer puffed out his cheeks. "It's irregular," he said, "and it's none too close, but given their age, I suppose we'd better. Go ahead, Hopewood. You can end your shift early." He told the wagon driver about the new plan and provided the address my father gave him. Then he steered my father inside, leaving Tom and me alone with Constable Hopewood.

The wagon rumbled off.

It was going to be a long, awkward five miles home.

Tom sat slumped in a corner, deep in his own tortured thoughts. With Polly's constable there, he couldn't say a word.

I pulled my packet of peanuts from my pocket and offered some to Constable Hopewood. He politely declined. Tom followed my lead, and we ate our salted nuts in somber silence.

Several times, Matthew Hopewood took a breath as if about to speak, then swallowed the words before they left his mouth. He was dying to ask me what we'd been doing there, I was certain, but he seemed to feel he ought not to ask me, a child. It suited me fine. I was in no mood to talk to him about it.

I made an effort to set aside my brooding over Mrs. Gruboil, to focus on the real question: where in that huge, dismal house could Mr. Poindexter be hidden? And how would we ever find him?

My fingers fidgeted idly with my coin purse, dangling from my wrist. I felt the stiff crumple of a folded bit of paper inside, and pulled it out once more. Secrets of Gretigwode Manor.

Of course! There it was, staring up at me, plain as day.

*The high tower was haunted by the ghost of some lady of the manor... During the English Civil Wars...noble captives were sequestered in the tower.*

"The tower," I told Tom. "He's in the tower."

Tom's eyes lit up. He nodded.

"What tower?" asked Matthew Hopewood. "Who's in a tower?"

Too late, I remembered my father's warning. "Say nothing." I stuffed the folded pamphlet back into my little purse and looked resolutely out the window. Constable Hopewood let out an aggravated sigh and looked out the windows on the other side.

The wagon plodded and sloshed on through roads becoming ever more soupy. Water streaked in dreary sheets across the small, grimy windows of the wagon.

Finally, the silence became unbearable.

"Seen Polly lately, Mr. Hopewood?"

"I had the, er, pleasure of your sister's company Tuesday last," he said stiffly, "for a few moments of conversation following choir practice."

Very proper of them. I wondered if that "conversation" had included more secret kissing.

"Polly never used to be one for singing," I said. "Funny how she's taken to it lately."

He turned pink. "I find it a very enjoyable pastime."

"To be sure," I said. "I understand you'll be joining our family for dinner tomorrow evening?"

He looked away. "Under the circumstances," he said, "I fear I must regretfully decline."

I wanted to give Matthew Hopewood a good poke in the nose with my fist. Weren't we good enough for him, now? Or does a constable not dare keep company with the daughter of a man who gets into trouble with the law?

The sky began to lighten, and the rain to lose conviction. Only a light drizzle dampened us as we climbed down from the police wagon near my home. Constable Hopewood had called up to the driver to stop some distance there. To spare our family the embarrassment of a police wagon stopping out front, no doubt.

He walked us toward the house. Polly, seeing him and us from a downstairs window, came hurrying out.

"Is everything all right?" she cried. "Maeve, where is Father?"

I hadn't thought about what to tell my family. I'd scarcely thought of them at all.

"Mr. Merritt is safe and well," the constable said.

"Oh, thank heavens," Polly sighed. "How, then, did you come to bring—"

I didn't linger to hear the rest of their conversation. I stalked inside, with Tom at my heels. Once through the door, I turned back to watch through the window as the constable concluded a very brief, very businesslike conversation with my sister, turned on his heel, and walked away. Polly stood frozen like a pillar, one hand pressed over her mouth, as if to hold back the breaking dam of shock and heartbreak and what she'd just learned. Slowly, she turned and approached the house.

I hurried up the stairs and to my room. Tom followed. I couldn't bear to face Polly just then.

I'd squandered my one chance to find Mr. Poindexter. Gotten my father arrested, and possibly, sacked from his position at the bank. And now, to top it all off, I'd cost Polly her future happiness.

And all from sneaking away from a tour group.

If they gave out prizes for reckless, stupid choices that caused the most far-reaching devastation to those one loved, I'd take the silver laurel. Perhaps I should call it my hidden talent. Maximum mayhem. Maeve Merritt, the human bomb.

And Tom. His wretched expression smote my heart. If we didn't find his dad, if we couldn't pry him out of the clutches of that evil, monstrous Mr. Fustian, what kind of future could Tom look forward to?

I had to fix this. I had to fix it for everybody. I had made this mess. One way or another, I was going to clean it up.

CHAPTER

20

I knew my mother and sisters would have a thousand questions for me, and that no good would come of me trying to explain what had happened. Either way, my mother would have hysterics, and either way, Polly would be devastated. The time would come when they would learn what they needed to know. That time didn't have to be right now.

"Let's get out of here," I whispered to Tom on the landing. "We can empty any clothes out of our carpetbags, but bring anything we might need to rescue your dad. Meet me here in a minute."

The first glimmer of hope I'd seen in too long flickered across Tom's face. "Be right back."

I dumped out my bag and grabbed a few things that might be helpful. A pair of scissors? A bit of paper? A pencil, a spool of string? What tools did one use to break into a home and rescue a man held prisoner? It wasn't as if I had many tools anyway, and I certainly didn't have much time.

I raided all my stash of money, which wasn't much, and stuffed it into my coin purse. Tom and I crept down the stairs and managed to get out of the house without anyone noticing.

"Now what?" Tom asked. "Do we fly to Dunstable?"

"Not yet," I said. "Let's get to the post office. We need to talk to Alice."

I wonder what people in Luton who knew me thought to see me walking down the street, bold as you please, with a tall youth with shocking carrot-colored hair, both of us carrying shabby carpet-bags. Word would get back to Mother, without fail, and there would be questions. I didn't care. We found the post office, which was still open, but barely, and I learned, after some careful calculating, that I had more than enough money to put a call through to Grosvenor Square. I handed it over to the clerk behind the counter, then gave my instructions to the operator.

After a long wait for Mr. Linzey to locate "Miss Alice," I finally heard her voice over the line.

"Maeve!" she cried. "Is that really you?"

"It's really me," I told her. We'd never spoken over the telephone before, though I was practically an expert, now, with two telephone calls to my name. "Alice, I don't have much time, so I need you to listen carefully. I have good news and bad. We went to the, er, place. We found a handkerchief there belonging to...you-know-who. And a calling card. And one of those pictures of Tom."

"But that's wonderful!" she cried. "Hand those over to Inspector Wallace, and he'll have to take this more seriously now."

"I can't," I said. "He's in London, and I'm here. It's Saturday afternoon, and I don't know how to reach him. Even if I did, I doubt he'd believe me."

"But your father was with you, wasn't he?" asked Alice. "Wouldn't the inspector believe him?"

"Um," I said. "Yes. He was with us. That's the bad news." I looked around to make sure no postal clerks were within hearing range, then whispered into the receiver. "*He was arrested.*"

She gasped.

"By Polly's own Constable Hopewood. We were searching around the house for clues, and Dad came looking for us, then they caught us, and Dad was the adult, so..."

"Oh, Maeve, no!" Alice moaned. "What will we do?"

"Tommy and I will go rescue Mr.—you know who—ourselves," I said.

"Maeve, you mustn't! It's too dangerous!"

"We have no other choice," I told her. "No one would ever believe me, and we can't afford to wait."

"I don't like this, Maeve." I heard a long sigh across the telephone wire. "There's nothing I can do to change your mind, is there?"

"No," I admitted. "But you can still help."

She groaned. "What do you need me to do?"

Good old Alice. She was the best friend to have in a jam, and since I got into a lot of jams, we were a good pair.

"I know it will be hard to make them believe you, but can you tell your grandparents all that I just told you, and ask them to relay it to the inspector? What's his name—you just said it—Wallace. Inspector Wallace. They have to come arrest him. Immediately. They've got to do something."

There was a moment's pause. I waited nervously.

"I'll do all I can," Alice said, "though I don't know if they'll believe me."

"I know I can count on you," I told her. "I hope I can give these to the inspector myself, but in case not, the, er, clues we found are in my writing desk in my bedroom."

"Oh, don't talk like that, Maeve," Alice said. "Stay safe, and give them to the detective yourself."

"There's one more thing," I told her. "Mrs. Gruboil. She's working in the kitchens at Gretigwode."

"She *what*?" I'd never before heard Alice actually squawk. "What's she doing there?"

"Helping Mr. Fustian, probably," I said. "Conspiring with him somehow. It's all I can figure."

"This is awful," Alice said. "Maeve, I have a terrible feeling about this."

So did I, but we had no time for feelings. "I've got to go."

"Wait, Maeve," Alice said. "I need to tell you something. That woman...Mrs. Fletcher? From the Orphan Committee, or whatever it was called?"

A cold, sick feeling came over me. "I remember her."

"She came to the house this afternoon," Alice explained. "At first she was very, er, flattering and fawning over my grandparents, about their beautiful home, and so on. Grandmother even took her to see the hothouse flowers. But when she learned Tommy wasn't there, but had gone to Bedfordshire for the day with you — someone not on her list—she became very disapproving. Almost rude. As though we were being careless with Tom's safety. Especially since Mr. Poindexter was nowhere to be found. Grandmother and Papa were offended, I think."

"Oh, no," I moaned. "What's going to happen?"

"I'm not sure," Alice admitted. "She said she'd be back tomorrow, and if Tom wasn't there, they'd file a report on him as a missing child. And if Mr. Poindexter wasn't there, they would consider that he had abandoned Tom. As soon as they located Tom, he'd be returned to the Mission School and Home."

I glanced over at Tom. He leaned against a wall, fiddling distractedly with the handles of his carpetbag. His mind, I knew, was on his fears for his dad. And now this.

"That's why we're going back," I told Alice, "to take care of this once and for all."

Alice was silent on the other end of the line.

"My time for the call is running out," I told her. "We're going back. Get the police to do something as soon as they possibly can."

"I will," she said, "if I can. It's late, but I'll try. Good luck, Maeve."

"Thanks." I hung up the receiver.

Church bells rang five o'clock as we left the post office. It would be hours yet before dark. I didn't dare attempt to fly. We'd be seen. We made our way to the Luton omnibus station and approached the ticket counter.

"How much for two fares to Dunstable?" I asked.

"Half a crown," the ticket master said.

I poked through the coins in my change purse, and my spirits sank. "I'm threepence short."

"Here," the man said, "didn't you ride to Dunstable this morning?"

I nodded. "We need to go back."

He chuckled through his walrus mustache. "What'd you do, fly back? Har! Har!"

Tom and I gave each other a look.

"Tell you what," he said. "Since you're such loyal customers, let's have what you've got, and we won't mind about threepence." He nodded toward the door. "The 'bus leaves in ten minutes. Might as well go get yourselves a seat." He paused. "D'you live in Dunstable?"

We shook our heads.

His bushy brows furrowed. "Then how will you get back home?" he asked. "This is the last 'bus run of the day."

"We'll fly," I told him. "Har, har."

It was past seven o'clock by the time Tom and I climbed the long, winding road that led to Gretigwode Manor. The evening air was warm and damp. The sky, still overcast, was already darkening with the setting sun, though it wouldn't be fully dark for some time yet. Three long carriage rides back and forth between Luton and Dunstable had meant nearly six hours of rattling in a horse-drawn conveyance. Now, lugging large carpet-bags a mile uphill, banging against our knees, sapped my energy and my spirits. What if we couldn't find Mr. Poindexter? What if somehow we couldn't get home? No one besides Alice knew where we were headed. If we didn't return, how long would it take before someone thought to ask Alice about us? Why would they? She was far away, in London. We couldn't safely walk home all night from Dunstable to Luton on dark country roads, not even if we knew the way.

I shook myself. *Stop that. This will work. It has to.*

A voice interrupted my thoughts. "Get your licorices, your peanuts, your marshmallows and toffees!"

Tom and I stared at each other. There, coming around a bend, was pesky Charlie.

"You two again!" he cried. "What'd you do, leave your umbrellas at the manor?" He whistled through his teeth. "There's no evening tour, you know."

"Then what are you doing, out selling?" I demanded.

"Heard you coming, didn't I?" He grinned. "I'm always open for business."

This popinjay would probably die rich. Maybe I should be taking notes from him. He had a bit of straw sticking out of his collar and in his hair. Maybe he was a scarecrow.

He leaned in closer. "Did you see who it was that got arrested during your tour? My sister says there hasn't been this much excitement among the household staff in a week. Not since—"

We waited.

"Not since what?" I finally asked.

"Never mind."

Tom took a step forward. "You can tell us, mate," he said. "Did something happen up at the manor a week ago?"

Charlie's eyes narrowed. "What makes you two so curious?"

Tom shrugged. "No reason," he said. "Just like a good bit of gossip, is all. It doesn't matter. Come on, Maeve. Let's go." We pushed past Charlie.

"Here, now," he said, jogging to catch up with us. "Buy some marshmallows?"

"Haven't a farthing," I said. "Sorry."

Tom reached into his pocket. "I'll take a licorice."

This piqued me. "You've got money? You could've said so, back at the station."

"You never asked." He grinned and surrendered his pennies, then opened the licorice parcel. I'm very fond of licorice. Tom is, too, and he has a habit of stealing mine.

He took a piece, and offered me one, then even offered one to Charlie. To my surprise, the candy seller took it.

"So," Tom said, "what *did* happen last week?"

Charlie wasn't one to let jaws stuck shut with licorice get in the way of a good story.

"It's late at night," he said, through smacking lips, "and the household's gone to bed, when all of a sudden, there's a knock, pounding at the door. The master answers, but my sister, she comes down in her housecoat, and she sees it all. The man at the door shouts at the master. He even has a pistol!"

Tom's licorice stopped an inch from his mouth. "Who was it?"

"Hang on," Charlie said. "I'm getting to that."

"Did the visitor use his pistol?" I demanded.

Charlie frowned. "Nah. I don't think so. The men on the staff showed up and put a stop to it. But my sister was scared out of her bloomin' wits. She asked Mr. Fustian if she should call the constables. No, says he, it's my long-lost cousin, and he's not well. I'll take care of him. But for everyone's safety, I'll keep him *locked in the tower!*"

Tom carefully avoided looking at me. "Then what happened?"

"He's there still," Charlie said. "You can see the light in the window at night. My sister says all the staff is atwitter, having a dangerous fellow locked in the tower. Sometimes she brings his meals up to him, but she doesn't go in. Mr. Fustian says it isn't safe. Only Thorne can take him his food and drink, and do the necessaries."

"Who's Thorne?" I asked.

"Huge bloke," Charlie said. "American. Made of muscles. Used to be part of a criminal gang in Chicago." Charlie was obviously enjoying himself. "My sister says the maids don't even dare speak to him, he's so mean."

*Ah.* I tried to sound casual. "I think I saw him on the tour," I said. "What does he do?"

Charlie shook his head. "Whatever Mr. Fustian wants done."

"That's odd, don't you think?" This gave me an idea. "Say, Charlie," I said in a low voice. "Does Mr. Fustian ever want...bad things done? Odd, or dangerous things?"

"Don't know about bad. But odd?" He laughed. "I'll say. He paid me five shillings a while back, just to let him take a photograph of me." He gazed with pride at his clothes. "It's where I got these new togs. He said I could keep 'em."

My skin prickled. "What was the photograph for?"

"He said it was a contest, for one of the photography journals," explained Charlie. "I lay on the floor, with the camera up toward the ceiling, and he had me move my arms and legs this way and that." He laughed. "Strangest five shillings I ever made."

"Definitely sounds *odd*," Tom said significantly. "Don't you think, Maeve?"

He had to be thinking what I was thinking. This must be a clue, somehow, to the mystery of the camera that could see the future. Though Charlie certainly didn't have Tom's face.

"Why," I asked, "would a picture of you, lying on a floor, moving your limbs about, win a photography contest?"

Charlie shrugged. "What do I care? I got my five shillings, didn't I? *And* new clothes."

New clothes probably weren't something this Charlie got very often.

"He told me to pretend like I was falling," he said. "He told me to act the part. Like I was in a theatrical. Only you wouldn't dare pitch people off a building in a theatrical, would you?"

Tom and I looked at each other once more.

"But you don't look anything like Tom in the face," I said.

Charlie made a face. "Who's bloomin' Tom?" he demanded. "And who said I looked like him?"

Tom laughed. "I'm Tom," he said, "and Maeve's thinking out loud. You should be glad you don't look like me. In the face."

Charlie wrinkled his nose. "You two are a pair of strange birds," said the marshmallow salesman.

"You aren't the first to think so," I told him.

By now, the sky was darkening fast. "Well," Charlie said, "I'd best get home. Say, you still haven't said what you're doing back up here."

"Stargazing," said Tom.

Charlie glanced at the lead-colored, flat night sky, wreathed in clouds. Not a single star.

"Sightseeing," I told him.

His eyes narrowed. "After dark?"

"It's amazing what sights you can see after dark," I said hurriedly. "'Evening, Charlie." And we hurried off before he could ask any more questions.

As soon as we knew he was gone, Tom nudged my arm. "Best threepence I ever spent."

I nodded.

"How could that Fustian put my face on Charlie's body?" he demanded.

"I don't know how," I admitted, "but now we know he did it. With science, not magic. And that's enough for now."

"Right-o," he said. "Are you ready?"

The only sounds on the air were the *cheep-cheep* of crickets. The night wasn't pitch-black, but near enough. Only the faraway edge of the sky showed any light. Anybody nearby, I told myself, was settling down for the evening. Indoors, I prayed. With the curtains drawn shut.

"I'm ready," I told him.

W e tucked our hats and loose items into our carpetbags, straddled them, and gripped the handles tightly.

"Come on, carpetbags," I said, "wouldn't it be fun to go have a look at who's up in that tower?" On an afterthought, I added, "But I don't suppose you can fly *that* high, can you?"

I felt a little shudder of glee between my knees, then gasped as the bag bolted up into the air. Tom shot upward beside me. We cleared the treetops in half a second and soared over the manor grounds. The two bags zoomed round and round each other like frolicking sparrows. I wished I hadn't eaten the licorice.

It was one thing to practice in a ballroom. Tearing through the night sky, over the gardens and fountains of Gretigwode Manor, was quite another. The night air smelled damp and fresh, like new-cut grass, but racing through it with gnats and mosquitoes colliding with your eyes made it hard to enjoy the atmosphere.

And then there was the height. *Don't look down.*

We barreled toward the house, which rose up before us as a mountain of black stone. The few lit windows here and there made it seem no less menacing.

"Let's go see the *tower*," I reminded the carpetbags. Rushing air snatched the sound from my mouth.

The carpetbags bucked forward and upward at such a sharp angle I feared I'd slide off. I gripped the handles till my fingernails cut into my palms.

We reached the tower, and those naughty carpetbags raced us around and around it. My head spun, my balance lurched to one side. I held on for dear life, not daring to look down. The tower's upper room did have a bank of windows, lit against the night, but we were spiraling too fast to see anything at all. I began to fear I would vomit.

"Can we *slowly* circle the tower?" I called out softly. "What do you say, carpetbags, eh?"

*Whoomp.* Our speed slammed from galloping stallion to groggy turtle. We nearly tumbled forward off the carpetbags, only just catching ourselves. We slowly orbited the tower, until the windows came into view. I was glad the air was so heavy and still. Otherwise winds would have buffeted at us, this high up.

"Let's pause here, shall we?" I cajoled the carpetbags. "Let's find out what's going on inside. Can you help us with that?"

We hovered and bobbed in the night sky, just outside the windows. I prayed we were far enough away from them to remain unseen. Yet we needed to creep closer in order to see and hear. A few panes of glass from the tower window were missing, which helped.

The windows were wide, crisscrossed with iron bars. A prison cell. From the days of the "noble captives" in the tower.

I heard Tommy's sharp intake of breath. Then I saw it, too. It's a wonder I didn't cry out.

Tied to a chair, a chair bolted to the wall, drooped the dirty, disheveled figure of Mr. Poindexter. One eye was darkly bruised.

"What's that monster done to him?" Tom hissed.

"Shh," I warned.

The room itself was mostly empty. A few old tables and chairs stood at one side, collecting dust. An old-fashioned lamp stood on one small table, sending long shadows around the circular chamber. A rickety staircase wound slowly around the wall, up toward the roof.

A man paced back and forth before Mr. Poindexter's seat. His gray hair stood out in a wiry mane about his head. He wore baggy trousers and a rumpled brown suit. He had a long face and beady eyes that glittered behind gold-rimmed spectacles. Something about him tickled the edges of my memory. Who *was* he?

It didn't matter. What did matter was the object he held in his hand: a flat, rectangular sardine tin.

Mermeros. My djinni. Mr. Poindexter's djinni or, I supposed, now the djinni of this odious Professor Fustian.

"Come now, Poindexter," the man said. "Don't be stubborn, there's a good fellow. Make the wish."

"Make one yourself" was his prisoner's weary reply.

"We've been through this," the stranger told him, with an air of exaggerated patience, as though speaking to a very young child. "I'm saving mine. That's why I need yours."

"I spent a wish getting here," Mr. Poindexter replied. "I already told you. If I use up my wishes, Mermeros will vanish."

"Which was very silly of you." Fustian made a *tsk* sound with his tongue. "Any sensible person would've taken the trains."

Mr. Poindexter's head hung low. "It was late on a Sunday night," he said hollowly. "The train I needed wasn't running. And you'd threatened my son." He sounded like a beaten man. "I wasn't thinking straight."

"Nothing that couldn't have waited until morning. Which only proves what I always say." Fustian waggled a finger at Mr. Poindexter. "Magic isn't for mere mortals to handle. Your *emotions*, my good fellow, got in your way. It takes a sophisticated thinker, and a calm, cool intellect—such as mine—to wield supernatural power."

A sort of a bark, what might almost have been a laugh, escaped Mr. Poindexter's lips. "A calm, cool intellect," he echoed, "such as yours."

Mortimer Fustian whirled about and darted in close to Mr. Poindexter's face. "Let's not forget," he cried, "who's in chains and who's in command, shall we?"

He reminded me of a certain type of girl I'd sometimes known at school. Desperate for importance, willing to be cruel to get it. Always terrified of being overlooked and ignored.

"Your emotions, *my good fellow*," mimicked Tom's father bitterly, "are getting in your way."

Beside me, Tommy grinned. "You tell him, Dad," he whispered.

Mr. Fustian backed away from Mr. Poindexter and paced the floor, muttering. He seemed to hit upon a thought, and returned to his supposedly friendly tone.

"Whether your squandered a wish, or no, it can't be helped," he said. "But you still can make your second wish. Come on. Be a good sport."

A good *sport*? This from the man who'd chained Mr. Poindexter to a chair and given him that black eye, with Thorne's help?

"Get your hired boxer or whatever he is," Mr. Poindexter said. "Get him to give you his wishes."

"I'm surprised at you," Mr. Fustian said. "I must say I'm disappointed in your intelligence. You can't seriously think I'd turn this priceless treasure over to a brute like Thorne! In two ticks, he'd turn against me." He rotated the sardine tin idly between his fingers. "No, my good shopkeeper. I fear, under the circumstances, I can only trust you."

"Yet you sent him to rob my shop," Mr. Poindexter said. "You trusted him that far."

"I wasted no time that day, did I?" agreed Fustian, as if Mr. Poindexter had been praising him. "I telephoned him from the Crystal Palace and gave him your address. But naturally, I couldn't tell him he was looking for a djinni. So I told him to look for lamps and bottles. I didn't yet know about sardine tins. Most unexpected."

"He destroyed my shop."

"Thorne *is* a bumbler," admitted Fustian sympathetically. "Strong but not very subtle. He requires careful management. Now, if you please, we return to the subject of the wish you're about to give me."

Mr. Poindexter took an exhausted breath. Had he been in that chair all week? Perhaps he had never been permitted to lie down and sleep. That poisonous professor!

"I won't do it," Mr. Poindexter said. "You're wasting your time."

Mr. Fustian sighed. "I'm a gentle soul," he said sadly. "A poet by nature. An artist at heart. It's not my fault your willful refusal to cooperate forces me to take extreme measures." He rested a hand on Mr. Poindexter's shoulder. "My dear fellow, I assure you this pains me more than it hurts you. *Thorne!*"

The last word was a loud cry. Fustian slid the sardine tin into his jacket pocket.

After a few seconds' pause, a door opened, and the gigantic strongman entered the room. "Yessir?" he growled.

"Make the telephone call," ordered Mr. Fustian. "Tell our man in London to seize the boy and bring him here, as instructed previously."

Tommy gasped.

Mr. Poindexter's head flew up. "No! You wouldn't!"

"Well, of course I wouldn't," Fustian said. "That's why I have Thorne do it for me."

Thorne, the colossus, bowed and left.

"You leave my son alone," Mr. Poindexter cried in a voice hoarse with suffering. "You're a fiend, to hurt an innocent child."

"I, the fiend?" asked Mr. Fustian smoothly. "I? Who am I hurting? I wouldn't hurt a mouse. If I simply bring a boy here, where is the harm in that?"

"You're barbaric," Mr. Poindexter said. "He's not property that you can steal."

"My dear fellow," said his captor, "everything is property. But you know, I always did think it would be a fine thing to have a son. A young mind to mold. A future to plan." He sighed. "Sadly, my devotion to my studies left me with little time for romance. I never did marry. Perhaps I'll adopt your Tom myself."

Beside me, on his carpetbag, Tom shuddered.

"He seemed like a fine young lad, that day that I shadowed you at the Crystal Palace," Fustian said. "A topper. Now, make this wish," he wheedled, "and I'll call off Thorne."

Mr. Poindexter glared at him through furrowed brows.

"What's more," said Fustian, "make this wish, and I'll let you go."

"Why should I believe you?" demanded Mr. Poindexter.

Fustian tittered. "What choice do you have?"

Mr. Poindexter shook his head slowly, agonizingly. "All right," he said. "I'll do it. But call off Thorne."

I heard Tommy's inhale. I knew he was about to cry out. I grabbed for his wrist and pinched it, hard. He turned to me with wild eyes. I let go of him and placed my finger over my lips.

"We need to let him know I'm safe," Tom whispered.

I shook my head. "If you do," I told him, "you might put your dad in greater danger."

"How?"

I tried to figure out how to explain it. "Fustian is using threats to control your dad," I told him. "Threats of harming you. If you prove to them that you're safe, and that that method won't work, wouldn't Fustian resort to more brutal means?"

Tom's face fell. "That rotten Thorne," he muttered. "Did you see my dad's black eye?"

Before I could answer, his carpetbag dropped a few feet.

"Come on, old fellow," he coaxed it. "Can we listen at the window a little longer? A favor, for me?"

His bag grudgingly brought him back up.

Mr. Fustian returned from barking instructions down the stairwell to Thorne. Then he crossed the bare room to where Mr. Poindexter sat. With a key from his waistcoat pocket, he unlocked the cuffs encircling his prisoner's wrists and ankles. He thrust the sardine tin toward Mr. Poindexter, then drew it tauntingly back.

"One more thing," Mr. Fustian said. "Thought you'd like to know. This has all been planned to the letter. Before you get any ideas of your own, know this: my London agent has now been telephoned and instructed to seize your son in five minutes, unless he receives another call to abort the plan."

Mr. Poindexter's bloodshot eyes burned with anger. "If you hurt my son, I swear to you, Fustian, I will find you. No matter where you try to hide."

Fustian shook his head sympathetically. "Believe me, my dear fellow," he said, "if there was any other way, I assure you, I'd employ it. This is *most* distressing, I know. Indelicate. Regrettable. But you'd best summon your djinni," he said. "You're running out of time."

Poor Mr. Poindexter's limbs were so sore, he could hardly stand. His fingers so stiff he could barely pluck the key from off the sardine tin and use it to peel back the top layer of metal. Fortunately, Mermeros, the djinni, didn't need much of a gap to escape his magic prison. As soon as the can was open, mustard-yellow fumes began billowing out of the tin in bulging waves that filled the space with noxious, fishy vapor. Tom and I even caught a whiff of it through the broken windows. That putrid smell, oddly enough, was the scent of happier memories for me.

The yellow mists swirled in a tornado-like column, forming themselves into a gigantic green body, big enough to make the mighty Thorne look like a member of the lightweight boxing class. As the mists cleared, Mermeros's great bald head came into focus, with its wide, white mustaches and his bushy eyebrows, his hoop earring, and his shark-tooth necklace.

My fingers twitched and my stomach fluttered. Ah, Mermeros! What hopes I'd once had for the great things I would do with you!

*You still have one more wish,* a little voice inside me said.

One glance back at poor Mr. Poindexter put an end to that.

From the lack of surprise in Mr. Fustian's face, it was clear that he'd met Mermeros already. Well, that made sense; Mr. Poindexter had been here for days.

Mermeros swelled himself even larger, till his tattooed arms bulged like tree trunks. He looked back and forth between the two men in the room, then glanced up and saw me, peeking in through the window. One bushy eyebrow rose.

I shook my head urgently. *No, Mermeros! Don't give me away!*

Mr. Fustian got right to business. "Now, Poindexter," he said. "You'll love this. You'll wish you'd thought of it yourself. Here it is. Make me this wish: Command your djinni to produce, for me, a map of the world, showing the precise name and location of all the world's magical objects, wherever they lie hidden."

Oh, *no*.

Mermeros acted as though he'd heard nothing. He addressed Mr. Poindexter.

"Are you a *prisoner* here?" he demanded. "You insult me. How am I to take orders from one who can't even command himself?"

"Oh, I *say*," cried Fustian indignantly, "that's not how this thing is supposed to work. I must say, Mermeros, old chap, I'm disappointed in you. You're to do as you're told."

Mermeros turned his sneering, fishy face toward Mr. Fustian. "Silence, mortal," he hissed. "You pathetic, mewling scribe, you distract and annoy me."

"'Mewling scribe,'" echoed Fustian. "How dare you, sir. I am a *scholar!*"

Mermeros's sneering lip curled. "An idle occupation for those too *weak* to conquer and command."

Good thing Mr. Abernathy wasn't here to hear this.

"You are to call me 'Professor,'" insisted Fustian.

Mermeros blinked leisurely. "I call you a maggotous grub, slinking and oozing beneath my feet, trailing slime in your wake."

The would-be professor turned purple in the face. "You haven't got feet."

Mermeros was clearly tired of him. "Let the bearer of my vessel speak freely." He darted closer toward Mr. Poindexter, like a fish swimming through the air. "I see you are a captive, and this *toad* presumes to hold authority over the one man on earth who commands *my* matchless power. Say the word, and I will shatter the walls of this prison cell and crush whatever schemes he plots against you."

"Remember!" shrilled the voice of Mr. Fustian. "Remember your boy! Time is running out!"

*He's afraid*, I thought, and well he should be.

Mr. Poindexter spoke. "I'm sorry, Mermeros," he said. "I must make his wish my own. He holds my son's life in his hands."

Mermeros glanced up at Tom through the window. "I can protect your son."

"In two minutes' time?" cried Fustian. "Can you snatch him from the grip of my hired man, all the way in London, in two minutes' time?"

Mermeros kept his bulging, fishy eyes trained upon Mr. Poindexter while he answered the odious Fustian's question. "I can protect your son," he repeated. "Easily." He glanced up at Tommy once again, then back again at Mr. Poindexter. "Trust me."

Tears ran down Mr. Poindexter's cheek. "I do trust you. But I don't dare take the chance that you might be mistaken."

"Don't do it, Dad!" Tommy whispered. He clutched my hand. "Maeve, we've got to tell him! Tell him I'm here, and I'm fine!"

I hesitated. Should he? Mermeros *could* save Mr. Poindexter. But what if something went wrong? Mermeros, I knew, was unpredictable. It felt too risky. Especially with that great troll, Thorne, waiting just downstairs.

"Shouldn't we let him make the map?" I asked. "He said, afterward, he'd let him go."

Tom pressed his lips together and said nothing.

Now Mermeros turned toward Mr. Fustian. "You don't know what you're asking, you amphibious salamander," he said flatly. "This is the most dangerous wish of all."

Mr. Fustian's hands trembled with excitement. "Crystal balls, magic carpets, enchanted swords, doorways to other realms!" he chanted.

"Yes," Mermeros said, "and toilets with goblins in the pipes. You will regret this."

"For years, they've scoffed at me. Called me a crackpot." Mr. Fustian actually *giggled*. A grown man, lost in his own fantasies.

"You will unleash upon the world powers and forces that are best kept hidden," warned Mermeros.

Fustian snapped back to the present with a vengeance. "May I remind you, I am the lord of this manor, and you are merely my, er, magical servant. Do as you're told."

Mermeros's brows bristled. His eyes glittered with malice. "I serve *this* man," he said, pointing savagely at Mr. Poindexter, "not you, and at his bidding I would drop you off at the South Pole without a moment's thought. *And* without a coat."

"Do it!" Tommy and I both whispered.

Mermeros's lips curled upward. The old codfish's sharp ears must've heard us.

Mr. Fustian jutted out his chin. As if he could intimidate a djinni.

"You don't know what you're doing," Mermeros said flatly.

"I'll be the judge of that," Fustian replied.

"You will," agreed Mermeros, with oily smugness, "when it's too late to save you."

"Enough of this!" Mr. Fustian, I was beginning to suspect, was what some call high-strung. "Make my map."

Mermeros glanced at Mr. Poindexter once more. The defeated man nodded once.

"Make the map, Mermeros," croaked Mr. Poindexter.

CHAPTER
23

Mermeros sighed and rolled his eyes. He cracked his neck
and his wrists. Muttering ancient curses under his breath,
he began to gesture with his hands as a scroll of stiff paper
unfurled in the air before him. He made flinging motions with his
hands, one after the other, and color began appearing on the map.
Greens, browns, and blues; lines and compass points and labels in
black, and red, and gold. Ornate mermaids in the water—perhaps
they were real, and not just decorative! Hippogriffs in tall mountain
caves. Even in the pool of dim light, and from this far away, I could
see it clearly—another marvel. It was a map of exquisite beauty.

It was also the most dangerous map ever made.

But oh, what I'd give for a good five minutes to study it!

Never mind.

We had to get Mr. Poindexter out of here. And Mermeros. And
that map. A man like Mr. Fustian mustn't be allowed to keep it. What
might he do to the entire world? The specter of cities burning and

seas rising to swallow towns and villages filled my mind. *Powers and forces that are best kept hidden.*

"We've got to stop this," Tom whispered. "How do we get in?"

"I don't see any door," I said. "We can't smash through these iron bars."

"Well, we certainly can't go through the house," said Tom. "Not with that gigantic Thorne at the bottom of the stairs."

Mr. Fustian, meanwhile, was gloating over his map. He cackled with delight. "Look at this!" he cried. "The whole world is positively loaded with magical objects! The United Kingdom is spangled with them. Ireland alone... Well, I suppose it stands to reason there'd be more in Ireland."

"Stands to reason," echoed Mr. Poindexter ironically, as if he cared.

Mr. Fustian produced a magnifying glass from his pocket and peered closely at the map. "Why, there's Dunstable! And my own house!" He looked up at Mr. Poindexter as though they were old friends. "You really must see this, Poindexter. It's extraordinary! When you look closer at an area, the most marvelous detail appears. I've never seen anything like it. How'd you do it, Mermeros, old fish? I can see close enough to know that there are..." He paused and frowned. "*Three* magical objects? Right here in my own home?" He scratched his chin. "It must be those totems from the Zanzibar trip."

"No," Mermeros said coldly. He cast a sly look my way, through the window. "It's a magic carpet. Well, two of them. You might say."

Mr. Fustian's eyes goggled. "You mean to say, right here at Gretigwode, there are carpets which can actually fly? *Two* of them?"

Mermeros crossed his huge arms across his chest. He arched an eyebrow for my benefit, then nodded. *How d'you do, old friend.*

"I'll gather them up immediately," he cried. "I'll instruct Thorne at once." He hurried to the door, and called to his hired strongman from the landing.

The carpetbag I sat upon quivered with impatience. They'd been good, these two bags. They'd cooperated.

Not any longer. My bag plummeted me down to the ground like a bolt of lightning, then scooped me up again. Tom's bag peeled away from the tower, tossed him in aerial loops, and caught him just in time. We found ourselves hovering side by side, some feet above the lawn, far from the house itself.

"Carpetbags," I told them. "You've been wonderful. We thank you. But we need your help just a little bit longer. Is there any way you can get us safely inside that tower room?"

The bags made no response, but drifted over the gardens indifferently.

"Let's go see, shall we?" I said. "Wouldn't it be amazing, Tom, if they could do it?"

Tom caught my meaning. "Amazing."

"Too bad they probably can't," I said. "I'll bet they're too tired."

*Zoom.* We were off once more. We soared over the roof tiles and up to the flat top of the tower. A low stone parapet encircled the tower's edge, crenellated to form battlements. I could just imagine defenders of the manor, back when robber barons waged war against each other across the land, hiding behind the battlements, then popping out to shoot arrows and pour boiling oil upon their attackers.

The carpetbags set us down upon the stones. I climbed off gratefully. But the roof? Why the roof? Were we supposed stomp a hole through the masonry?

The moon shifted in and out from behind the clouds, giving me just enough light to see an area where the flagstone roof looked different. I headed over to investigate.

"Tom," I whispered. "It's a trapdoor!"

He joined me. "Those round stairs must come up here."

"What do we do?" I asked him. "If we go charging in, we could end up as prisoners, too. Then we won't be much help to your dad."

Tom's voice was grim. "We've come this far," he said. "We've got to at least let him know that I'm all right." He paused. "If we can get him up here on the roof, we can fly him away on the carpetbags, can't we?"

"They carried me and Alice," I said, "so I would think so. Let's do it. At the very least, they would slow our fall." I gulped.

I felt for the iron ring in the door. It was crumbly with rust, but the door rose on squealing hinges when I pulled hard. I was sure the sound would bring Thorne with a hatchet, but nothing happened. Creaky old houses.

"You go down," I told Tom, "and show yourself to your dad, if you can get his attention without Fustian seeing. I'll stay here and keep watch on you and on the bags."

"Good," he said. "That way, if anything happens, you can go get help."

The stairs leading up to the doorway looked none too secure from where we knelt atop the tower. Tom took a cautious step down, and then another. He crouched there, partly concealed by the rafters, but visible to anyone who bothered to look up.

Tom was walking into a lion's den, and no one knew we were here except for Alice. Oh dear.

Down and down crept Tom. I lay down on the stones and leaned my head over the opening to watch. Mr. Fustian stood in the doorway that led downstairs, still talking to Thorne. From his low voice, it seemed Thorne must be right there upon the landing, but Mr. Fustian made sure not to let him see the djinni inside.

Mr. Poindexter stood, dejected, leaning against a wall. Mermeros floated over by the bank of windows, looking out at the night sky. Perhaps he was wondering where we'd gone.

"Dad!" Tom whispered.

Mr. Poindexter looked up and around the room, then gave up and leaned against the wall once more.

"Dad!" Tom repeated. "Up here!"

Mr. Poindexter looked up and saw Tom. Bewilderment, shock, joy, and then terror unfolded on his weary face, one after another.

"How?" he mouthed silently. He pushed at the air as though pushing Tom away. "Not safe! Go! Go now!"

But Tom wouldn't give up. "Come on!" he whispered, beckoning urgently. "Trust me!"

Mermeros turned about lazily. He glanced at Tommy, and then up at me. "Ah," he said. "The ragtag infants have decided to join the party. And why not? Why not make my humiliation complete? I am already degraded by granting wishes for a weak, imprisoned man on behalf of a delusional maniac. Why not bring in the urchins, too?"

*I've missed you, too, Mermeros.*

Mr. Fustian turned back at the sound of Mermeros's voice. "What's all this chatter? What's going on?"

"Nothing." Mr. Poindexter assumed the tired look he'd had before. "Just talking to Mermeros."

"Well, don't," Mr. Fustian said. "It aggravates me. Keep him quiet. And don't get any ideas."

"You said you'd let me go, once you had your map," Mr. Poindexter said.

"Change of plans," sang the so-called scholar cheerily. "I'm afraid, my good tradesman, that you know too much. It pains me to inconvenience you, but you're much too dangerous to let go. I had police here earlier today, poking around and asking questions about you." He paused, as if concerned. "Don't take it hard, old man. You understand, don't you? Surely you see how much of an annoyance your mere existence is to me?"

"I just want to get back to my boy," pleaded Mr. Poindexter. "I'll never say a word. You can keep your djinni."

"Tchah," sneered the offended Mermeros. He liked it better when people fought over him. He and his precious ego.

Tom blinked once, twice. He rubbed his eye with his sleeve. *See, Tom? Your father loves you and wants you for your own sake. Not because of some bargain over Mermeros.*

"Please," Mr. Poindexter begged. "Let me go."

"Afraid not," said the repulsive collector. "Excuse me. I have other plans to attend to."

He turned back to the door. Mr. Poindexter sent a pleading gaze at Tom, trying once more to wave him away, to order him to flee. But Tom wouldn't have it. He beckoned all the more urgently to his father.

Finally, curiosity got the better of Mr. Poindexter. He tiptoed toward the stairs, with Mermeros's sardine tin still in his hands. He now saw me peeking through the trapdoor. I got in on the beckoning action, waving him toward us for all I was worth.

It worked. He decided to take a chance. His gaze darted back and forth. Carefully, he placed one foot on the bottom stair. It made no noise. Another step, and another. Mermeros, tethered as he was to the flat tin in Mr. Poindexter's hand, trailed along for the ride.

Tom beckoned till I thought his arms might fall off.

His father decided. He made a run for it and scrambled up the stairs.

I jumped to my feet to hoist Tommy up, and then Mr. Poindexter.

The first thing he did, upon reaching the top, was to enfold Tommy in his arms.

"Oh, Tom," he sobbed, "I've been so frightened for you."

For a moment, Tom had no words. He just held on tight. Finally, he spoke.

"I'm fine, Dad," he said. "I'm right here."

Mermeros, it must be said, rolled his eyes and groaned, the great grump.

While this touching scene unfolded, I slammed the trapdoor and stood upon it. *I* am not without softer feelings, unlike certain fishy persons. But first things first.

Finally Tom and Mr. Poindexter drifted apart.

"*How* did you get up here?" babbled Mr. Poindexter? "How are you here at all? Is there a ladder? Who's helping you? How did you know to come here? Are the police on their way?" Then he froze. He looked around at the scene—the tower, the ramparts. He stepped closer toward the edge and looked down. His face paled in horror.

"Tom," he whispered. "You can't be here. You're in terrible danger."

Poor Mr. Poindexter. If he did have a tormented, hunted look about him, who could blame him, after all he'd been through?

"No, I'm not, Dad," Tom protested. "I know about the picture. It's fake. I'm not sure how he did it, but it's not real."

"You can't say for certain."

"I can," said Tom. "Fustian took a photograph of a boy from the neighborhood. Bought him clothes that looked just like mine."

A terrific crash sounded on the wooden door. It rattled all the way from my feet to my teeth. Mr. Poindexter and Tom hurried over to stand on the trapdoor too.

It didn't matter. The door wrenched open so hard that we tumbled off it. Its hinges broke and dangled from the screws that had held them in place. Huge arms tossed the door aside. The man in black leaped onto the roof.

Mr. Fustian came scrambling up after him. "What have we here?" he cried. At the sight of Tom, his eyes grew wide. Then he smiled like a cat with a bowl of cream. "How delightful," he purred. "So good of you to come to us. Spares us the trouble of finding you."

"Finding him?" cried Mr. Poindexter. "You mean, you never even knew where—?"

"Who do you want first, Boss?" growled Thorne, American mobster. "They're sitting ducks up here. I can nab 'em all."

I inched my way closer to where our carpetbags sat gossiping on the flagstones. Tommy followed my lead, taking his dad by the hand and inching the other way around the circular tower's top. *Smart move, Tom.* Those orphan boys at the Mission Industrial School and Home knew all about how to divide and conquer in a fight. If we went separate ways, Thorne could only catch one of us.

"Are you really from Chicago?" I asked Thorne. "How fascinating!"

An attempt at diversion might've worked. You never know. In this case, it didn't. Mr. Blacksuited Thorne had forgotten about us and was staring at the floating green apparition hovering closely behind Mr. Poindexter.

"*What* in the *Sam Hill* is that?"

I couldn't see what a Mr. Samuel Hill, or any other fellow, had to do with anything, but then, I haven't met many Americans.

Mermeros swam toward the flabbergasted Thorne. "Greetings," he murmured. "Are you considered strong in your part of the world?" He simpered and twirled the outrageous loops of his mustaches. "How amusing."

"You shut your mouth," roared Thorne. "You ain't so much. You ain't even got legs!"

"Thorne, my good man," said Mortimer Fustian, "your opinions aren't required at present. Be so good as to stop blabbing and fetch me the boy."

"You are a man of might and valor," purred Mermeros to Thorne. "Why do you let him order you about? Seize my home from these two aged weaklings, and my power will be yours to command."

"What's your home?" asked Thorne. "You live in the neighborhood?" I hate to say it, but his intelligence did not inspire confidence.

"Enough of that," cried Mr. Fustian. "Grab Poindexter and the boy before they do something idiotic."

Like make a wish and banish Mermeros.

"What are you scared of, Mr. Fustian?" I taunted. "Oh, I see. You need Thorne to do your dirty work, and you need Mr. Poindexter for his djinni. You can't do much on your own, can you?"

"Be quiet, girl," ordered Mr. Fustian. "I could tell you were a cheeky little hoyden from the moment I first laid eyes on you at the Crystal Palace."

Aha. "You were the sleeping old man," I said. "You were faking it. Eavesdropping."

"Not so very old." He threw back his shoulders and attempted to smooth his hair.

"Old as Methuselah," I told him, "and worse looking."

I know. That wasn't nice. Nor strictly necessary. Alice would've fainted on the spot. But my stalling had worked. We'd reached the carpetbags. Tom and I each grabbed ours.

"Thorne, you ox, get that tin of sardines," cried Mr. Fustian, "and *get that boy!*"

A gleam of understanding flickered—eventually—on Mr. Thorne's beefy face. His eyes narrowed, and he barreled toward Mr. Poindexter and Tom.

Mr. Poindexter planted himself before Tom. I placed myself before Mr. Poindexter, and got bowled over in the melee. Twenty stones' worth of angry American is nothing you want charging you at the rim of a high tower.

There was a clash of arms and legs. A scraping of rock crumbling against rock. A scuff, a shove, and a cry as Tom, wedged between two battlements, slipped and fell to the ground below.

CHAPTER

24

"T om!" shrieked Mr. Poindexter. "*No!*"

I wasted no time, but leaped through the gap in the stone parapet after him.

"Maeve!" cried Mr. Poindexter. "Mermeros, save those children!"

Oh, *no*. Mr. Poindexter's third wish. Now Mermeros would vanish!

The ground raced toward me. A rushing wind flapped my hair and clothes in my face.

It wasn't the wind rushing. It was me.

"Let's catch Tom, shall we?" I bellowed at the carpetbag. "Just in case. Are you fast enough?"

The carpetbag bolted with such a jerk that my body slammed in midair, then darted upward. It couldn't have been as unpleasant as landing on the terrace would've been, but it wasn't an experience I'd care to repeat.

A whoosh of movement rushed past me one way, then again. It was Tom, circling me like a shark around its prey.

"Are you all right, Tom?" I called softly.

"Fine," he said. "Carpetbag caught me. My poor dad. We'd better go tell him."

"Wait," I told him. "I'm not sure we should let Fustian and Thorne know we're still alive."

"But my father!" cried Tom. "He thinks I'm... Maeve, don't you see? It's that photograph come true! Remember? The camera that could photograph the future?"

I gulped. He was right. Poor Mr. Poindexter!

"I think," I said, "we can still help him more if they don't know we're coming. Don't you?"

He nodded slowly. "I see your point."

"Let's fly around behind the house and creep up on them from high above, where they'd never think to look. We need to see what they do to your dad." I took a deep breath. "Your father made his final wish to send Mermeros to save you."

Tom's head drooped. "He didn't even need to." He gritted his teeth. "That foul professor! He's wasted all of Dad's wishes. Now Mermeros is gone!"

"I know," I said. "It's rotten, but it can't be helped. Let's go check on your dad."

We soared wide around the manor house, circling high till we had a bird's-eye view of the tower's top.

Mr. Poindexter sat on the roof with his back to the parapet. He looked shattered. It broke my heart to see him so desolate. I waved at him, but it was pointless. The blackness of the night had swallowed us up.

"Look!" whispered Tom. "Mermeros is still there!"

Professor Fustian peered down between battlements, searching, no doubt, for some sign of the fallen boy and girl. He held the sardine tin around which Mermeros hovered. Could he have snatched it away before Mr. Poindexter cast his wish? Did that last wish, therefore, not count?

Thorne stood, breathing heavily, clenching and unclenching his fists. "I didn't take this job to hurt kids," he growled. "You never said nothing about that."

"Why did the girl jump after the boy?" wondered Professor Fustian aloud. "Positively extraordinary." He turned about, scratching his scalp. "And how *did* they get up here in the first place?"

My blood boiled. He didn't even care that we might be dead. Some vaguely scientific curiosity was all he could feel.

Such a man, with neither a soul, nor a conscience, should never have the power of Mermeros at his whim to command. And he certainly, definitely, absolutely mustn't be allowed to keep that map of magical objects. If even Mermeros was afraid of some of them... We had to get Mr. Poindexter out of there. And then, we had to stop Fustian. Steal Mermeros *and* the map. I couldn't see any other way.

He turned back from the parapet. "Go on, Thorne," he said. "Chain our pathetic friend here back to his chair, then go down to the garden and see about the, er, unpleasantness."

Meaning us. What would happen when they discovered there was no unpleasantness to find?

Still muttering and cursing under his breath, Thorne hoisted Mr. Poindexter up by one arm. The poor man stumbled along, making no protest. They disappeared down the hatch and into the tower room. I wanted to cry.

It had been my idea to come tonight. Yet I had neither the plan nor the means to rescue Mr. Poindexter, and now I'd only made things worse. Was there *anyone* I cared for whose life I hadn't ruined today?

Yet Mermeros was still here. And so was that map. And so was Tom's father, my own good friend. My dear old partner in crime.

If I had to commit a crime to get him free and fix this mess, I would.

CHAPTER

25

om and I swooped down on our carpetbags, looped around the grounds, and dismounted, for lack of a better word, near some shrubs at the perimeter of the gardens.

"I'm so angry I could spit," Tom said.

"Not at me, please."

"I could scream!"

"Me too," I told him, "though I wouldn't advise it."

"We've got to get Dad out of there," Tom said. "Tonight." He paced back and forth through the foliage. "I know. When Fustian and Thorne go to bed, we go back up through the roof and fly off with him."

Something wasn't adding up in my brain. Everything had been so harried these last few moments. *You're missing something*, my mind kept telling me.

"Let's find a place to sit down and think," I said. "Before we go charging off any which way. Let's make a plan."

I could tell Tom chafed at this proposal—a man of action is our Tom.

"You sound like Alice," he said.

"I do wish she was here," I admitted. "She does some of the better thinking among the three of us. No offense."

"None taken."

A bobbing speck of light in the distance silenced us both. It grew larger as it swung back and forth toward us. We crept back behind the bushes, clutching tightly to our carpetbags.

"It's Thorne," Tom whispered. "Searching for something."

"For us," I said. "For what's left of us."

Tom gulped. "Right."

We kept still. Thorne trudged back and forth, compassing a wider and wider radius. I almost snickered. Did he think a gigantic wind had blown us fifty yards away from the tower?

But I didn't dare laugh.

Closer and closer he came. I prayed that the shrubs hid us from his view.

"Close your eyes," Tom whispered faintly.

A smart call. Lantern light might reflect in our eyes. I clamped mine shut.

It was a horrible, dreadful, unspeakable wait. Crouched near the ground, with nothing but a flimsy bush to hide me. My body curled in a ball, my eyes clenched shut as though that could somehow save me. I didn't dare move. Hardly dared to breathe. And all the while, *cheep, cheep, chee-eep* sang the crickets. A nightingale chattered and trilled nearby, and an owl answered, *whoo, whoo* from a distance.

And still that brutish, hulking colossus didn't move. What was he doing, sniffing for our scent?

*Whoo, whoo,* called the owl once more.

I thought of Morris the owl. Maybe that was him, reassuring me. Of course it couldn't be. He had a broken wing and couldn't fly; he was safe, miles away in Tom's guest bedroom at Grosvenor Square in London. But he'd come to my aid before. Nothing would surprise me anymore.

Finally we heard Thorne turn and trudge off through the grasses. I counted to ten, then opened my eyes just in time to see him enter the house through a side door.

I let out all the air that had been stoppered up inside me.

"He's gone," said Tom. "But let's wait a bit to make sure it's safe to go see Dad."

Lights winked off one by one in the house as the household settled down to bed. Over in the stables, dim light still shone. Grooms, probably, currying down the horses for the night.

"What do you think Fustian will do next?" I asked Tom, partly to pass the time.

"Go look for magical objects, I guess," he said.

"And what will he do with your dad?" I asked. "I mean, if nobody were to rescue him?"

He paused. "What do you think he'd do, Maeve?"

I hesitated. I had several possible theories, and I didn't like any of them very much. "I-I think he won't want to keep him here at his home anymore. Constable Hopewood and the other copper came this morning, asking questions. Somehow, his prisoner's son and his friend showed up today, by way of the rooftop, no less. If I were Professor Fustian, I think I'd be worried about that."

"He didn't seem worried to me," muttered Tom. "He's a cocky devil."

"Well, he's that, too," I said, "and odd. But he's clever, and he's cautious. He won't want to take the risk of keeping your father here for long. Look how he's taking his time with his wishes. He's shrewd, making your dad give up one of his. Checking all the rules first." I sighed. "He's being a lot smarter about it than I was."

"But he's evil," protested Tom. "You're awful, but you're not evil."

I laughed. "Thanks."

Tom fumed in silence. "I hate him, you know that?" he said. "I just lie in bed at night, thinking how much I hate the monster that did this to Dad. And to me. I don't understand how there can be such selfish, wicked people." He laughed bitterly. "And I grew up in the Mission Home. I thought I knew evil already. My old schoolmasters were saints compared to him."

"Djinnis seem to bring selfish people in droves," I said.

"Like me?"

Well, it *was* how we'd met.

"And like me," I said. "Professor Fustian is dangerous, as far as your dad is concerned," I said. "And to the world, as far as that map is concerned."

Tom shook his head. "I can't think about the map right now," he said. "I can't worry about the world. I've got to save my dad."

"I understand," I told him. "But once your dad is safe, I'm going after that map. And Mermeros, too. Thorne or no Thorne."

Finally the light in the tower went dark as well. The only light in the house was a single candle that moved past a window. A woman's form, in a nightdress and cap. One of the servants, looking for something, maybe.

It felt as though an hour crawled by, but it was probably more like fifteen minutes. Finally I could endure waiting no longer.

"Let's hurry up there now," I said. "Let's keep wide away from the house until we're high enough that nobody can see us. Let's go visit your dad's window, right now, and let him know we're all right. We'll figure the rest out then."

"Carpetbags," I crooned, "wouldn't it be fun to fly up to that tower one more time and have a word with Tom's father?"

The bag in my hand wiggled, for all the world like a terrier who's been offered a walk.

We took our seats and launched once more into the sky. Our clothes flapped in the breeze, while night air whistled through our hair.

"You know," Tom said, "I think I could really get used to this."

"Me, too," I said, "though the wind does blow up one's skirts."

Tom leaned to one side and did a full roll on his carpetbag. It was a good thing he wasn't wearing his hat.

Well, that was all it took. Tom's carpetbag decided it was playtime. It shook him free and zipped underneath to catch him as he fell, flailing, to the ground. It was the ballroom all over again, with much farther to fall. Tom had gotten the more rambunctious bag, but I could tell my own bag was getting ideas.

"Please, carpetbags," I cried. "Won't you help us save Tom's dad? When he's back, Tom and I will take you out somewhere to play. We'll find a place where you can really run free. But not here. Not now. Would that be all right?"

Tom's bag placidly caught him and brought him back to where I hovered.

"It's all in how you talk to them, isn't it?" he groaned.

"They like to think it's their decision," I said. "That's my theory."

We reached the tower and hovered outside the windows as before, but now the inside room was pitch-dark. We waited, straining to listen for what might be going on inside. Was Mr. Poindexter alone?

Someone was in there. We heard noises that had to be human—breathing? Moaning? Crying?

Oh, the poor man! Here we'd been capering about in the air—not our idea, mind you—while he sat here, suffering.

"Dad," Tom whispered. "Dad, is that you in there? It's me, Tom!"

We heard a small sound, like shuffling or scraping feet. "*Tom?*"

"It's me, Dad!" cried Tom softly. "I'm here. Outside the window. I'm all right."

"It can't be you," protested Mr. Poindexter faintly. "I saw you fall!" A sob caught on his throat. My eyes filled with tears.

"I fell," Tom said, "but I didn't land. I'm right as rain. We had some, er, magic help. Please believe me, Dad."

There was a long silence. When he finally spoke, Mr. Poindexter's voice was pitiably sad. "I can't see you," he said. "I-I'm hearing things."

"You're not," Tommy called. "We're really here."

His voice faltered. "Are you a ghost?"

I hadn't expected this.

"Mr. Poindexter," I piped up, "it's me, Maeve. We're really here, Tom and I. We're as alive as ever."

He hesitated. "*Maeve?*"

"Think about it," I said. "If this was a hallucination or a ghostly visit, would you expect to hear from *me?*"

Mr. Poindexter began sounding more like himself. "One never knows when you'll show up, young lady."

"Thanks." I smiled to myself. "If I could get in there, I'd prove to you that we were real. Are you alone in the room?"

"I am."

"Then we're coming in," said Tom. "We'll come down through the roof, as before."

"They've hammered it shut with boards and nails. Thorne just left." He paused. "Though that shouldn't matter if you're ghosts."

Tommy started laughing. "We're not ghosts, Dad!"

"Is that so?" Mr. Poindexter was actually growing irate, which was probably better for him than despairing. "Then how do you come to be floating outside my window?"

"Magic carpets," I told him. "If we can get you out, we can fly you home."

"Even if you were real, you couldn't do it," he replied, "because I'm chained and locked, and the trapdoor is boarded shut."

"We'll go get the police," Tom said. "Keep your chin up, Dad. We'll come back in the morning, first thing."

"You do that," Mr. Poindexter said. "And, Tom?"

"Yes?"

"In case you're not real..." Mr. Poindexter's voice broke. "I just want you to know how sorry I am. For everything."

Tom laughed. "Good *night*, Dad."

We let the carpetbags loose to scamper through the air around the grand old house one last time. Just as we looped around the rear, heading for the main entrance, we saw a large, elegant carriage, pulled by six horses, come sweeping up the drive. At this hour of the night?

A sickening thought occurred to me. "Maybe Mr. Fustian has sent for a driver to carry your dad away," I told Tom. "Maybe we're too late!"

We veered left and swung low to spy on the coach unseen.

A footman stepped down and held the door open. A figure hopped nimbly out.

"*Maeve*," it cried in a low voice. "*Tom*. Are you here? Are you flying about? Please come down. It's me, Alice."

*ell*. There are surprises, and then there are surprises. I have tremendous faith in Alice, but I have to say, I never expected to see her arrive here and now. She'd outdone herself. And bowled me over completely.

We swooped down to the front drive and landed on the gravel beside her. And not a moment too soon, for my sister, Polydora, was just climbing down out of the coach.

"Maeve!" she cried. "Oh, thank goodness you're all right!" She wrapped her arms around me, then held me at arm's length. "Maeve, for shame! It was *very* wrong of you to leave as you did, without a word about what had happened to Father, nor where you were going."

Mr. Bromley and Inspector Wallace climbed down from the coach while Polly scolded.

"Polly," I asked her, "how are you *here*?"

"Hmph," she said. "With Father, er, unavailable, someone has to look after you, haven't they?"

"Well, yes," I sputtered, "but how did you come with the Bromleys?"

Alice came to my sister's rescue. "We stopped at your house," she said, "to fetch the clues you'd left in your writing desk."

"I was frantic with worry for you." Polydora wiped her eyes with a handkerchief. "Mr. Bromley kindly allowed me to come along. Maeve, you have no idea how we've worried today. Mother is an absolute wreck."

I hung my head. She was right. My attempts to solve this riddle and save Mr. Poindexter had gone precisely nowhere. And look at all the harm I'd done.

I became aware of another pair of shoes standing on the gravel. I looked up to see, of all things, Mr. Abernathy, my tutor. What next? The Royal Household Cavalry?

"Mr. Abernathy!" I whispered. "Why are you here?"

"I came along for the ride." He grinned. "I must say, I'm glad to see you're all right. When Miss Alice told us about your conversation on the telephone, I had to come. I admit I couldn't pass up the chance to get to the bottom of this business about old Morty Fustian and his so-called djinni."

"Inspector Wallace." I turned toward the detective. "I'm glad you came."

He muttered to himself, then answered me. "I hope I'll have cause to say the same."

"Let's don't just stand here," Tom pleaded. "My dad's in there.

He's up in the tower. They've got him chained up. A big American bloke has given him a black eye. That professor is a fiend. We've got to go arrest them."

"You've seen this?" inquired Inspector Wallace. "How?"

Before I could answer, the horses whinnied, and a dog from inside the stables barked. Soon we heard another sound of hoofbeats and wheels on gravel.

A police wagon pulled into the drive. In the dark, I couldn't tell at first who climbed out of it, until they came very near.

"Dad!" I cried. I wrapped my arms around him, then froze when I saw his traveling companion. "*Constable Hopewood?*"

I turned to see Polly. She wouldn't look directly at her— former?—beau.

My father took me by the shoulders. "Are you all right, Maeve?"

I nodded. "How did you get out of jail?"

My dad smiled ruefully. "Young Matthew here came back to the police bureau this afternoon and made sure the magistrate heard my case. Stayed all evening. The magistrate dismissed the charges on lack of evidence."

"Nothing was stolen, you see," explained "young Matthew," as if he needed some justification. "We were still at the local bureau when Inspector Wallace telephoned , asking for police support. I volunteered to come."

"You went *back* to the bureau?" I asked the constable. "Your Saturday shift was over."

"It was," he replied. "But I thought Mr. Merritt needed help."

"I can almost forgive him," my dad teased, "for arresting me."

Polly turned away. She made a point of not looking at our father, nor at the constable. Perhaps Dad was ready to forgive Matthew Hopewood for arresting him, but Polly wasn't.

"This is all very touching," Inspector Wallace said drily, "but we're here at his hour on rather slim evidence suggesting a man is being held prisoner inside this home. I suggest we get back to business."

The arrival of a coach and six, and a police wagon, in front of a large manor home, long past dark, does not go unnoticed. Lights had begun blinking on in the windows of Gretigwode Manor. A small light appeared in the upper loft over the stables. Any minute now, Mr. Fustian's footmen and grooms would venture out to investigate.

"It's not 'slim' evidence," declared Tom. "We've seen my dad. We've talked to him. He's chained in the tower. They're being awful to him."

"They're in the tower?" demanded Inspector Wallace, "and yet, you've seen him? Did you enter through the house?" He rubbed his temples. "That's breaking and entering..."

"No...o...o," I said. "I guess you would say we, er, climbed." Through the air.

Mr. Wallace frowned as he glanced up at the tower. He shot grim

looks at Mr. Bromley and at my father. They both directed their
gazes back at Tom and me.

"He's there," Tom insisted. "If you go in, you'll find him. Just as
we said."

Nobody looked convinced.

Tom took a deep breath. "This isn't a game," he told the gathered
adults, with barely contained anger boiling underneath courtesy.
"You may not believe in djinnis, but my dad's in there, chained to a
wall, with an eye like an eggplant, crying himself to sleep, because
he thinks..." Tom almost lost control, but mastered his voice once
again. "He thinks I've fallen to my death off the tower."

"Why would he think that?" asked Polly's constable. "Is he
suffering from nervous strain?"

"Of course he is," I cried. "Wouldn't you? He *saw Tom fall*. Because
Tom did fall. And I jumped after him."

Inspector Wallace's voice crackled. "Off that tower."

I couldn't blame him for doubting me. But I'd still had about
enough. "That's right."

"And he didn't die because...?"

I sighed. "Because he had a magic carpet. Um. Bag."

Do people actually gnash their teeth? Apparently they do. I'd
always thought that was just a manner of speaking. Mr. Wallace
might need to have a word with his dentist.

He turned to Mr. Bromley. "My dear sir," he said. "I would do anything, truly anything within my power to help you, especially since you've always been such a good friend to my father, but I can't... The bureau can't... If word got back that I showed up, late at night, to investigate this—this well-to-do, respectable gentleman—"

"I wouldn't say 'respectable,'" cut in Mr. Abernathy. "In Oxford circles, he's a certifiable crackpot. His name is mud."

Mr. Wallace's nostrils flared. "To investigate this...gentleman," he continued, "on the basis of a child's magical fancies, I would damage the reputation of Scotland Yard, not to mention endanger my own job. Djinnis? And now, magic carpets?"

"Bags," I said, then wished I hadn't. "Carpet*bags*."

My father cleared his throat. "Mr. Wallace," he said, "we found Siegfried Poindexter's handkerchief in his umbrella stand, and his calling card, and another copy of that horrible picture of young Thomas, here, falling, in one of his belowstairs rooms. Nothing magical about that. We found that evidence here, today."

Alice produced the items in question from her coat pocket.

"Yes," said Mr. Wallace bitterly, "and you were arrested for trespassing."

"Because Mr. Fustian was ill-tempered and unreasonable, and wished to make some sort of example of us," I cried. "It wasn't Daddy's fault in the slightest. His *arrest*,"—I glared at Constable

Hopewood—"was a disgrace and an outrage." I pointed toward Matthew Hopewood. "He was there. Ask the arresting officer."

Wallace turned to Matthew Hopewood. "Constable?"

The man in question dug the toe of his boot into the gravel drive. "I do believe Miss Maeve has summed it up correctly."

Polly smiled in spite of herself.

"While we stand here talking," I told them, "Professor Fustian is no doubt doing something diabolical to Tommy's dad, or else plotting to scurry him away from here and do him a mischief. He said as much. He said he couldn't set him free, because he knows too much."

"*Professor* Fustian?" barked Mr. Abernathy. "Ha! If he's a professor, I'm the Archbishop of Canterbury."

"A handkerchief and calling card aren't much evidence to go on," Inspector Wallace said.

"But *we've seen him*." Tom was almost in tears. "Why does nobody believe us?"

Alice stepped forward. "I believe you, Tom."

Mr. Bromley coughed. "Mr. Wallace," he said, in his most conciliatory voice, "don't you feel you have reason enough to knock at the door and ask some questions?"

He paused for a reply, but none came.

"We've come this far," Mr. Bromley added gently.

Some of the fight went out of Inspector Wallace. He sighed and turned back to Tom and me. "A magic carpet*bag*?" he repeated. "These bags at your feet are magic carpet*bags*?"

We nodded.

"Can you prove it?"

"*Pardon* me."

The voice came from a distance. We looked up to see a middle-aged man approaching from the direction of the manor house. He carried a lantern in one hand and walked in the stiff, dignified, offended manner of a butler at a grand, old English country house. Though perfectly dressed, he gave an air of having been rooted out of bed and ordered to put on his daytime clothes once more, faster than he would have liked.

"Good evening," my father and Mr. Bromley both said together.

"Good evening," replied the butler icily. "My employer, Mr. Fustian, requests that you be so good as to state your names and provide a reason for why you have decided to gather upon his private property, unannounced, for a late-night conference."

Before Inspector Wallace could find words, our classical tutor, Mr. Abernathy, spoke up.

"You tell Morty Fustian," he said, with a twinkle in his eye, "that Hamish Abernathy, from the good old Oxford days, came all this way to find out what's all this folderol about a djinni. If you please."

CHAPTER
27

We stood in the vestibule of Gretigwode Manor. By late night, the dimly lit old pile had an even more haunted, ghostly air than it had during the midday tour. Only one lamp sputtered upon a low table.

*Morty Fustian.* Somehow you couldn't quite fear and tremble at the thought of some villain's wrath when you know his schoolfellows called him Morty.

Footsteps sounded from up the stairs. The coldly disapproving butler climbed the stairs to greet their owner. Mr. Fustian met the butler on a landing and spoke a word or two to him, handed him a bag or valise of some kind, then descended the staircase, eyeing us. I took advantage of the shadows to slide behind Dad and out of sight, and hissed at Tom to do the same behind Constable Hopewood. Fustian was bound to notice us eventually, but he didn't need to see us at first. We clasped our carpetbags close to our bodies so they wouldn't poke out noticeably.

"Hamish Abernathy?" said our gracious host. "Is that you? The years haven't exactly been kind to you, have they?"

What a pig!

"Who's this rabble you've brought along?" he went on. "Your poor relations?"

I took it back. Calling him a pig was an insult to pigs.

"Never mind that," cried Mr. Abernathy. "How've you been, Morty? Haven't seen you in ages. Fancy you being the master of Gretigwode Manor!"

Morty Fustian goggled at him. "You don't believe I'm fool enough to believe this is a social call, do you, Hamish?" He shook his head. "Rather late at night to stop by unannounced and reminisce about the dear old school days." He nodded toward the rest of the party. "One doesn't usually bring the police along, either."

"Now, Morty," my tutor said soothingly. "What's all this I hear about you holding a shopkeeper prisoner here, all for some rumor of a djinni in a bottle?"

Fustian's gaze darted uneasily toward the other listeners.

"We're not schoolboys anymore, Morty," Mr. Abernathy said gently. "We have the gray hairs to prove it. Isn't it time to leave story-book fancies behind?"

Mr. Fustian scowled. "I don't need your patronizing lectures, Hamish," he said. "I didn't need them at school, and I don't need them now."

"I was only trying to help, back then," Mr. Abernathy said quietly. "The things you'd insist on saying about magic... The other chaps were making fun of you left and right."

A slow smile spread across Fustian's face. "They were wrong then, and you're wrong still," he said. "You all thought I was crazy to believe in magic. Turns out *I* was the one who was right."

Mr. Abernathy sighed. "Morty, you can believe what you will. But if you have anything to do with this Mr. Poindexter's disappearance, let him go."

Mr. Wallace's patience seemed to snap. "Mortimer Fustian?" he said. "I'm Inspector Wallace from Scotland Yard."

Our genial host stiffened, then put on his smug smile once more.

"Another copper, but this one in a suit," observed he. "This other one, here, in the brass buttons, came by earlier in the day to ask impertinent questions. Back for more, I see?" He tapped his chin. "As it happens, I've just now caught one of my new kitchen staff prowling around the manor's bedrooms and private offices. Robbing me blind right under my nose! You can't find good help nowadays. I locked her in one of my supply rooms downstairs, but now you, Constable, can arrest her and take her away."

*Mrs. Gruboil.*

"Locking someone in your home against their will is a serious offense," the inspector said. "I advise you to let her go immediately."

"By all means," Fustian said carelessly. "You may have her. I certainly don't want her. She's not even a very good cook. Constable, if you'll follow me, I'll lead you to her."

Matthew Hopewood, who'd been looking rather dazed, snapped to attention and followed Mr. Fustian down the corridor that led to the basement stairs. I remembered it from our ill-fated tour this morning. Matthew swaggered in an extremely official-looking manner, no doubt for Polly's benefit.

A few moments later, Fustian returned. Inspector Wallace wasted no time getting to business.

"Mr. Fustian," he began, "we have received reports—"

"That's 'Professor,'" corrected Fustian.

"Hmph," snorted Mr. Abernathy.

"*Reports,*" said Inspector Wallace, "which we deem—er—credible, that you are holding a man against his will in this house."

"That, my man, is an outrageous accusation," said the lord of Gretigwode Manor. "I demand an apology."

"You're holding a cook against her will," my father said in a low voice.

Fustian glowered at him.

"We *hoped,*" the detective continued, "that you would be so good as to prove the statement false. Your cooperation in our effort to lay such a troubling charge to rest would be a great courtesy on your part."

"And if I refuse?" drawled Fustian.

Inspector Wallace stayed as cool as a cucumber. "Then we would regret your decision and be left to wonder what reason you could have for hindering a legitimate investigation."

"Which I am within my rights to do."

"Certainly," replied Inspector Wallace. "We rely on your decency and sense of civic duty to assist us."

"Stuff and nonsense," declared Mr. Abernathy. "Now Morty, you listen here—"

"Is there a reason, Inspector," Fustian asked, "why you felt it necessary to bring with you schoolgirls and spinsters…"

A little choke of humiliation sounded from Polly's throat. Spinster? If I'd been in reach of Fustian just then, I'd have kicked his shins.

"Washed-up scholars and petty clerks?"

Mr. Abernathy. Dad.

My fingers curled into fists. *Focus, Maeve,* I told myself. Set Mr. Poindexter free. Then perhaps I could take a poke at Fustian's jaw.

"What next?" continued the eloquent "professor." "The entire chorus line from the Alhambra Theatre? Why not bring them, too?"

"We are concerned parties," said Mr. Bromley, "interested in the welfare of the missing person."

"Couldn't this meddlesome inquiry have waited until tomorrow morning?"

"Not if someone's safety was at stake," said Alice simply.

"Little maids should be seen, and not heard," said Fustian.

"Bad show, Morty, bad show," cried Mr. Abernathy. "This young lady is my star pupil. She speaks as well as any lad, and better than most men."

*Huzzah, Alice!*

Fustian heaved a heavy sigh. "Well, come on, then," he said. "Most people who want the tour come on Saturday afternoons, but as you seem to think it's my *civic duty*, I'll oblige you. Where did your mysterious 'sources' seem to think I was keeping my poor victim?"

Inspector Wallace sounded embarrassed. "In the tower."

"Naturally," said Fustian. "Just what novelists would lead you to expect. Well. Would the females and the star pupil prefer to wait down here while I satisfy the good officer's curiosity? There may be cobwebs. No? Suit yourselves. To the tower we go. Unless you're afraid I'll lock you up, too."

The butler returned with a candelabra for Professor Fustian, and the rest of the group followed our host up the stairs. If he'd seen Tom or me, he gave no sign of it.

A cold feeling stole over me. Was Thorne up there, waiting to give us all black eyes?

We climbed one tall set of stairs, and then another to reach a garret, and then another staircase to the tower's upper room.

Cobwebs swayed in the dark, draped like buntings from rafter to rafter. Professor Fustian opened a door to reveal another dark flight of stairs, this one made of rough, unpainted wood.

One by one, we filed up the stairs. This should be the moment where we proved we were right, found Mr. Poindexter, and set him free. It should be a moment of triumph. Why, then, were the hairs on my arms prickling with alarm and warning?

Nobody said anything. No cries of "Mr. Poindexter! *There* you are!" Or "Oh, Morty, how *could* you?" And certainly not "Mortimer Fustian, you're under arrest."

Dad reached the top of the stairs, and I crept up behind him. Inspector Wallace, with Tom as his silent shadow, had already reached the top.

The room was dark, so I took a chance and peered out from behind Daddy. There stood Fustian, holding up his candelabra. Its wavery light swam about the room, showing dusty tables and chairs as before, but no prisoner. *No Mr. Poindexter.*

Of course not. Fustian would never willingly lead us to where Mr. Poindexter actually was. What could he have done with him in so short a time?

The look of triumph on Fustian's face made me want to... Never mind. "*Now* are you satisfied?" he crowed. "Now, I suppose, a law-abiding gentleman might be allowed to return to his bed?"

Tom stepped out from behind Inspector Wallace.

At the sight of Tom, Fustian's sardonic air faltered a moment. "*You!*"

"That's right," Tom said. "Me."

"How did you...? How...?"

Inspector Wallace took a step forward. "You *know* this lad?"

"He knows me," said Tom, "from about an hour ago. Atop this very tower."

Professor Fustian still seemed in a daze. "But I saw you fall..."

"What's going on here?" cried Mr. Bromley. "Something very strange is afoot."

"Tell the truth, Morty," our tutor pleaded. "Do the right thing. This is a sorry pass. Things look very suspicious for you."

The professor held his candelabra high. "Suspicious for *me?*" he repeated. "You come disturbing my peace in the middle of the night, telling me there's a prisoner in my tower—as you can see, there's clearly none—and you say things look suspicious for *me?*" He gestured toward Tom. "I've never seen this young man before in my life."

"That's a lie." Tom's voice lashed like a whip. "What've you done with my dad? He was here half an hour ago. Where is he now?"

"Besides," Alice said, "you just said you saw Tom fall." She thrust her photograph toward him, as if presenting shocking evidence before a judge. "And this photograph of Tom was found this morning in your house."

I decided it was time for me to set down my carpetbag and pop out from behind my dad. "Hullo, Professor," I said. "Fancy seeing you again so soon."

His eyes bulged a bit. "Not *you* too!"

"Me," I said.

His gaze fell upon the carpetbag at my feet. He came closer and bent low with his candelabra. The others in our party gaped at him.

"A carpetbag," he murmured. "A *flying* carpetbag."

There was an awkward silence among the adults.

"So *that's* how you survived falling."

"Morty," pleaded Mr. Abernathy, "my dear fellow, there's no shame in admitting it. Your work has placed you under a nervous strain. You need time off. Perhaps a nice vacation in Lausanne. Or you might take the cure in Tuscany."

"Arrest him," declared Mr. Bromley. "Haven't you proof enough, Inspector?"

"No," said Inspector Wallace curtly.

"He's got my father!" cried Tom. "He's not here where he's supposed to be. He's not home in London where he's supposed to be, because this fiend kidnapped him. What more evidence do you need?"

I scampered up the stairs to the trapdoor. "If you look here," I called down to Inspector Wallace and the others, "you'll see where he's only just barely barricaded this door with boards and nails. Just tonight. After we came in through the ceiling."

Professor Fustian glared at me.

"And here," cried Tom, "is where the chair was where my father sat. If you look, you can see how the dust is disturbed."

"The boy is lying," Fustian said. "There's nothing at all to see here."

Tom plucked something from the rough wall and held it high. "That's a bit of torn cloth from my dad's trousers."

Inspector Wallace watched the proceedings through narrowed eyes.

"This looks fishy, Morty," cried Mr. Abernathy. "What have you to say for yourself?"

A fit of giggling suddenly came over Mortimer Fustian. "Fishy?" he chortled. "Fishy? Hee, hee!"

My dad and I looked at each other.

I took in the assembled group. Mr. Bromley, Mr. Abernathy, Inspector Wallace from Scotland Yard, and Tom, Alice, and me—all stood staring openmouthed as Fustian the fiend unraveled before our eyes.

"A terrible business," said dear old Mr. Bromley, shaking his head. "Inspector Wallace, haven't we seen enough to, er, take action?"

"No," the inspector replied, "because we haven't seen Mr. Poindexter. He isn't here. But I believe we now have sufficient grounds to ask a magistrate to grant a warrant, and—"

"Gentlemen," cried Professor Fustian, holding up his hands, "there's a very simple explanation for all of this. If you'll excuse me one moment, I'll go get the, um, thing I need—"

"Your djinni, I suppose," said Mr. Abernathy.

"Most amusing," tittered Fusitian. "It's easiest if I just... Wait right here, won't you? I'll be back." And with that, he hurried down the stairs, leaving us all in the dark.

"Well, that's a fine thing," said Mr. Abernathy. "He forgot to leave us so much as a candle."

We heard a click, and then Polly's gasp.

"What in thunder..." said the voice of Inspector Wallace.

I pressed through the darkness until I found the wall with the door. I slid my hands across its dusty surface until I found the door. I tried the knob.

Just as I'd feared.

Outside, the sound of iron horseshoes ringing against gravel floated through the missing windowpanes.

"Mortimer Fustian has locked us in," I said. "I think that's him we're hearing outside, about to make his escape with Tom's dad."

Good *night*," groaned my father. "We walked right into that one."

"Kidnapping!" added Mr. Abernathy.

"False imprisonment," growled Inspector Wallace. "Impeding an officer of the law in the execution of his duties."

"Behaving *extremely* rudely." Strong words, coming from Alice.

If the pitch-black tower room had been unnerving before, now it became a nightmare chamber. Inspector Wallace found the door and began pounding on it and yelling in his most intimidating official manner. Polly and Alice, lending their higher voices to the task, set up a yowling for help that would've offended a chorus of stray cats. Gretigwode Manner was far from its nearest neighbor and surrounded by woods, and it was the middle of the night. But somebody somewhere must hear us. The servants, at the very least.

I made my way back to my carpetbag and grasped its handles.

"Come on, old chum," I whispered. "Let's go get a look out that window."

With others around me fuming and hollering, my carpetbag and I drifted slowly upward, over to the window. By the bit of moonlight peeping through the clouds, I saw the dark world of Gretigwode Manor slumbering below.

Something brushed against my leg.

"Sorry," said a voice. "Should've known I'd find you here."

"Ahoy there, Tom."

The shouting and bedlam in the room made it hard for us to hear each other. On the bright side, nobody else heard us, either.

We peered out of the window together. Had any of the screaming and pounding worked?

The only light downstairs was the glimmer above the stables. An awfully risky place to keep a light burning, with all that straw about.

"Could we smash our way out of the windows?" asked Tom.

"We'd have a hard time getting through the bars," I said. "Someone should hear us and come soon."

"Why haven't they already, then?" asked Tom. "Why haven't the servants come to get us out? They must hear us. Seems like they could hear us in America. And every minute we stay stuck here"—Tom swallowed hard—"my dad gets farther and farther away."

"Wherever your dad goes," I said, "we'll find him. Fustian won't get away with this." I paused to listen to the pounding and shouting from the outraged detective at the door. "He's angered the wrong people. That was foolish of him."

"Yes, well," said Tom, "he's not worried about policemen anymore. He's got Mermeros. And a map guiding him to every other powerful object in the world."

"I have to admit," I said, "that was clever. I wish I'd thought of it."

"Thank goodness you didn't," said Tom. "Maeve. I'm afraid."

My heart broke. "I know," I told him. "I don't blame you."

"What's he planning to do to my dad?" Tom whispered. "I can't see any way this could end well."

"We'll stop him," I vowed. "He can't have gotten far."

"If Dad doesn't come back," Tom said, "I've made up my mind. I'm running away. I won't go back to that orphanage."

"Don't talk nonsense," I said.

"I heard what Alice told you," he said. "Those telephones are loud."

I hung my head.

"You might've told me, Maeve," he said, "about that Pearl Fletcher woman showing up at the Bromleys'. It's *my* fate, and I'm your friend."

"Your dad's coming *back*," I said. "Tonight. No matter what." I looked down at the dark, swaying trees once more. "The light in the stable's gone out."

Down below us, our imprisoned party seemed to be flagging. Polly and Alice let their calls go silent. Inspector Wallace left off pounding and shouting. The air of dejection and discouragement felt palpable, even in the dark.

"Perhaps he's vacated the house," said the voice of Mr. Abernathy. "Gotten all the servants out."

"In a matter of minutes?" said Inspector Wallace. "I doubt it."

"Maeve?" my father called to me. "Are you still here?"

I whispered to my carpetbag, and it brought me gently down to the floor without bumping into anyone, which is more than I could've done myself in that dark room.

"Here, sir," I told him.

"Good," he said. "I hadn't heard your voice in a while. That usually makes me nervous."

*Very funny, Dad.*

"What happens now?" Alice asked. "Will they find our skeletons up here someday?"

"Oh, my darling girl, certainly not," cried Mr. Bromley.

I knew Alice well enough to know she'd been joking. It amused me to think her own grandfather didn't.

"Rivers and Patchett" (Mr. Bromley's coach driver and footman) "are bound to grow suspicious before long. They'll knock on the door, and if no one comes, they'll go in search of the police."

"That could take hours," my father pointed out.

"Mr. Fustian has made a very grave mistake," Inspector Wallace's voice said, "if he thinks the police will overlook this stunt of his."

"How could he be so thick-headed as to attempt it?" wondered Mr. Abernathy. "No one would give Morty Fustian top nonors for intellect, but I wouldn't have thought he'd be so foolish as this."

"He did it," I said, "because he has an all-powerful djinni." I thought of the map. "And other magical tricks up his sleeve. So he thinks there's nothing you can do to him."

"Djinni or no," said Inspector Wallace, "Britain's not large enough for him to hide from me. Once we get out of here, I'll track him down like a bloodhound. I'll—"

"Track him down," interjected Tom, "like you should've done yesterday? When it was my dad he'd imprisoned in this tower, and not you?"

A horrible, shocked silence fell over the entire group of captives.

Had Tom just made a catastrophic blunder? Usually that was my job. Tom was right, of course, as right as Solomon. But he still needed the policeman's help. Powerful adults, from what I could tell, rarely took kindly to a direct challenge from a young person. Not like that. Not with others around to witness. And especially not when the kid's criticism was bang on the dot.

"Young man," the inspector said at length, "you are correct."

I let out a sigh of relief.

"Yesterday, I didn't feel we had enough evidence to do more than we did," Inspector Wallace continued. "But if it had been my father, or someone I loved, locked up in this tower, I would want the authorities to believe me sooner and take action sooner. I'm sorry we let you down."

For a moment I feared Tom wouldn't give the inspector an answer. Finally he spoke, though not without some difficulty.

"It's good of you to say so, sir," my friend said. "I know you were only doing your job."

"Yes, well," muttered the inspector, "as soon as I get out of here, I'm going to start doing my job in a way Mortimer Fustian won't appreciate, I'll wager."

"Good show," cried Mr. Abernathy.

"That's the spirit," added Mr. Bromley.

There was a sound at the door. Conversation froze. Polly gasped. We dangled in space at the sweet-chiming clink of a metal key clicking into a lock.

CHAPTER

29

The door opened, and Constable Hopewood stormed through, holding a lantern.

"Oh, Matthew," cried Polly. "Thank God."

But her Matthew wasn't alone. Mrs. Gruboil, still in her cook's uniform, her hands shackled before her, followed after him, looking murderous. Behind her came a young woman, dressed in a white nightcap, clutching a faded housecoat tightly around her frame. She, too, held up a candlestick before her as if it might ward off evil spirits.

"Polydora," Matthew called in deep concern. "Are you all right?"

Mr. Abernathy stepped forward. "I do declare," he said, sizing up Mrs. Gruboil, "if it isn't the baroness!"

Inspector Wallace rubbed his eyes. "Pardon me?"

My father clapped Constable Hopewood on the shoulder. "Good to see you, son," he said. "Took you a bit to get here."

Constable Hopewood looked rumpled and disheveled.

"Fustian locked me in, too," he said. "With this person. Mrs.

Gruboil. In that same room where I arres—er, where I found you here this morning."

Polly appeared at his side. "How did you get out?"

Matthew made a face. "The bureau," he admitted, "may owe Mr. Fustian a new door."

Polly beamed at him. The rift between them, it seemed, was more than mended.

We turned to the young woman who had followed Mr. Hopewood and Mrs. Gruboil in.

"G-good evening," she stammered. "None of you wants to hurt me, do you?"

"My dear young woman," cried the gallant Mr. Bromley, "why on earth would we?"

She lowered her candlestick somewhat. "Aren't you...violent?"

"Merciful heavens," Mr. Bromley said softly. "What have you been told?"

She gulped. "That you were the violent sort. Rough. Like Mr. Thorne. But you're...you're gentlemen, aren't you?"

"And ladies," said Mr. Abernathy. "We wouldn't hurt a fly."

A head poked out from behind her.

"*Charlie?*" Tom and I both cried.

The young woman's face registered shock. "You know my little brother?"

My father's mustache twitched. "It's the marshmallow man. We met yesterday."

She whirled upon her brother. "'Ere!" she cried. "You're still at it, are you? Out selling to the visitors, come to the manor? What've I told you about that, you little imp? Mister Fustian'll have my head on a platter if he catches you at it again."

"Charlie," I said, "what are you *doing* here?"

"Rescuing you, ain't I?" he said. "Saw the whole thing. Saw you come, but not leave. Heard you screaming. Saw Mr. Fustian leave, and tell the stable hands to tell the housekeeper in the morning to let out the people in the tower, *but not before*. So I came and got Maud up and told her to give that copper the key and let you out."

"Why on earth would you see all that?" I asked. "What were you doing in the stables?"

"I don't understand," said Mr. Abernathy. "Didn't you, miss, also hear us making noise, from within the house?"

"'Course," said Maud, looking at the constable as if this were a silly question. "But Mr. Fustian, he told all us domestics we weren't to interfere, not even if you made ever so much noise. Said he'd take care of it in the morning. It was more relatives, he said, a whole caravan of 'em arrived in the night, he said—dangerous ones, wrong in the head."

"And you *believed* him?" demanded Mr. Abernathy.

Maud's face was pale in the candlelight. "Beg pardon, sir," she said.

"I didn't see you folks come in. Mr. Fustian, he…" She swallowed. "He's a strange one, and he's not a good person, I know it. But he pays my salary." She looked pleadingly at him. "Things go best for all of us when we believe his tales." She stood up a bit taller. "Anyway, he said you were all just like the one that's been staying up here all last week. *He* made a lot of noise, too. We got used to it." She bit her lip, then seemed to think of something hopeful. "At least Mr. Fustian already went and took that first relative of his to a hospital. Just now."

"To a *hospital*?" wailed Tom.

She shrugged. "It's what he said."

"Come *on*." Tom turned toward our group. "We've got to go find my dad. We can't wait any longer."

Everyone gathered their coats and hats.

"Who's your dad?" Charlie asked Tom.

"The man who's been making noise in the tower all week," Tom said bitterly.

"Oh," said Charlie's sister, in a much more friendly voice. "You're family, then? With the Fustians?"

"No," Tom said. "It wasn't a dangerous relative you were hearing all week. It was a man your boss held here as a prisoner. My dad."

Her eyes grew wide. "Oh…"

"Told yer they weren't relatives," Charlie told Maud.

"Watch your mouth," she hissed.

Constable Hopewood took a look at Mrs. Gruboil, still smoldering in resentment in her handcuffs, and paused. "What do I do about her?" he asked. "I need to take her to the bureau and process her arrest. She's been charged with attempted burglary."

All eyes turned to Mrs. Gruboil. She glowered at us, saying nothing.

"If you stop at the station," Tom said in exasperation, "Mr. Fustian will get away."

"We can't drag her to London on a manhunt that will likely last till morning," Inspector Wallace pointed out.

I stepped forward and spoke. "Let her go."

Mrs. Gruboil startled. "Lemme *what*?"

"Let her go," I said. "She won't be any further trouble."

Mr. Abernathy turned to me. "I thought she was chasing after this so-called djinni just as hard as Morty was," he said. "That's what she told us. Why, Maeve, would you want her let go?"

I studied her face. Was I making a great mistake? I had to hope not. True, she'd broken the law by snooping, but she hadn't tried to hurt anyone.

"I think she responded to an advertisement Mr. Fustian placed in the papers asking for information about a djinni," I said. "I think she told Fustian what she knew, in return for some promise on his part. Payment, or one of the wishes, or something."

The so-called baroness's eyes bulged. "Here, how'd you know that? Did he tell you?"

"No," I said. "He didn't need to. I think Fustian tricked Mrs. Gruboil, so she put on her cook's uniform and took a job here to try to get Mermeros back."

"Trying to rob your employer is still a crime," pointed out Constable Hopewood.

"But she never did take anything," I argued. "She only has Mortimer Fustian accusing her, and we know he's a liar."

Tom hopped from one foot to another. "Can we go, please?" he begged. "He's getting away with my dad!"

"Let her go," I said once more. "I don't think she'll cause trouble for us, or for Gretigwode Manor, again."

Inspector Wallace, Constable Hopewood, and the other men exchanged glances.

Wallace shrugged. "Fine by me," he said.

Constable Hopewood unlocked the cuffs and stepped aside to let Mrs. Gruboil take her leave.

She looked at me. One long, probing, incredulous look, and then bolted down the stairs and out of sight.

"Ladies, gentlemen," Inspector Wallace announced, "we have a kidnapper to catch. Let's be off."

CHAPTER

30

E veryone gathered their jackets and hats and filed through the door and down the stairs. Charlie's sister Maud went first, holding the candle, but Charlie lagged toward the back with Tom, Alice, and me.

At the sight of Alice, even in this dim light, his eyes bulged. "Haven't seen you before, er, miss."

She smiled, and held out her hand. "I'm Alice."

"Pleased to meet you, Miss Alice," he gurgled.

Good *night*. Not this, not now. Romance was becoming a pebble in my shoe. Was Alice pretty? In an angelic way, if you went for that sort of thing.

"This makes me the hero, don't it?" Charlie crowed. "You'd be up there all night if it weren't for me."

"Maybe," I said. "Why *were* you in the stables, Charlie?"

Charlie looked away.

"He lives there," Tom said quietly. "Up in the loft. But Fustian's not supposed to know. Right, Charlie?"

Charlie glowered, then gave up the struggle. "How d'you know?"

Tom was quiet for a moment. "I'm an orphan, too," he said simply. "I didn't always live at the charitable home. Before that, I lived on the street."

Charlie jutted out his chin. "I don't live on the street," he said. "I keep to my little loft in the stables. Maud, she looks out for me."

Tom nodded. "You're lucky to have her."

We'd reached the main floor of the house by now.

"You won't tell on me, will you?" Charlie said. "You won't tell Mr. Fustian about me? Maud'll get sacked."

Tom shook his head. "'Course not."

We filed through the grand vestibule. "Tom," I whispered, when I had a chance at his ear, "how'd you figure it out?"

Tom pushed his way out the front door. "I know a survivor when I see one."

We reached the drive. The night was still dark, but the clouds had cleared enough for a three-quarter moon to light our way, in company with a smattering of stars.

Charlie made a beeline for Mr. Bromley's horses. He spoke gently to them and stroked their necks.

The rest of our group stood in the drive. Mr. Bromley's footman hurried over to greet us, while his driver readied the horses to leave, shooing Charlie away.

"What do we do now?" my father asked. "Do we track Fustian down?"

"He's gotten a long lead on us," muttered Inspector Wallace. "He could be anywhere. We don't even know which way to start."

"Where would he most likely go?" asked Constable Hopewood.

"We'll notify Scotland Yard," said Wallace, "and they'll send notices to all the county bureaus in the country to be on the alert for him."

"By then, he'll be gone," I said. "He's leaving the country. I'm sure of it. We've got to rescue Mr. Poindexter tonight."

My father rested a hand on my shoulder. "Tonight is nearly over, Maeve. This is the best we can do."

I called out to Charlie. He'd begun to make his way back toward the stable. At the sound of my voice, he turned back. "Yeah?"

"Who was with Professor Fustian when he left tonight?"

He blinked. "Mr. Thorne, the big bloke," he said, "and a sorry-looking fellow. Bald. Roughed-up."

"My dad," Tom said darkly.

"Jim Bauer drove," added Charlie. "They took Jock and Thunder."

"What?" asked Inspector Wallace irritably. "Are those dogs?"

"Dogs!" Charlie laughed aloud. "They're the fastest horses in the stable. Hitched to the post chaise. They'll fairly fly tonight."

My father and Mr. Bromley looked at each other grimly.

Mr. Bromley gestured toward his coach and six. "I'll venture we could give them good chase," he said, "*if* we knew where they were going."

Sometimes, it boggles my mind how adults can be so daft. We'd already told them we had carpetbags, but they didn't believe us. Even though every detail had proven our story right. And we had an informant in our midst, but as he was young, of the servants' class, they never thought to ask him.

"Charlie," I said, "did Mr. Fustian say anything about where they were bound?"

Charlie looked puzzled. "To the sea, of course," he said. "He's heading for his boat. The...*Meducine's Head*, I think."

Mr. Abernathy frowned. "The *Meducine's* Head?"

Alice smiled. "I think he means *Medusa*."

"By Jove," said Mr. Abernathy. "Well done, my pupil."

"Remember, Dad?" I asked my father. "On the tour. The tour guide said the professor likes to spend time yachting in the Mediterranean."

"So he did," my father said. "Fancy remembering that."

It just figured that Monstrous Mortimer Fustian would name his boat after a Gorgon with snakes for hair, so ugly that one glance would turn anyone seeing her into stone. Though, I must admit, in my studies with Mr. Abernathy, I liked Medusa a good deal better than most of those lovestruck nymphs in silly dresses and sandals.

"Well, come on, then," I said. "Tom and I will find Fustian's post chaise and tell you where to go. Ready, Tom?"

"But how on earth…?" cried Polly. "Maeve, whatever can you mean?"

There was no point explaining. Tom and I straddled our carpetbags and leaned down to coax them.

"What do you say, carpetbags?" I asked. "They don't believe you can fly. Shall we put on a show?"

We launched upward, spiraling around each other like the stripes on a barber's pole. Cries of shock and horror reached our ears, coming from the ground below.

"Coo!" cried Charlie.

"Egads!" cried Mr. Abernathy.

"Merciful heavens!" cried Mr. Bromley.

"Maeve!" begged Polly. "Come down immediately!"

"Gorblimey!" cried the carriage driver.

"All right up there, Maeve?" called my dad.

"Fine, Daddy."

"All right, then."

I turned to Tom. "Why don't you see if you can find a post chaise barreling its way south, toward the city, and come back and tell us how to follow it." I paused. "If he isn't heading south, try east, but it ought to be south."

"Which way's south?" he asked.

"Fly high enough," I told him, "and you'll see London. That's south."

Tom nodded, whispered to his bag, and zipped off with a *whoosh*. I gulped. I'd never yet seen the carpetbags travel that fast. I hoped Tom was holding on tight.

"Come on, carpetbag," I whispered, "let's go see what they're up to down below." I looped in circles around the coach.

Those on the ground were locked in argument, or rather, in several arguments.

"I can't believe what I'm seeing," babbled Mr. Abernathy. "It absolutely defies all the known tenets of science."

"We don't know where he keeps his yacht," the inspector said.

"How're they doing it?" cried Charlie. "Where can I get one of those bags? I've got my earnings, saved up in my shoe..."

"Maeve," Polly cried once more. "Get down at once! Matthew, make her come down."

"Remember Icarus," cried Mr. Abernathy. "Man wasn't made to fly. The gods do not ordain it."

*My wings aren't wax, and they won't melt in the sun*, I thought. *And I'm not a man, anyway.*

"It's bound to be London," my father said. "One of the marinas on the Thames."

Mr. Bromley's voice rose above the rest. "We can pursue this professor, and his hired gangster, but I must insist that the, er, women and children be dropped off somewhere safe first. Your home, perhaps, John?"

"I'm fine, Grandpapa," Alice protested. "Let me come. I want to help."

"Mr. Merritt," said Mr. Abernathy, "how are you not worried for your daughter?"

Dad glanced up at me. "I have many worries for Maeve," he said, "but falling off a carpetbag isn't one of them."

"Unthinkable, my dear Alice," Mr. Bromley continued. "If anything ever happened to you, I shudder to think!"

"Nothing will happen," Alice protested.

"Oy, Maeve!" cried Charlie, hopping up and down. "Take me!"

At times like these, it was a relief to float above the din.

Just then, Tom whizzed over the treetops and down over our gathering. He dismounted on the drive. I joined him.

"They're on the turnpike, racing south," he said. "The roads are pretty quiet now. If you hurry, you should overtake them before they reach the city."

"We'll stop in Luton to leave the young ladies at the Merritt home," insisted Mr. Bromley. "I can't bring Alice into danger."

"If you do, they'll get away," said Tom simply. "They'll disappear into the city and reach the boat before you can stop them."

Everyone, it seemed, had opinions. Loud ones. It's a wonder to me that adults ever get anything done at all.

Alice ran to me. "Maeve," she whispered, "take me with you. On your carpetbag."

I stared at her. "First Charlie, then you," I said. "Your grandfather would never forgive me."

"I'll never forgive you if you don't." It was the harshest threat I'd ever heard from Alice. "Take me with you. Then Grandfather will have to chase after us. They'll have no choice but to rescue Mr. Poindexter."

The Bromleys would uninvite me, without a doubt. My blissful life in Grosvenor Square would end tonight. But to bring Mr. Poindexter back—Tommy's father, and my old partner in crime— there wasn't even a question.

"Hop on," I told her. "You'll have to sit in front. Pull the handles toward you, so you can grab onto them between your knees. I'll hold on to you."

"But my skirts!" she exclaimed.

"Bother skirts," I told her. "Hoist them up. At a hundred feet high, there's no one to see."

"Do I need to, erm, steer?" Alice asked.

"Not really," I said. "The bag is in charge."

We got ourselves ready. Mr. Bromley turned just as I addressed the carpetbag.

"You marvelous carpetbag," I said, "Wouldn't it be fun if you took us both to London to find Tommy's dad? You want to help Tommy, don't you? And you can carry both of us, can't you?"

"Alice, *no!*" cried Mr. Bromley.

He was too late. We left the ground behind in a breakneck rush up to the skies, clearing the trees, the roofs, even the top of Gretigwode Manor's two towers, in seconds.

Alice squeaked in terror. Her weight slid back toward me. I gripped the bag between my knees and wrapped my fingers tightly around both my wrists. My arms were already clutched around Alice's waist.

"You bring her back down!" cried Mr. Bromley.

"Poor Grandpapa," Alice said. "I'm being quite terrible, aren't I?"

"You're being brave," I told her. "Let's go tell them what we're doing."

The carpetbag obligingly brought me low enough to see the folks on the ground. Charlie was arguing with Tom, it seemed, but everyone else was begging me to release Alice. As if I had somehow kidnapped her and forced her to come with me!

Precious Alice, and Rotten Maeve. I get blamed for everything.

"Grandpapa," Alice called, "I'm going. We're going to find Mr. Poindexter. We'll lead the way, and you can follow."

More shouts and protests. Some scrambled into the carriage, while others reached up into the air helplessly as though they might pull us down by the ankles.

"Get to the turnpike," Tom called. "Hurry!"

"Let's go, Maeve," Alice said, "before I change my mind. I think I'm about to be sick."

"Don't be," I warned her. "It will all fly in my face. How about London, then, eh, carpetbag?"

Gretigwode Manor fell away beneath our feet until it was a mere dollhouse. Its canopy of trees soon hid the house, and its dark deeds, from sight.

CHAPTER
31

"Whatever you do, Alice," I told her, "don't close your eyes. This is the view of a lifetime."

"You say that a lot," Alice said. "You said it when Mermeros took us to Persia."

I laughed. "Stick with me, and you'll cram a lot of lifetimes into one."

It *was* the view of a lifetime. Of a thousand lifetimes. The sky had cleared. Overhead, a luminous moon, and stars upon stars, spread over the entire bowl of sky, while dark Britain, with its hills and farms and rivers, stretched and slumbered beneath us, between splotches of town and city lights. Such a sky! Rim to rim, brimming with light! Whole constellations, whole galaxies of stars. I could reach up and pick them like apples.

To think that most people would go to their graves never seeing more than a wedge of sky, never realizing what glorious heavens they swam through each night while they slept.

"We're the luckiest girls who ever lived," I told Alice.

"You're right," Alice said. "We are."

She *was* looking. Alice is full of surprises.

"*Wheeeeeee!*" cried a voice, rushing up from behind. "*Hoooo-eeeeeee*, lookit me!"

They came into view and rode alongside us. It was Charlie, perched at the fore of Tom's carpetbag. He gripped the handles and bounced up and down on the bag as if he were a tot riding a pony for the first time.

"Cut it out," cried Tom. "You'll knock me off."

"We're flying!" Charlie screamed. "*Flyyyyy-*ing!"

"Yes," I shouted over to him. "And the people below are sleeping. Less of the shouting, all right?"

"Lookit that!" Charlie yelled. "Looky looky lookit! That's London!"

The sprawling patch of pinpricked light rushed nearer.

"Tom," I called out. "Why did you—"

"Easier to bring him," Tom yelled back, "than to put up with his badgering."

Charlie the salesman. He had one skill, and he used it well.

"What do you see, Tom?" I cried.

He leaned over to get a good look ahead. "That's the turnpike, up ahead," he said. "And that's Mr. Bromley's carriage."

A tiny toy carriage crawled along the dark ribbon of road beneath us.

"Do you see Mr. Fustian's chaise?" I asked.

"No," said Tom. "I'll go find it. Can you stay back enough to see me and keep an eye on our party?"

"I'll stay back," I shouted, "but I won't see you far in the dark."

"Stick to the turnpike," cried Tom. "If anything changes, I'll find you." He and Charlie zoomed ahead and were soon swallowed by the night. Beneath me, the Bromleys' carriage maneuvered its way through the streets of Dunstable, heading for the main route south.

We soared along. I let Alice enjoy the view while I kept a close eye on our carriage, urging the carpetbag to speed up here and there to see if I could bring Tom into view. Finally the carriage found its way onto the highway. It was empty at this hour of night, so the Bromleys' driver let the six horses run.

I'll say this for flying two people on a carpetbag built for one: Alice blocked most of the windy blast that would've buffeted my face.

"Do you suppose Grandpapa will ever forgive me?" Alice asked.

"Of course he will, when this is over," I told her. "Right now, though, he's probably suffering agonies."

"Oh dear," moaned Alice. "Perhaps it was wrong of me to do this."

"None of that," I said firmly. "You were a true heroine. Tell you what: let's find Tom and make sure we're still on track to find Fustian's chaise. Then we'll fall back, fly low, and show ourselves to your grandfather. Maybe then he'll be less afraid."

She nodded.

"Oh, carpetbag," I called, "wouldn't it be fun to catch up to your twin and say hello to Tom and Charlie?"

The carpetbag agreed. We catapulted forward, slicing straight across the winding curves of the road. We could hear Charlie whooping and hollering long before we saw them. At least someone was having fun.

Down on the dark road below, a pair of lanterns bobbed, swaying from the roof of a fast-moving chaise.

"Is that them?" I asked Tom.

"Yes," called Tom. "I flew low to make sure. This one"—nodding toward Charlie's back—"nearly gave us away. Can't keep his mouth shut."

"Well, we knew that about him," I said. "Our carriage is on the highway now. How much longer do you think Fustian will be on it?"

"Until the city limits, I guess," said Tom. "Are we gaining on them?"

"I hope so," I said. "I'll go give my dad the message."

Tom nodded. I explained my needs to the carpetbag, which turned me around quite obligingly.

We flew in a loop so we could swoop down low and pass by the Bromleys' carriage from the rear. We hovered right alongside them. They didn't see us. I peered inside to see faces drawn with worry, by the light of a small traveling lantern. Polly sat next to Mr. Hopewood, so I supposed she wasn't suffering too badly. My father looked all right.

I did the scariest thing I'd done yet that night and let go of Alice's waist to reach over and rap on the carriage window.

My dad opened the window. Mr. Bromley sprang up and leaned his head out.

"Alice, my child, are you all right?"

"Wonderful, Grandpapa," she told him. "You should try this! It's marvelous!"

He closed his eyes in relief. They sprang open once more. "Come down, young lady, and we'll ride in the carriage. No more of this dangerous business."

"I'm *fine*," she told him. "I'm not coming down until we have Mr. Poindexter, safe and sound."

"Be careful, Maeve," my father said.

"I will, sir," I told him. "They're still on this highway, up ahead. You're on the right course. We'll let you know if anything changes."

We peeled away and pushed back toward a high lookout point.

The thrill of flight is one I'll never grow tired of. But a night of no sleep had worn me down. I found myself nodding and bumping my forehead into Alice's braids.

"I do believe we're gaining on them, Maeve," Alice cried. "I can see both vehicles now. And there are Tom and Charlie, up ahead. I wasn't sure at first, but I can see them in the moonlight. Look!"

She pointed downward. I saw a darker splotch of shadow race over rooftops, turnstiles, and fields. Tom and Charlie's moon shadow.

"Do you think Grandpapa will catch up to them?" Alice asked.

"I hope so," I replied.

"Mr. Fustian's horses were fresh," Alice said, "but Grandpapa's already made one long trip this evening. They may tire out sooner."

I blinked the sleep out of my eyes. Couldn't give in to doubt now.

"If the police fail to catch up to Professor Fustian in time," said Alice, "then what?"

I took a deep breath. "Then we'll have to save Mr. Poindexter ourselves."

"Oh dear," she said. "I was afraid you'd say that."

On we flew. The carriages below us seemed to crawl. So did time. Whenever I felt tired, I thought of Mr. Poindexter.

Off to my left, a faint glimmer of gray began to lap the edges of the night.

"Maeve!"

I looked up to see Tom circling around us.

"Fustian's chaise is nearly to the city," he told me. "Looks like they're keeping to the west of Regent's Park. Aiming for Marylebone."

"Got it," I told him. "I'll go tell my dad and Mr. Bromley."

"We might lose them, Maeve," Tom said. "The smoke is thick. I've got to stay low, right above them. Can't leave for a second. You might lose me."

I looked down. He was right. The congestion of the metropolis was fast upon us. Already other vehicles began to take to the roads. Not many, but enough that I could see it would soon become difficult to know which was which.

"I'll tell Dad," I said, "then I'll come back to you two. We need to stick together."

I fell back and looped down once more to fly close to the Bromleys' coach window. This time, my father was watching for me. He had the window open before I needed to knock, and leaned out to speak with me.

"How goes it, Maeve?" my father called. "What's the report?"

"They're reaching the city," I told my father. "Keeping west of Regent's Park, aiming toward Marylebone."

"Makes sense," said Dad. "I'll tell the driver."

"Tom's flying right over them," I said. "We're afraid of losing them in the city. And not being able to find you. The city's waking up. More vehicles are on the road already. It will be harder to spot which one is you."

My father stroked his chin. "What do you propose?"

I glanced over at Polly, asleep on Constable Hopewood's

shoulder. My mother would have fits about the impropriety of it all, but Dad took a much more pragmatic view of things.

"Polly's scarf," I told him, in a burst of sudden inspiration. "Can you tie it, somehow, to the top of the carriage? It will flap, like the tail of a kite and help us to find you from above."

He nodded. "I'll try not to break my neck doing it."

"Thank you," I said. "He must be bound for the river. I hope we can come back and tell you where, but—"

"But if you can't, we'll find you," he said. "If all else fails, go back to Grosvenor Square."

I got a little misty, and it had nothing to do with highway dust in my eyes. "Thank you, Dad," I told him.

He looked surprised. "Of course I'd want to help find Mr. Poindexter."

"No," I said. "Well, yes, that too. But thank you for...for trusting me."

He smiled. "Maeve Merritt," he said, "I trust you more than almost anyone I know. To do everything, that is," he added, "except stay out of trouble."

I grinned.

"Now, go find Tom," he said. "Bring word if you can, but if not, we'll find you."

I saluted, nudged my carpetbag, and leaped into the sky once more.

## CHAPTER 32

Tom was right. Once Fustian reached London proper, he took a convoluted route through the warren of dark streets, pressing his way toward the Thames. It almost seemed as if he was trying to shake off pursuit. Yet he couldn't know we were following him. Could he?

It made me nervous.

We stayed high enough that no one should see us. The morning was still gray and dim enough that no one should see a handful of kids whizzing through the sky. I hoped.

We flew side by side now, keeping careful watch. You'd be surprised how much cabs, coaches, and carriages look alike from above.

"What's Maud gonna say in the morning when she finds me missing?" Charlie wondered aloud.

"You should've thought of that," said Tom, "before you hitched a carpetbag ride."

Mr. Fustian's driver pulled up, at last, at a building near the wharves on the river. A club on the banks of the Thames. St. George's Yachting Club.

Mists rose off the water. Docks extended out into the river, with long, sleek boats, covered in canvas, bobbing in the undulating water. The air smelled of wet ropes and fish.

Tom beckoned to me silently. He found a place to land, some thirty yards or more away from Professor Fustian's carriage. We touched down on a slippery wooden boardwalk and crouched behind a pair of empty barrels. The slop of water against the quay covered our footsteps and voices. I hoped.

"Everybody all right?" asked Tom.

We flexed our numb fingers and rolled our stiff shoulders. Yes, we were all right.

"Your grandfather's carriage... They'll never find us here, will they?" Tom whispered.

Alice shook her head. "Not in time."

"I'll go tell them," I said, reaching for my bag.

"I'll do it," offered Charlie.

"No thank you, laddie," I told him. "You're not getting your hand on these bags."

He looked offended. "Don't you trust me?"

"Not a lick."

Alice peered through the barrels. "Maeve," she said, "I'll go. You should stay here. You're much...quicker on your feet. You know what to say. You're needed here."

I've said it before, and I'll say it again: they don't make many braver hearts, nor truer friends, than Alice Bromley.

"Do you mind flying?" I asked her.

She bit her lip. "I do," she said. "But I'll manage it."

Tom's expression melted. "You'd do that for me, Alice?"

She gazed at him in surprise. "Of course I would, Tom. Just as I know you would for Maeve, or for me."

Tom was at a loss for words. Fortunately, I was not.

"Go now, then," I said, "while they're not looking. Tell them, St. George's Yachting Club, and if you see any landmarks along the way, remember them."

"St. George's Yachting Club," she repeated. "St. George's."

I continued my instructions. I felt like a parent dropping a child off at school. *Don't forget your coat and mittens.* "Hold on tight, Alice, and trust the carpetbag. It won't let you down." I caught myself. "Well, it might. But if it does, it'll catch you."

This, I realized, was probably the wrong thing to say. Alice's face was gray as she straddled the bag, bent low, and whispered to it. It rose softly, slowly, gently into the air. Maybe these bags understood the temperament of their riders. Alice was someone everyone wanted to be nice to. I was the sort of person to drop from forty feet up.

She floated through the sky and disappeared into early morning fog and smoke.

*Good luck, Alice.*

We turned our attention to the activity at the pier. Mortimer Fustian was barking orders at someone who seemed to be in the employ of the yachting club. The so-called professor looked ghastly after a night of no sleep—his clothes, even more rumpled, his hair standing on end. He wore a canvas courier bag slung over one shoulder and across his chest. That must be where he kept Mermeros's sardine tin, and his magic map. On his person at all times. It's what I would do.

We saw the silhouettes of two persons still seated inside the chaise. Thorne and Mr. Poindexter.

"Tom," I hissed, "do we dare steal that chaise?"

He took a deep breath. "With Thorne in it?" he said. "I don't think so."

"I guess there's nowhere to go but in the river, anyway," I said. "By the time we got the chaise turned around, they'd have us."

One worker began pulling the canvas tarps off Fustian's yacht. I could now see the words "Medusa's Head" in oddly beautiful lettering along the side of the boat. Another worker stacked boxes of supplies on the pier next to *Medusa's Head*. A third boarded the boat and poured a liquid into a nozzle. Water, perhaps? A funny odor wafted across the waterfront to tickle our noses. Probably not water. Petrol?

"This is bad, Maeve," Tom whispered. "They may never get here in time."

I nodded. "I know."

"What do we do, if it's up to us?"

I tried to think of a plan. My brain felt as foggy as the London sky. We'd come this far. We must do something. But what could we do? They were powerful adults, with authority, money, muscles, and maybe even weapons. We were two kids and a carpetbag. Three, if you counted Charlie, which I didn't.

"If your coppers manage to nab Mr. Fustian," Charlie murmured, "he'll go to prison, and my sister will lose her job, won't she?"

Oh, *no*. This we didn't need.

"Maybe not," I said brightly. "Maybe the house will go to his next of kin, and they'll keep the household staff."

Charlie frowned. "I just came along for the ride," he said. "And the pretty lass, but now she's gone. Take me home, all right?"

"Pretty lass!" I fumed. "We're on a rescue mission, and that's all you can think about?"

"We'll take you home," said Tom, "when my dad is safe."

"You know," said Charlie, "I could go tell 'em you're here."

I clenched my fists. "What do you want, marshmallow boy?"

"Half a crown'd do the job," he said. "If you've got it."

"Why, you—" I muttered. "What I'd give to knock you into the river!"

"Wait." Tom turned to Charlie. "For half a crown, would you help us?"

Charlie's eyes narrowed. "What d'you mean?"

"What *do* you mean, Tom?" I was so angry at Charlie, I could spit.

"Mr. Fustian," said Tom. "He knows you, doesn't he?"

"'Course he does," said Charlie. "I told you. He paid me to take my photograph."

"Right," said Tom. "So, you go out there and call to him. He'll be mightily confused why you're here. Draw him away from us, farther down the quay. So that he's on the other side of his carriage from us. So he can't see us rescuing my dad."

"Why would I do that?" demanded Charlie.

"For half a crown," I told him.

"And when Mr. Fustian asks me how I got here?" demanded Charlie.

"Tell him anything," I said. "Tell him you flew here for all we care. But, Charlie?"

"Yeah?"

I jabbed him in the shoulder with one finger. "If you go out there, and call to him, and betray us, and tell him were here to rescue Tom's dad, *I'll* tell him you've been hiding out in his stables, burning candles up in the hayloft."

His eyes grew wide. "You wouldn't!"

I glared at him. "Are you sure?"

He blinked. "I think, mebbe, you would."

"Good thinking."

"Go distract Mr. Fustian," ordered Tom.

"Money first," said Charlie.

"There's two of us," I hissed, "and one of you. First you work, then you get paid."

Charlie laughed. "You think I'm afraid of a *girl*?"

Tom snorted. "If it's *this* girl," he said, "you should be."

"Fine," said Charlie. "You drive a hard bargain."

He tiptoed along the quay toward the chaise. He passed it. So far, so good. Fustian, criticizing the work of his lackeys, didn't notice him. Charlie looked back at us, and we waved at him to go farther. Finally, when it seemed he'd gone far enough, we nodded.

His voice, when he called out, echoed across the water to us.

"Ho, Mr. Fustian," he called. "Mr. *Fustian*! It's me, Charlie Mulligan!"

Mortimer Fustian froze for a beautiful second. I wished I was a photographer with a Kodak camera of my own to capture the look on his face. He turned about slowly and saw Charlie there, waving to him. I had to hand it to the marshmallow rogue. He would earn his fee.

Fustian strode the length of the pier and banged on the door of his chaise with the flat of his hand. The door opened, and Thorne stepped out stiffly, as though he'd been sleeping. He followed his employer over toward where Charlie stood.

"Now," I whispered. "Let's go."

"No," said Tom. "I'll go. You stay."

"What do you mean?" I snapped. "None of this chivalry nonsense. Two are better than one. You know that."

"I do," said Tom. "And I'd rather you did come. But in case this goes wrong, I need someone here to see what happens. Someone who can protect the carpetbag, and use it to go get help."

There was sense in what he said. I had to admit it.

"Fine," I said. "But hurry."

While Charlie babbled nonsense, stalling for time, Tom slipped along the quay, darting from pillar to post, so to speak, hiding behind anything that could afford him a bit of cover. He reached the door of the chaise and opened it.

He climbed in. I waited, counting under my breath.

He didn't come out, and didn't come out. What could be wrong? Was his father sick? Was someone holding him prisoner there? I was just about to abandon my hiding place and run to investigate, when the door opened once more, and Tom climbed out, coaxing an exhausted, frail-looking Mr. Poindexter to lean on his arm and come along.

Mists off the river swirled in and obscured my view. They were coming. They would make it. We could get Mr. Poindexter to safety. That was the crucial thing. Everything else—the sardine tin, the map—none of it mattered so long as Mr. Poindexter was all right.

A cry froze the blood in my veins.

The mist cleared. There stood Thorne, holding Tom by the collar with one hand, and a sagging Mr. Poindexter with the other.

I ducked low. I wanted to cry; I wanted to scream. I wanted to take my magic carpetbag and fly it like a cannonball, straight into that bull-like Thorne's chest.

Morty Fustian came hurrying toward the carriage. "Where's the girl?" he cried. "Where this wretched redheaded boy is, that repellent girl can't be far behind."

I gripped the handles of Tom's carpetbag for dear life. I needed to be ready to spring.

Thorne stood there with his captured prey in each hand, with the air of a soldier waiting for his orders.

"Put them on the yacht, Thorne," he said. "Lock them in the hold. Charlie!"

Charlie Mulligan appeared at his side. "Yes, sir, Mr. Fustian, sir?"

"Hop into the chaise," he said. "James will drive you home."

Charlie climbed into the equipage with the dejected air of one who's been cheated out of half a crown.

But I had no time for Charlie. They were locking up Mr. Poindexter. Locking up Tom. Where, oh, where could Mr. Bromley's party be! We needed Inspector Wallace and Constable Hopewood. We needed the arm of the law, and the additional arms of Mr. Abernathy and my own father.

But they didn't come. Maybe Alice never found them. As the city awoke, how could a flying girl pick out one coach among a thousand?

It had been a fool's errand. This whole venture was. We'd failed.

But as Thorne pushed Tom's head down underneath the hatch, into the bowels of the small yacht, the *Medusa's Head*, I knew that, fool's errand or no, with help or all alone, I would have to see it through.

Morty Fustian was as twitchy as a rabbit in a spring garden. Charlie's and Tom's appearances had rattled him. That much was plain. There must be a way to work that to my advantage. His fear galvanized him into rapid, almost frenetic motion, scurrying to get the yacht loaded, untied, and prepared to leave.

His haste would not work to my advantage. Every second's delay might bring help our way. But still, it didn't come.

I had only the slap of the water against the wooden jetty to soothe my rattled nerves. My head ached, and my fingers didn't want to obey. Now, when I desperately needed all my faculties, they abandoned me.

I unbuckled the carpetbag. Perhaps something in here could help, or at least suggest an idea. By pale morning light, I was surprised to see the items I had packed. A pair of scissors. Some paper. A pencil, a spool of string. *My* bag? Somehow our bags had gotten switched, and Tom had ended up with mine. Alice, then, was flying Tom's rambunctious carpetbag. Oh dear.

The two dockworkers pushed the *Medusa's Head* out into the water. Mr. Fustian yanked several times on a long, thin chain. The roar of an engine noise shattered the quiet of the morning. He turned the wheel, maneuvering the *Medusa's Head*. As it turned out to sea, to the Thames's wide basin, I saw a propeller furiously churning the water. To my horror, I realized Fustian wouldn't simply sail away. He would fairly fly across the water, powered by a modern petroleum-powered engine. No police boat would be able to catch him.

The only way to get him back, I thought, would be to make him want to come.

*That was it.*

He had lured Mr. Poindexter to bring Mermeros's sardine tin to him in just the same way. Not with force, not with open threats. Not with language that committed an obvious crime. He'd gone fishing for a sardiney djinni by throwing down a lure for an innocent shopkeeper—safety for the son he valued above all things.

Mr. Poindexter loved Tom more than anything in the world. Mortimer Fustian had no heart to love another. That was plain. But I knew what he valued. I'd better get it now, before it went far beyond reach.

The *Medusa's Head* was now chugging out in the open channel of the river. The morning was light enough that anyone looking would see me. I couldn't worry about that anymore. It was Sunday morning. The docks were mostly quiet.

"Best and bravest of carpetbags," I purred. "Wouldn't it be a great joke to go out onto that boat and rescue our Tom and his dad?"

The carpetbag squirmed with anticipation.

I cast one desperate glance along the whole marina. No sign of help. It was all up to me.

We soared out over the water. Morning sun glittered lavender and gold upon its waves and swells. Spray baptized my face. Just the cold, refreshing shock I needed to jolt my brain awake. I tried not to think about all the things Londoners dumped and flushed into the Thames.

We drew near to the boat, my carpetbag and I. The hum of the engine echoed across the river from shore to shore. Good. Mortimer Fustian, standing on the deck, operating his vessel, wouldn't hear my approach.

He piloted his vessel from the ship's wheel, in the rear, or *aft*, deck. A high mast, suspended by taut ropes and pulleys, dominated the deck, but none of the sails had yet been raised. Fustian relied on the power of his noisy engine to evade capture by Her Majesty's government. No doubt he would raise the sails and enjoy the leisure of an ocean voyage once he'd left the mouth of the Thames, and Great Britain, far behind. For now, he piloted his yacht through the river, squinting into the rising sun.

"Here," I told my carpetbag. "Let's land here."

I stepped softly onto the deck a few yards behind Fustian. Keeping a tight grip on my carpetbag, I crept toward him.

He didn't hear me. He made no move. No loose deck boards squeaked beneath my feet. The *Medusa's Head* was clearly kept shipshape and in racing trim. Its engine thrummed beneath my feet.

There. He was right there. The strap of his courier bag lay diagonally across his back. I reached into my carpetbag for the scissors.

"There you are, Miss Maeve," he said. "I've been expecting you."

I froze.

He hadn't even turned around! Had he already traded one of his wishes for...supernatural powers? Eyes in the back of his head?

Then I saw it. A mirror. A wide, curved mirror was mounted before him. Perhaps it helped him see other vessels coming up behind him in crowded waters. Vessels, and schoolgirls.

Foiled by a simple mirror.

I turned. St. George's Yachting Club was gone from sight. No one could see us. No help could find me now.

A dry gulp stuck in my throat.

"Of course, I like nothing better than good company aboard ship," said Mortimer Fustian. "But as you can see, the Thames riverway is filling up with vessels. I need to concentrate. Thorne!"

Oh, no.

"We may run into difficulties with provisions, if unexpected stowaways keep appearing," he said conversationally. "You haven't got that little pest, Charlie, in your back pocket, have you? Or that irritating little blond girl?"

I took a step closer. He still hadn't turned around. I had only seconds before Thorne arrived.

"What are you going to do with them?" I demanded. "With Mr. Poindexter and Tom?"

Another step.

Mr. Fustian's gaze darted back and forth from the river, to his own foredeck, to oncoming vessels. "*Do*?" he repeated. "I'm no killer, if that's what you mean." He sighed. "We scholars are so tragically misunderstood."

Another step.

"If you don't plan to kill them," I said, "what will you do?"

"Leave them somewhere, of course," he said. "And you. Somewhere far away, where you won't be a nuisance to me. Where it will take you a good long while to find your way home."

"Mr. Poindexter isn't well," I said. *Step.* "If you leave him somewhere, who knows what might happen? Your rough handling of him has weakened his health."

"He does seem to be rather a broken man," agreed Mortimer Fustian. "I'm disappointed in him."

"I wonder how you would look," I said, "after being tied to a chair for a week and beaten up by Mr. Thorne."

*Another step.* I could reach out and touch the hem of his jacket now. I was directly behind him.

I heard the creak of hinges, followed by the noxious sound of Thorne's harsh American voice. "You wanted something, Boss?"

I couldn't see Thorne, hidden behind Fustian as I was. I prayed he couldn't see me.

"Yes, Thorne," said Fustian. "When you've finished securing our, er, guests, I need your help with something up here."

"Back in a minute, Boss. This boat's making me sick." The hinges creaked once more. It must be a hatch door leading belowdecks.

So. The invincible Thorne had no sea legs. He couldn't handle the swells.

My hand located my scissors, sliding about the bottom of the carpetbag. I slid my fingers through the handles and pulled them out slowly. Would Fustian see what I was doing in his infernal mirror?

"What do you even want with a djinni, Professor Fustian?" I spoke softly, hoping to disguise just how close I was to him. Carefully, I reached the scissors toward the strap of his courier bag. "You have plenty of money."

He turned his wheel counterclockwise. "They tell me, Miss

Maeve, that you were the first in recent times to discover Mermeros," he said. "Surely you aren't such a simpleton as to think money is the only use for such an ancient, magical being."

"Of course not," I said. "But that's what most people seem to want him for."

I slid the farther blade behind the canvas strap. How could he not know I was here? Perhaps, if I could no longer see his mirror, he could no longer see me. It was designed to spot boats in the distance, not pickpockets standing directly behind him. Yet how could Fustian not hear me breathing?

"Then you and I," he said, "are different from most people."

The riverway filled more and more with boat traffic. It took all of Fustian's concentration to steer, thank goodness.

I squeezed the handle of the scissors. They barely gained any purchase at all against the reinforced canvas strap. They weren't the sharpest blades. Just a pair I kept in my writing desk.

"Tell me," Fustian said, "what you used your wishes for."

*Crunch.* I sawed at the strap, severing only a few threads of fabric.

"The first wish was foolish," I said. "An act of revenge."

*Crunch.* A few more threads; hardly enough to make a dent.

"An understandable passion," said Fustian. "I have a long list of former colleagues—colleagues, pah! They were never in my league!—who need to be taught a lesson."

I sawed away at the strap. The motion of the boat underfoot jarred my hand and threw off my balance.

"It wasn't worth it," I said. "It turned out to be a complete waste of a wish."

"We'll see about that," said Fustian darkly. "Your second wish?"

"A trip to Persia," I said, "to learn more about Mermeros and the kingdom from whence he came."

*Crunch.* Finally, it seemed, I was making some headway. Curse these dull scissors! I was nearly halfway through. I prayed Fustian couldn't feel what I was doing. If he did, he showed no sign.

"Aha, you see," cried Fustian, "you and I *are* alike, Miss Maeve. Where others seek treasures, *we* seek knowledge. The highest prize. The mysteries of the ancient world far surpass any mere rubies and sapphires."

Yes, well, I'd been hoping to find a few pots of rubies and sapphires, along with a smattering of knowledge, but I kept that fact to myself. My hand ached as I sawed away with my scissors. All the while, Fustian piloted his vessel expertly. I'd say this for him: he was a superb yachtsman.

"Is that why you made the map?" I asked him. "Of magical objects, instead of, say, buried treasure and such?"

"Precisely," said Fustian. "We who seek knowledge and wisdom answer to a higher call. Why are you standing so close behind me?"

I gulped. "To hear you better," I said. "Over the noise." I chopped with all my might.

"Stand where I can see you," he ordered. "This is very strange, talking in this way."

*Crunch, crunch.* Would this never end?

"Forgive me," I said. "I need shade. The sunlight bothers my eyes."

I was so close, I could see every line in the pattern of his tweed jacket. I could smell his brand of soap, though right at this moment he could stand to use a bit more of it.

"You could come with me, Maeve," Fustian said. "We'll leave the others behind. Be my assistant and heir, when I'm gone, to all my fantastic discoveries. Mysticism and marvels! Incantations and amulets, unexplored! Paradoxes the ordinary human mind cannot comprehend. You are obviously a girl of unusual intelligence and daring."

I smiled grimly. "My schoolmistresses, as a rule," I said, "would disagree. Though Mr. Abernathy seems to like me well enough."

"Abernathy. Pah! He's a disgrace," cried Fustian. "Speak to me no more of Abernathy."

"Suit yourself." Nearly there! The strap was almost severed in two.

"I wonder," Fustian mused, "if you might not, yourself, have a sort of gift. An uncanny knack where magical objects are concerned."

I blinked. What was this bizarre idea that had taken hold of both Fustian *and* Alice?

"You are unblinded by greed." Fustian kept singing my praises. "Unlike most mortals."

Ha! Hold out a sack of doubloons, and try me.

*Chop, chop* went my trusty scissor blades. *So close.* "It seems to me," I said, "that greed comes in several forms."

"You could wield magic that makes our little Mermeros a petty fish by comparison."

"Don't tell him that," I said. "Mermeros has very sensitive feelings."

The hinges creaked open once more.

"Hey! Boss!" bellowed Thorne. "Look around! That rotten girl's stealing your stuff!"

*Snap.* The canvas strap fell in pieces. I snatched the bag away and leaped onto my carpetbag. My faithful leather-handled friend soared into the air, above the mighty Thorne's great, grabbing reach. I had them. I'd won. I'd secured the bait.

Mortimer Fustian turned and looked at me.

"I've got Mermeros and the map," I cried. "If you want them, come and get them."

A most hideous grin stretched across Fustian's foul face. "Have you?" he asked. "Are you sure?"

A blade of river spray arcing up from the hull of the *Medusa's Head* splashed over me, matching the cold, clammy, sick terror in my heart. I fumbled with the buckle on the bag. It was empty. No sardine tin. No map. Nothing but a notebook and a wadded-up handkerchief.

Thorne leaned over the handrail and heaved the contents of his stomach overboard.

"A brave effort, Miss Maeve," cried Fustian, no longer my great admirer, "but, as with all your other pathetic attempts, it has failed."

I wiped stinging water from my eyes.

He spoke to Thorne, who nodded and returned on shaky legs belowdecks.

"Go home, Maeve," called Fustian. "There's nothing more for you here. I'll leave your friends somewhere—Constantinople, maybe, or Peking. With luck, you'll see them again in a year or two."

The sun hung over the horizon, huge and orange, sizzling down upon the water, burning the river mist away. I whispered to my carpetbag, and it brought me up into the sky. The long, slivered-almond shape of the *Medusa's Head*, with its mahogany deck and skeletal riggings, shrank beneath me, along with my brave words, and all my hopes.

I'd go back to the shore. Maybe the police would have arrived. I could fly back. With Inspector Wallace. But the *Medusa's Head* tore through the water like a stallion. Could I even catch up with it? And how did a policeman arrest two men on a boat, with nothing but a carpetbag and a schoolgirl to back him up?

Yet again—again and *again* and again—I had failed.

My carpetbag kept pace with the yacht. I looked down upon Mortimer Fustian, directly below me, and I very nearly spit upon him. I'm the last girl in Britain you'll ever call ladylike, but even I had my limits.

The sun roiled. It would be a scorcher of a day. The miniature, puppet-like figure of Fustian, below, pulled off his jacket and rolled up his sleeves. He dropped his jacket on the deck. A blinding flash of sunlight seared my vision.

My breath caught in my throat.

*There.*

"Carpetbag," I whispered, "can you help me? Can we do it? Like a bullet? Do we dare?"

The bag wriggled with glee. *Hold on*, it seemed to say. Then down, down like a shot, we barreled for the *Medusa's Head*.

F ustian never saw me coming.

I wasn't sure I'd survive to tell it. The carpetbag raced like a rocket. I thought I'd end up crashing through the deck *and* the hull, and meeting my end on the Thames's mucky, littered bed.

The whine we made, slicing through the air, reached Fustian's ears too late. I'd already grabbed his jacket, and the shiny sardine tin that had slid out of its breast pocket, with the blue and green map folded like a Chinese fan inside.

He turned about in horror just in time to see me launch off from the deck and back into the sky.

"Thorne!" he screamed. "Thorne!"

"Come back to shore, Fustian," I cried. "Back to your yacht club, and surrender your prisoners, if you want your djinni and your map back."

"You'll never give them back," he screamed. "It's a trick! It's a trap!"

Thorne popped up from belowdecks, looking green about the gills.

"You think no one else keeps their promises," I cried, "because you never do."

"Do you think I'm an idiot?" he cried. "Thorne! Get my fishing gear!"

Fishing? Was he planning to snag me with a fishing hook and reel me in? Just to be safe, I flew a little higher and hung farther back behind the boat.

"You won't win, little girl," snarled Fustian. "I'll reach the Channel and get away before anyone can catch me. The *Medusa's Head* is the pride of the seas."

It was a very nice boat, but frankly, I doubted that.

"It's your choice, Professor," I told him. "Come back and trade your prisoners. Or I'll send Mermeros after you like a hurricane with a toothache. You decide."

I took off, high into the clouds, hoping other sailors wouldn't see me. But not so high that I couldn't see what happened with the *Medusa's Head*. On she chugged, out to sea, toward the Channel and France and escape from justice.

I reached into the pocket of the jacket for the sardine tin. Time to employ Mermeros? Once I spent this last wish, he'd be gone for good. If I must, I would do it. But if it could at all be avoided...

The *Medusa's Head*'s prow veered to starboard and cut across the Thames's wide basin. Mortimer Fustian's wiry gray hair flapped in the breeze as he steered his yacht around. A tug coming up the river, against the current, pulled on its ship's whistle in some alarm, but Fustian cranked his engine into high gear, finished the turn, and churned ahead, leaving the anxious tugboat far behind.

"Come on, carpetbag," I told my faithful companion. "Let's go back and find your friend, and mine."

The *Medusa's Head* was fast, but my carpetbag was faster. We soared over the Thames, skimming the clouds, and settled ourselves gently upon the quay at St. George's Yachting Club, landing on the docks and into the eager arms of Polly, Alice, and my dear old dad.

"He's coming," I told them. "Quick! Hide, or he'll never come to shore. Where are the officers? Are you ready to arrest him?"

"I don't understand," asked Inspector Wallace. "Why is he coming back?"

I almost answered him, then bit my tongue. "I persuaded him," I said. "I have something he wants. He's got Mr. Poindexter and Tommy in the hull, along with that great ox, Thorne."

"They already know that," said a familiar voice. "I told 'em."

"Charlie!" I cried. "You stayed! Why didn't you go home with Fustian's driver?"

He gazed at me in pitying bewilderment. "Simple," he said. "Your mate Tom owes me half a crown."

The *Medusa's Head* chugged into view.

"Hide, everyone," I hissed. "You have to surprise him."

The plain sight of Mr. Bromley's coach and six ought to have given the game up to anyone sensible, but Morty Fustian, it seemed, was beyond sense or reason. As the *Medusa's Head* pulled into its slip along the pier, anyone on deck could only see me, standing there, holding out a sardine tin and a folded parchment map.

Just like the old times. Mermeros's tin wriggled in my fingers, calling to me. The map buzzed with the promise of wondrous adventures and hidden delights. No wonder Fustian would risk all to have them.

*You and I are alike, Miss Maeve.*

Mortimer Fustian's expression, when he climbed off his yacht, was murderous. "You give those back to me this instant," he cried. Which, in my book of threats, is distinctly lacking. Unimaginative. He disappointed me. But I must make some allowance for nervous strain.

I held my twin prizes over the edge of the water. "Prisoners first," I said, "or I drop them into the Thames."

He halted in his tracks, staring at me through wild, bloodshot eyes.

"Thorne," he called. "Bring the wretched pair."

We glared at each other for an unpleasantly tedious minute or two while Thorne maneuvered his quarry up above deck. Mr. Poindexter was weary, and Tom, ready for a fight. When he saw me, standing on the quay, dangling Fustian's hopes over the edge of the water, his face lit up like fireworks at the Crystal Palace.

"Come this way, Tom," I called to him. "Bring your dad to safety."

Thorne relinquished them with disgust, and wiped his hands upon his black trousers. Tom draped his father's arm over his shoulder and steadied him as they slowly made their way to solid ground. As they passed by me, Mr. Poindexter paused and gripped my hand with such a look of gratitude that I wanted to cry right there on the spot. And I *don't* cry.

"Now," Fustian told Thorne, "go get the girl."

"Get her yourself," growled Thorne. "I already told you. You're twisted. I didn't take this job to hurt kids."

Morty Fustian gnashed his teeth—another gnasher for the scrapbook—and charged toward me.

I lowered the sardine tin and map over the water.

"You'll never drop them in," he said, advancing toward me. "You value them too much."

I backed away. Each step brought me closer to terra firma and farther from the water's edge.

"You're right," I said. "I can't."

"Then keep your promise," he said. "I gave you back your friends. Give me back my things."

Another step, and another. Away from the dock. Away from the water and the *Medusa's Head*.

"The problem about these things," I said, "is that they aren't yours. Not by rights. You stole them, violently, from Mr. Poindexter. This was his djinni, and the map was his second wish, which you forced upon him by threatening Tom."

I pocketed Mermeros and tore the map into long strips. It broke my heart. My hands shook. I tasted gall.

But no one should have a map like this. Not even me.

Fustian shrieked at the sight of me ripping the strips into tiny bits and, tossing them high, scattering them upon the breeze.

"You lying little *sneak*!" he screamed. "Give me that!"

Frantically, he snatched at the bits of parchment fluttering through the air, and found himself gripped in the arms of Constable Hopewood and Inspector Wallace.

"You're under arrest," said Constable Hopewood, "for kidnapping, assault, theft, threatening, intimidation, interfering with police, false imprisonment—"

Mortimer Fustian thrashed against their grip. "It was the American," he cried. "Look at the big brute! He made me do it all!"

Mr. Abernathy stepped out from his hiding place with a gleam in his eye. He shook his head, *tsk*ing his tongue.

"Bad show, Morty, bad show," he said. "What will the old crew back at Oxford think of all this?"

Mr. Fustian's eyes were wild. In a feat of strength of which I wouldn't have imagined him capable, he broke away from the two larger officers and scrambled back along the quay. He snatched my carpetbag and ran with it the full length of the dock.

"Fly me away!" he cried. He leaped off the edge, straddling the bag like a pony.

The carpetbag, unimpressed, flipped upside down, dropping Mortimer Fustian into the Thames with a splash, then flew back to my side like an obedient terrier.

A terrier who could fly.

Never mind.

It's all in how you ask them. They like to play and be treated like friends. And they like to think the hijinks are their idea.

CHAPTER
35

"Fish him out of there, would you, Matt?" Inspector Wallace asked Constable Hopewood. "I'll go see to the American."

The constable lowered a rope into the water and pulled Fustian up easily. Turning around, I saw Polly watch him with swelling pride. At his muscles, or whatever it was that made girls weak in the knees about their gentleman friends. I felt a great snort of laughter welling up inside of me, and turned away before I could embarrass my swooning sister with it.

Thorne, to my surprise, put up no resistance. He was only too keen to get off that boat, and to tell anyone who'd listen that it was all Fustian's idea. He'd only been following orders. He would never *dream* of hurting a kid. That wasn't the kind of boy his mother had raised to manhood, back on the farm. Etc. In no time they sat on the docks, back to back, their wrists tied behind their backs, squabbling with each other.

Mr. Poindexter sat inside the Bromleys' coach, with Tom beside him, his arm wrapped protectively around his dad. The sight of

Tom's shocking red hair nestled next to Mr. Poindexter's bald head put a lump in my throat.

Mr. Bromley had apparently procured some foodstuffs in the dining room of the St. George's Yachting Club, which was probably no easy task at this hour of the morning, but he and his wallet managed it. He was hovering close by, urging food and drink upon poor, tired Mr. Poindexter.

When Mr. Bromley's attention turned elsewhere, I held out the sardine tin to Mr. Poindexter, who took it gratefully and slid it into his pocket. His gaze met mine once more.

"Are you all right?" I asked him.

"Nothing time won't mend," he said. "I don't know how to thank you, Maeve."

I shook my head. "All the credit goes to Tom," I said. "I just came along for the ride."

Tom grinned and shook his head. I backed away to give them their privacy. My good, good friend, and my partner in crime, back together where they belonged.

Alice stood nearby, politely conversing with the unflappable Charlie Mulligan. The two carpetbags sat nestled at her feet. How did mine make its way over here without my notice? Those rascally bags! It really was a marvel to me that Mr. Poindexter had never caught them frolicking before.

Could Alice's theory be right? Fustian had said it too. *Was* there something about me that woke up magical objects from their slumber?

Poppycock.

"Well, Charlie," I asked him, "have you been paid your half a crown yet?"

He turned pink.

"What's this?" asked Alice. "Does Maeve owe you money?"

"Not I. Tom owes it," I told her. "*This* one required payment in order to help stop Mr. Fustian and Mr. Thorne."

Charlie darted frantic looks my way, begging me to cease and desist. I was too irked with him to care. I *mostly* flowed with the milk of human kindness just then, but not enough to overlook betrayal from this marshmallow-selling rat.

Alice reached into her pocket for her coin purse. "I'll take care of that, Mr. Mulligan," she said sweetly. "Tom has other concerns at present. Here. Half a crown."

Charlie held out a protesting hand. "That's all right, miss," he told her gallantly. "I was only joking. 'Course I was glad to help."

I rolled my eyes. Fortunately for Charlie Mulligan's pride, Alice didn't notice it.

"Well, I call that extremely good of you," said Alice. "Friends ought to help one another, oughtn't they?"

"You said it right." Charlie swelled up like a tick, ready to pop. "Friends ought."

Good *night*.

But for once I kept my mouth shut. I decided to let it pass. I was too tired, and too glad, and too rosy in my general outlook on the world just then to give that rascal Charlie the verbal drubbing he deserved. I would let him put on his little show of gallantry for Alice Bromley, Lady Fair, this once.

Mr. Bromley stepped away from the coach and turned and met my gaze. My heart sank into my boots. Time to face my guilt head-on.

"Mr. Bromley," I said, "will you ever forgive me?"

He rested his hands on both my shoulders. I had no choice but to meet his gaze.

"Miss Maeve," he said, "you give me a fright that I don't know how my poor old heart could withstand."

I hung my head. "I know," I said. "I'm sorry."

"But," he said, "you knew what you were doing. And Alice is safe and well. And a bit of a heroine herself now, thanks to you."

I smiled. "Alice has always been heroic. She's made of strong stuff."

He beamed with pride. "She surely is. She is the comfort of my later years."

I grinned. "Not so much later, sir, if you don't mind my saying so."

He laughed. Then his face turned serious. "Miss Maeve. If I may.

I hesitate to ask you, but if you wouldn't mind, that is to say, I...I would never wish to be anything less than forthright, however—"

I patted his arm. "Don't worry, Mr. Bromley," I said. "Alice's grandmother will never hear about her carpetbag flight from me."

He shuddered in relief. "I'm grateful to you. I knew I could count on your discretion."

I nodded. "I keep my secrets well, Mr. Bromley."

He eyed me sideways, a bit nervously. "I believe it, Miss Maeve. Thank goodness you are, how shall we say, on the home team?"

"Very much." I laughed. "Home team through and through."

Mr. Bromley joined Alice in her conversation with Charlie, leaving me free to wander off a bit and stretch my legs, alone with my own thoughts. Everyone else had their occupation at the moment. Constable Hopewood supervised the criminals in his most official manner, with a very appreciative audience in my eldest sister, bless her soon-to-be-married heart. The other adults mingled in conversation. Inspector Wallace was nowhere in sight; he'd probably gone in search of a telephone to summon a police wagon.

The sun, climbing high in the sky, danced in golden sparkles off the peaks and crests of the rippling surface of the Thames. I shaded my eyes with my arm against the brightness. My eyes reminded me once more that they hadn't properly closed the night before and requested permission to inform me that they were longing for bed.

A glint of whiteness caught my eye. I turned to see.

Wedged under the bottom of a pile—one of the wooden posts atop the docks that boats tied their moorings to—fluttered a scrap of paper, rattling in the breezes off the water. I bent and picked it up.

My heart fluttered like the paper. It was a scrap of thick, creamy parchment. A bit of map, beautifully etched in brown, and green, and blue. A smattering of gold stars sparkled across it. Ornate letters rolled off the scrap.

T-L-A-N-D

*Scotland.* A scrap of a map revealing magical treasures concealed in eastern Scotland.

I slipped it into my inside coat pocket.

*Thank you, Mermeros.*

<br />

CHAPTER

36

M r. Wallace departed in the police wagon with Mortimer Fustian and with Thorne, who, as it turned out, was named Willhoughby, Willhoughby P. Thorne, which discovery forever stripped him of any further power of intimidation in my mind, be his muscles ever so large, or no. Though he allegedly sprang from the great criminal metropolis of Chicago, it seemed that he'd actually been born and raised on a farm near a sedate American town called Schenectady, which sounds to my ear like a failed sneeze. So there you have it. Frightening looks aren't everything.

At Mr. Bromley's insistence, we all returned to their home at Grosvenor Square to eat and rest. There wasn't really room for us all in the coach, so my father, Polly, and Constable Hopewood escorted Charlie back home by way of the trains, promising to return later on, after a bit of sleep.

I wondered and worried about what would happen to Charlie if his sister's employer ended up in jail. My father later explained to me that whether in jail or no, Mr. Fustian would maintain staff at Gretigwode Manor to look after the place. Charlie's sister, he believed, would remain employed. "And probably," my father added, "relieved to have her eccentric employer elsewhere for a while." Tours would still come, and Mr. Fustian's horses would still need tending, so Charlie's stable-loft home, and his brisk trade in licorices and marshmallows should remain undisturbed.

The grand Sunday dinner, originally scheduled for this evening at my parents' home, was to be moved to the Bromleys' home. Mother might regret a wasted grocery bill but she would never miss an invitation to dine with the illustrious Bromleys.

Back at Grosvenor Square, Mr. Bromley saw us inside and arranged a late breakfast for us. He sent one of his footmen to fetch spare clothes from the flat above the Oddity Shop for Mr. Poindexter, then sent each of us to bed.

I thought I'd be much too agitated by the morning's excitement to sleep, but no sooner did my head hit the pillow than I vanished into the Land of Nod. When I awoke, it was four o'clock in the afternoon. Alice had already finished her bath and dressed, and had drawn a bath for me.

I sank into the tub, thinking, thinking. So much had happened in the last two days. I could barely make sense of it all. I'd need to write it all down in my journal. I wasn't a great journal-keeper, but if my previous adventures with Mermeros, Alice, and Tom were any indication, some memories were too wondrous to be allowed to fade. I needed to hold on to them, every shred, every snippet. Plus, my journal had its own little lock and key. Just the right place to preserve my precious scrap of magical map.

The bath felt heavenly. Alice had sprinkled in some lavender bath salts—possibly a hint about my hygiene—and they were soothing and delightful. I splashed around a good deal, then got down to business washing my hair and sudsing up the rest of myself. A night of flying through southern Britain's dust and bugs, along with a few splashes from the Thames, leaves a girl grubbier than you might think. I was a much happier person when I emerged from my room half an hour later, freshly braided and dressed in clean clothes.

"There you are." Alice greeted me on the landing. "Your family arrives soon. Mr. Poindexter and Tom have been asking for you."

We hurried down the stairs to the second floor and knocked on Tom's door. He called us in.

"—do something about Charlie," Tom was saying to his father.

I surveyed the room. Morris the owl perched, as before, on a curtain rod. He ruffled his feathers by way of greeting as we entered the room. The carpetbags, I noticed, were stuffed under the bed. Napping too, I shouldn't wonder. Perhaps they wouldn't antagonize the poor bird now.

Mr. Poindexter sat up in an easy chair by the fire with a blanket over his lap. He was still tired, it was plain to see, and the bruise on his face was still ugly, but rest, food, a bath, and peace in place of terror had done wonders for his appearance. He held out his arms to me, and I ran to embrace him. This had never happened before, but it felt as natural as jam on scones.

"Maeve," he said simply. "Maeve."

I pulled away. "It's good to have you back, sir."

He smiled. "It's good to be back."

We pulled up footstools and sat close beside him before the fire.

"What was that you were saying, Tom," I asked, "about Charlie?"

His face colored somewhat. "I was telling Dad that I'd like to do something for Charlie."

I bristled. I wished the poor lad no harm, but I wasn't as ready to forgive him.

"Why did you trust Charlie, Tom?" I demanded. "He was rotten. He nearly betrayed us."

Tom sighed. "It's not entirely his fault, Maeve."

"Yes, it was," I protested. "He nearly gave us away to Fustian. He could've gotten us hurt."

"He's a survivor," Tom said once again. "I know how a survivor thinks. When there's nobody in the world there to help you when you land in the soup, you have to look out for yourself, above all else."

I pictured Tom living on the streets. The Mission Industrial School and Home for Working Boys must've seemed like heaven, compared to that. And if the Mission Industrial School seems like heaven, you know you're in trouble.

"Having a friend," continued Tom, "*being* a friend, being loyal to someone else, even if it might get you into trouble—those are luxuries a street kid can't usually afford."

Friends are *luxuries*? Like gold and jewels and fancy carriages? I thought anyone could have friends.

Tom was right. I'd take my friends over jewels and carriages any day.

Mr. Poindexter ruffled Tom's hair. "I'm proud of you, son," he said. "We'll find a way to do something for Charlie." He turned to Alice and me. "I have so much I want to say to each of you," he said, "about your splendid courage and heroism in rescuing me. But first, I think, we have an urgent matter to discuss."

We turned to him inquiringly.

He pulled the silver sardine tin from his pocket. There were the ornate letters I knew so well: "Sultana's Exotic Sardines, packed in salted oil, imported exclusively by the Eastern Trading Company, Liverpool." My spine.

"I'm very worried," Mr. Poindexter said. "Last time Mermeros came out into the world, very few people saw him. Few were made aware. Yet from those few, look at the trouble that has unfolded."

Alice used a poker to stir the fire. "I still don't understand," she said, "who this Mr. Fustian even was, and how he learned that you had Mermeros."

Mr. Poindexter sighed. "This all began when Mr. Fustian, who was visiting the museum exhibits at the Crystal Palace the same day that we were there, overheard Maeve and me talking about a djinni."

"That would certainly catch his attention," observed Tom.

"*Whoo, whoo,*" said Morris the owl.

"As it happens," continued Mr. Poindexter, "I'd dropped one of my calling cards, so he learned my name and address. He heard me say that I was saving the djinni for Tom, as I already had everything I needed." He smiled ruefully. "He told me the story five times at least. Aside from worrying about you, my boy, the worst part of being locked up in that tower all week was having to listen to Fustian. I never knew such a fellow for yammering."

I laughed.

"As I say," continued Mr. Poindexter, "Fustian learned I had a son. He perceived—quite rightly—that if I valued my son more than a djinni's power, then my son would be my weakness, so to speak. The way to get my djinni from me would be to threaten Tom."

"But that photograph," protested Alice. "That horrid story. What a diabolical thing to do."

"No doubt," agreed Mr. Poindexter. "I don't believe it was his plan at the first. He photographed Tom to make sure he could identify him to that monster, Thorne. A more straightforward kidnapping was his original intent, I believe. The idea for the stereoscope, and that elaborate story about the camera that could photograph the future, came later."

"It's imaginative, at any rate," I said. Even a villain deserved his due.

"So he followed us around the rest of the day at the Crystal Palace," said Tom, "taking pictures of us on the amusement rides?"

"It was atrocious," cried Alice.

"I know," agreed Mr. Poindexter. "It quite turns the stomach. One of the pictures was of you, Tom, on the Topsy-Turvy Railway, screaming in terror."

"I wasn't in *terror*," protested Tom. "I was having a grand time."

"As you say." Mr. Poindexter nodded obligingly, but I caught the twinkle in his eye. "Fustian is quite skilled with photographs. In fact, I gathered from other remarks he made that he has used tricks with photographs to try to publish forged accounts of magic to magazines in the past. So he used Tom's face and Charlie's body to make the photograph that frightened me so and brought me racing to Gretigwode Manor."

I had figured out some of these details, and so had Tom, but this was Alice's first time learning what had really transpired.

"My point is," continued Mr. Poindexter, "in addition to all the fuss with the photographs, Mr. Fustian placed those advertisements in all the London papers. He received two responses from people who knew about Mermeros: Mrs. Gruboil and that Rooch fellow from last winter. Your 'ginger-whiskered man,' Maeve. That means none of this is a secret. With his information, along with what strangers were willing to tell him for a small fee, this odious person soon had all the information he needed to set a trap for me that nearly cost me all I hold dear."

Tom kept his gaze fixed on the fire. I looked away to give him his privacy.

"Those were witnesses to Mermeros the last time around," said Mr. Poindexter, "and not the only ones."

It was true. In our earlier entanglements with Mermeros, we ended up with an entire chorus of rascals trying to get their hands on my djinni, of which Mr. Rooch and Mrs. Gruboil were merely minor members of the ensemble.

"And now," I cut in, "many, many more people have seen carpetbags fly. Or seen Mermeros."

"Oh dear," whispered Alice. "We're in terrible trouble, aren't we?"

Tom looked up at his father expectantly. He trusted him completely to know what to do. Just as I trusted mine, and, in his own way, my dad trusted me.

"I think we might need magical help with this," said Mr. Poindexter, "before matters run completely out of hand."

"A wish?" asked Alice. "From Mermeros?"

He nodded.

"I would do it," I said, "but that would banish Mermeros forever." I hesitated. "Is that, perhaps, what we should do?"

"So it would seem," said Mr. Poindexter slowly, "although I hate to. Maeve, you and I are in the same position. Neither of us dare cast another wish."

"I'll do it, Dad," cried Tom. "I've got three wishes. I can spend one on this."

"Let me, Tom," said Alice. "Save your wishes. I don't mind."

Tom turned toward her. "But, Alice," he said, "you could have a turn, too, with Mermeros. You'd want your wishes just as much as I'd want mine."

Alice shook her head and smiled. "I don't think so," she said. "After all I've seen, wishes frighten me. You keep yours, Tom. I don't need anything. Please, let me help with this."

Tom nodded, and Mr. Poindexter handed her the sardine tin. I remembered a time when Alice had the chance and the need to use Mermeros to cast a wish, but she was too frightened . Too frightened to fly, yet willing to do it to save a friend. Who's more brave, the one who conquers her fears, or the one without enough sense to fear in the first place?

My bet's on Alice.

She pried the key carefully off the bottom of the sardine tin and fitted its flat slit over the thin metal lip of the top. Once, twice, three times she cranked the key back. That old familiar fishy stench filled the room. I hoped to goodness it wouldn't bring Mrs. Harding running to fumigate.

Mermeros burbled out of his sardine tin in a spume of thick yellow vapor, folding upon itself like ribbon candy until his massive green bulk loomed above us. The glow of the fire shone through his incandescent shape. It was still rather unsettling, and I'm used to Mermeros.

"Good afternoon," said the great fish. "I see we are taking turns. Passing the djinni about like a bottle around the campfire, eh? I warn you, such games nearly always end in *gruesome death for all parties.* People think they'll cooperate and share my power, until ruthless greed sets in."

Alice sat up straight and tall upon the embroidered cushion of her footstool.

"Good afternoon to you, too, Mermeros," she said clearly. "I think we'll skip the gruesome deaths today. It's my turn to make a wish."

Mermeros peered at her nonchalantly down the length of his nose. "Ah," he said. "Well, you have vexed and aggravated me less than some of your kind. I will grant you that."

"Thank you," she said primly.

He rubbed his great green hands together. "And what would you like, young mistress?" he said. "A carriage spun from filaments of diamond? Gowns laced with pearls and woven from strands of gold? A unicorn?"

Alice didn't blink as the great tyrant goggled his fishy green eyes upon her.

"No, thank you," she said. "I would like you to... Wait. Did you say 'unicorn'?"

Tom's eyes grew wide. If even Alice could be tempted to make self-serving wishes, no one was safe.

"I did indeed," purred the great sneak.

Alice shook herself slightly. "Never mind. Here is my wish. I would like you to cause all those who have learned about your existence—"

I choked, realized the dreadful mistake that was about to take place.

"—excluding ourselves," Alice said, realizing it, too, "to forget that they've ever seen you or heard of you."

The great sea-lion's shoulders sank. He deflated down to a third his ordinary size, hovering right at Alice's eye level, blinking at her like a forlorn baby seal.

"You wish me to use my power," he repeated faintly, "to cause humans to *forget* me?"

Alice's face melted into sympathy. "It's for your own good," she said. "And for everyone's safety. Look at the great harm Professor Fustian did to Mr. Poindexter, all to try to steal you. Look at the dangers Maeve and her family faced, last time around."

Mermeros stuck out his fishy lower lip. "Yes, but that's what makes things *entertaining*," he said. "Mortals come, and mortals go, but I am here forever. Practically speaking. The more people fight over me, the more—"

"The more your ego is stroked, you great inflated whale," I cried.

Alice's eyes grew wide. "Maeve, *shh*," she whispered. "Others will hear you!"

Mermeros puffed himself up to full size, folded his massive arms across his tattooed chest, and glared at me. "It can't be done."

"What do you mean, it can't be done?" I demanded.

Mermeros wouldn't look at me. "Tell your companion," he told Alice, in a sniffing sort of way, "that I only answer to you."

Alice turned to me. "He says—"

"I heard what he said."

"Mermeros," Alice said, turning back to the djinni, "are you quite sure? Why can't it be done?"

Suddenly the ruthless djinni became as pious and proper as a parish curate. "I can no more wipe away people's memories than I can wipe off their arms and legs," he said. "It's unfair and hurtful. It's wrong."

My goodness. Right and wrong had never gotten in Mermeros's way before.

"Think of it this way," said Mermeros, watching me archly. "The villains who've been arrested—if nobody remembers me, nor even the idea of me, how long can you keep them in prison? What crime would your magistrates charge them with?"

I hadn't thought of that.

"The young couple," he said, "who are more besotted than ever through their recent adventures. Take away the memory of me, and it all becomes a confusing muddle in their minds."

"How do you know all this?" I demanded. "You were locked up in the sardine tin for most of those goings-on."

He favored me with a fishy smile, baring all his pointy teeth. "If you think, Girl Hatchling, that that sardine tin actually contains me, then you know nothing at all. It is—how shall we say—an illusion of a container, to spare you mortals undue terror, and to give me a place—for lack of a word your mortal minds can understand—to rest."

"Sounds like you're tired of rest, though," I told him. "Sounds like you wish more people would invite you out to play. So you can be entertained, watching their lives unravel as they fight over you."

"*My* wishes," hissed Mermeros, "are my own private affair." He sucked thoughtfully on his pointed teeth. "But, yes. You are correct."

At least he admitted it.

Alice wrung her hands. "So, there's nothing at all that we can do?"

"Nothing I can see," said Mermeros loftily. "This is a problem of your own creation, and its solution will be yours to manage also. Will that be all?"

Alice turned imploringly to each of us. "What do you think?"

Mr. Poindexter shook his head sadly. "It's a muddle, to say the very least. More likely, a diabolical mess."

"We'll figure it out," said Tom stoutly. "Together, we'll make a plan."

Mr. Poindexter rumpled Tom's bright-orange hair. "That's right, my lad," he said. "Self-confidence. That's the ticket."

Downstairs, we heard the doorbell ring.

"Your family's arriving, Maeve," said Alice. "It's time for the party to begin. I guess I'd better send Mermeros back to his rest."

"Wait," I told her. "Wait just one moment. I'll be right back."

I jumped off my stool and tiptoed out into the hallway, making very sure no one could look over my shoulder into Tom's room and see its magical contents. While Mr. and Mrs. Bromley received my family in the downstairs foyer, I crept up the stairs to the room Alice and I shared and found what I sought. I slipped back downstairs and into Tom's room, holding the item behind my back.

"Yes?" sneered Mermeros. "What is it?"

"You're magical," I said, "right, Mermeros?"

He blinked his great fishy eyes in deep disdain. "Obviously."

"Which is how you can shrink yourself small and live inside the sardine tin."

"As I have attempted to explain to your weak brain," he said, "it's not that simple."

I ignored his jab. "But you can take things with you, can't you?"

His nostrils flared. "Things?" he repeated. As if I'd said, "germs."

"Things," I said. "Like your clothing. Your earrings. Your shark-tooth necklace."

He glared at me under furrowed brows. "Why?" he demanded. "Do you wish me to dress in your era's repellent fashions?"

Oh my. This opportunity was too good to pass up. But if he tricked me into making a wish—then again, it wasn't I who'd summoned him—what to do...?

"I don't believe you could," I said, with a dismissive wave of my hand. "You wouldn't know a thing about 'fashion,' as you call it."

*Pop.*

The sight that greeted my eyes will give me fits of hysterical laughter at wildly inconvenient times from now until my dying day.

There was Mermeros, enormous and green, dangling in the air, dressed from head to—well, to whatever was the lower end of him—in a tightly tailored suit cut from ludicrous purple and brown tartan plaid. A mauve waistcoat trimmed with velvet and studded with ebony buttons adorned his barrel chest, over a cream-colored shirt, with an orange silk cravat artfully clustered at his throat. He wore a monocle screwed into one eye and twirled a walking stick with one hand. His billiard-ball head sported a gray top hat so tall, it brushed against the ceiling. Best of all—or worst, actually—his glorious white mustaches were now joined by a massive pair of white muttonchop whiskers sprouting out from each side of his face.

He thrust out his chest proudly, rotating this way and that to show his costume to its best advantage. He was proud of himself, the old peacock. So much for calling modern menswear *repellent*.

Tom made a sort of strangled sound. Alice, who is much too polite to laugh in anyone's face, developed a fit of coughing.

It took me a minute to get my own face under control.

"I've wronged you, Mermeros," I finally told him.

"You should never underestimate my talents," he informed me.

"I should say not," I agreed. "You look quite...er..."

"Dapper," supplied Mr. Poindexter. "You make a dapper djinni, sir."

He peered at me with his monocled eye. "Why all the questions," he demanded, "about my ability to keep *things*?"

I laughed. "I have a present for you."

He blinked. "A present?"

I nodded. "Something to pass the time. To amuse yourself with. And to remind you that you are never forgotten."

His gaze darted away, and back to me, then away again. He was dying to know what his present was. Silly old fish!

"I am not in need of *amusement*," he said. "*Time* is not of concern to me."

"Oh," I said. "In that case, never mind."

"Hmph," he said.

I backed away. "I suppose you probably wouldn't even know what to do with it," I said. "It's probably too dark in there, anyway."

"It is in no way too dark for my comfort in my ancient domicile," thundered Mermeros. "Don't speak such infernal nonsense!"

It took everything in me not to laugh out loud. "I'm sorry, Mermeros," I said sweetly. "Would you like your present after all?"

He sighed. "If you insist on giving it to me, I won't be so ungracious as to refuse."

"Well, then," I said, "here you are. A token of our friendship. And my thanks."

His eyes goggled at my words. I used the moment to hand him my gift. A bound leather copy of *The Arabian Nights' Entertainments*. An English version of Monsieur Galland's *A Thousand and One Nights*, published by Milner and Sowerby. My father had given it to me, and I'd squeezed every drop out of this marvelous collection of stories, long since.

The book sat in Mermeros's gigantic hands like a postage stamp. He stared at it, though, as if it were an engagement ring.

"For me?" he whispered.

"All for you," I said. "To thank you for all you've done for us. You haven't been as good as you could be, I'll wager, but you've no doubt been better than you might've been."

He was too busy leafing through the illustrated pages. "What did you say?"

I grinned. "Nothing. Read it carefully, Mermeros. You'll find several tales of djinnis inside," I said. "Tell us next time whether or not you think they're correct."

Mermeros closed the book and tucked it inside his great purple plaid suit coat. He gave me a ridiculously formal bow. "Thank you, Girl Hatchling," he said. "I am not accustomed to receiving gifts."

"I hope you enjoy it," I told him. "We'll have to figure out, with our weak brains, what to do with you. But meanwhile, you can enjoy a cracking good read."

"Alice, dear!" came Mrs. Bromley's voice through the doorway.

Alice began frantically cranking the lid to the sardine tin shut. Most sardine tins, once opened, could never be closed, but this one, for a thousand (and one) reasons, was different. Mermeros bulged out for an instant, then shrunk himself down into a purple plaid dollop and slipped back inside.

"Thomas," called Mrs. Bromley. "May I come in? Are Alice and Maeve in there?"

"Come in, Mrs. Bromley," Mr. Poindexter called. "We were just visiting."

She opened the door. To her eyes, we were just four friends, talking around a fire.

"How cozy," she sighed. "Oh, Mr. Poindexter, I am just too, too glad to see you safely back with us. But come, if you're able, and children, you come, too. The party's just beginning, and it won't be the same without you." She slid her arm through mine. "Maeve, dear, your whole family is here. Even your married sister is here with her new husband, and dear Polly is here with her constable, and I—well, the way they're both looking at each other—I just have such a *feeling* about tonight!"

I smiled. "Me too, Mrs. Bromley," I said. "Me too."

Her brow furrowed. "Oh," she said, "I almost forgot. Thomas, that unpleasant woman, Mrs. Fletcher, is here inquiring after you. You know, from the Orphans' Committee. Shall I send her away? I don't suppose either of you are feeling up to company just yet."

A slow smile spread across Tom's face. "Mrs. Bromley," he said, "would you mind sending her up? I'd like to introduce her to my dad."

# Author's Note

One of the most delicious aspects of researching this book was studying the history of the famed Crystal Palace, one of the more memorable stars in a constellation of mass-entertainment attractions that began to shine in the Victorian era. Though the Crystal Palace is no longer, it remained, for at least a generation after it tragically burned to the ground in 1936, a living memory of thrills, magic, wonder, and delight.

As I write this, in the year 2021, entertainment is an established industry; we're well aware of theme parks, pleasure cruises, and vacation spots dotting the globe. That wasn't always the case.

The three main reasons why mass entertainment could spring up during the nineteenth century (the years 1800–1899) were extra money, extra time, and expanded modes of transportation.

Great Britain transitioned from a largely farming economy to a largely factory or industrial economy at a rapid pace during the long years of Queen Victoria's reign, which began precisely sixty years before this chapter of Maeve's adventures began. This change brought new prosperity into the lives of much of the nation's population. (Much of it, but, we must remember, not all of it. Wretched poverty still existed then, as it does now.) Still, many in the working classes could now reasonably expect to have a bit of money to spend on pleasure and fun, after paying for food, shelter, medicine, clothing, and other things necessary for survival, and a bit of time left for pleasure when the workday or work week ended.

More people could afford to buy books—and more people had enough education to read them—so new authors and publishers of popular fiction thrived. The novel—the very thing you're holding in your hands—became the dominant literary art form, leaving poetry and drama behind. Charles Dickens, widely regarded as the father of the modern novel, was a Victorian author. The "penny dreadful" crime novels Constable Hopewood accused Maeve of reading (a charge which she did *not* deny) emerged during this time. More people could afford a ticket to see a show, and theaters and music halls sprang up around the nation, and not only in London. With railroad trains criss-crossing the nation, people could easily travel to entertainment spots throughout the country. More people could set aside a day to spend at the seashore, and at theaters, boardwalks, and carnival attractions at beach destinations up and down the coasts.

More people lived in towns and cities than ever before, working at smoky factory jobs and living in small apartments. When they had a day off, they longed for greenery, scenery, and a breath of fresh air. Popular "pleasure gardens" sprang into being. Often these had once been grand estates with fine houses, woods, ponds, and gardens. With the addition of ticket booths, dining pavilions, dance platforms, vendors selling food, and musicians providing atmosphere, these pleasure gardens became places where people of all classes liked to stroll about, admiring the flowers and fountains, rowing in the pond, sampling the entertainment, and running into friends unexpectedly. Special attractions such as hot-air balloon "aeronauts," jugglers, magicians, and novelty acts added wonder to the fun.

To imagine what it was like, you might remember the "Jolly Holiday" animated sequence in the film *Mary Poppins*, if you've seen it. Bert, Mary Poppins, Michael, and Jane put on festive clothing in cheery colors and spend a day strolling about a scenic outdoor setting, admiring the flowers, trees, and birds. Occasionally, as luck would have it, there would be a carousel to ride, a horse race to watch, or an outdoor restaurant selling "raspberry ice, and then some cakes and tea." Flip that scene from a cartoon to real life, travel there by train instead of jumping into a chalk picture, add lots more people, keep the carousel horses bolted in place, turn the singing penguins into human waiters in suits and ties, and you've got the idea.

As you might imagine, for people hoping to find romance or

meet a special someone, a public pleasure garden could be a place to find a new friend; for those who already had a special someone, a pleasure garden could be a lovely place to spend an enjoyable day together, just as our Polydora and her Constable Hopewood did.

The Crystal Palace was a pleasure garden, and more than that. The building itself didn't get its start at the Sydenham Hill location where Maeve and her friends visited it. It first appeared in London's Hyde Park for the 1851 Great Exhibition, the first true World's Fair.

The Exhibition required a building that could house all the merchants, artists, and displays that would be its main attractions. Outdoor booths wouldn't do for an event on such a grand scale, lasting five and a half months. An architectural design contest was held to choose the right building. In the end, it wasn't an architect but a gardener, Joseph Paxton, whose idea won. Prior to that point, the idea of a gigantic building made of glass had been virtually unheard of. The Crystal Palace, in a way, was a massive and elegant greenhouse or hothouse, similar to those gardens kept to grow flowers and strawberries in the winter and to start garden seedlings early in the spring.

The Great Exhibition and its fairylike glass building were a grand success. Thanks to an expanded railway network that made a day's outing possible, more than six million people from all over Great Britain visited the Exhibition in the nearly six months it ran.

They bought food, souvenirs, and train tickets along the way. They explored the booths rented by merchants and manufacturers eager to show their soaps, fabrics, fine dishes, and tools to the entire nation. This was highly effective advertising for new products. Visitors browsed, sniffed, tasted, and shopped. Clearly, there was money to be made in combining many types of entertainment, attractions, and shopping under one roof. In fact, the inside of the Crystal Palace might remind us a great deal of our shopping malls today, complete with glass roofs, food courts, entertainment (video arcades and movie theaters), and lots of new merchandise on display.

An interesting dotted line connects the Crystal Palace to theme parks as we know them now. The Crystal Palace was first erected for that 1851 Great Exhibition and World's Fair. The city of Paris had begun holding industrial expositions prior, but, inspired by the success of the London Great Exhibition, launched "Expositions Universelle." The 1889 Exposition Universelle (or World's Fair, as English-speakers called it) in Paris featured its own architectural and engineering marvel: la Tour Eiffel, or the Eiffel Tower. It was constructed for the fair, and the intention was that it, too, would be disassembled afterward, just as the Crystal Palace was.

The city of Chicago didn't want to miss out on the excitement and the income to be made from a World's Fair, and in 1893 launched its own, called the World's Columbian Exposition (or

Expo). In an astonishingly short period of time, workers cleared land on the southern shores of Lake Michigan and erected a temporary city for the expo, with buildings housing exhibits from around the world. This Expo featured its own engineering marvel: the first Ferris wheel. Almost overnight, it seemed, this magical city of glittering white lights, music, fun, and laughter sprang up on the shores of Lake Michigan, only to be taken apart when the expo was over.

One of the workers involved in building the expo was a contractor named Elias Disney. He would later tell his children about the glittering white city, the Ferris wheel, and the exhibits where families could learn together while relaxing, eating, playing games, and having fun. These stories left a deep impression in the imagination of one of his children, whom Elias had named Walter Elias. You know his name better as Walt Disney. Today Disney theme parks, inspired by those stories from Walt's father, are found around the world.

When the 1851 London Great Exhibition was over, the building was taken apart, leaving piles of plate glass and mounds of cast-iron frames. Eventually a group of investors purchased the building's materials and used them to build a permanent exhibition-like experience at Sydenham Hill. The great building was expanded, redesigned, and reassembled on a new foundation. A dedicated train line was built to connect directly to the Crystal Palace, with a glassed-in walkway connecting the station and the building, so that not even rain would keep visitors away. Two stations, in fact, were built to serve the Crystal Palace. One remains in use to this day. Joseph Paxton himself helped design the beautiful gardens, grounds, and fountains in the park surrounding the building.

Thus was born the Crystal Palace, both a permanent exhibition and a pleasure garden that would delight generations of British visitors from 1854 to 1936, when the building was destroyed by a fire. It hosted gatherings, jubilees, concerts, and conferences. For many years, it boasted an indoor aquarium, which was the largest in the world when it opened to the public, but that had closed by the time Maeve and her friends arrived.

At the start of the nineteenth century (the 1800s), the chance to enjoy the beauty of a large, scenic garden would have been a luxury only the wealthy could afford on their private estates. Tickets to an opera, ballet, play, or concert would have been affordable to only a small segment of society. An expanding entertainment industry, along with better working and living conditions for much of Britain's population, brought these pleasures within reach for millions of people.

Something magical happens when we share fun and delight with others. The hush over a large crowd during an amazing performance is electric. The roar of laughter at a comical show is contagious, and somehow, the screams of thrilled terror on a roller coaster ride make most of us eager to get in line for our turn, just like Maeve and Tom. (I confess I'm more of an Alice in that respect. I'll try it once, then probably go looking for a lemonade stand.)

Large-scale entertainment spaces become the source of some of our happiest and most vivid memories, just as they were for the generation that grew up loving the Crystal Palace. Today we're very familiar with large spaces where enormous gatherings are possible— shopping malls, convention halls, stadiums, large theaters, auditoriums, and concert halls. We have the Victorians to thank for many of them.

As I write this, the world is still in the grips of the coronavirus pandemic, which has limited the types of large gatherings that feel safe and appropriate to hold. Many of our entertainment spaces have gone temporarily dark and silent, collecting dust. I hope that will soon change, just as I hope those who have suffered from this pandemic will receive comfort, healing, and hope. We need our places and our moments of joy, festivity, and fun, and our times where we celebrate the spectacle and skill of athletes, performers, and wondrous works of creativity, engineering, and art. And we need to share those joys with others.

Until then, and always, thank goodness for stories.

# About the Author

Julie Berry is the author of the *New York Times* bestseller *Lovely War*, the Printz Honor and *Los Angeles Times* Book Prize shortlisted novel *The Passion of Dolssa*, and many other acclaimed young adult and middle-grade novels, as well as several picture books. She holds a BS from Rensselaer in communication and an MFA from Vermont College. She lives in upstate New York with her family.